THE SECRET LIFE OF SUNFLOWERS

MARTA MOLNAR

DEDICATION

This book is dedicated to all the women who keep on fighting.

With my sincere gratitude for endless patience and friendship to Sarah Jordan and Diane Flindt. For unfailing support to Jill Marsal. For invaluable help to Linda Ingmanson, Toni Lee, Mary-Theresa Hussey and Margie Lawson. For steadfast friendship and support to Patsy Keller. For early feedback to Deb Posey Chudzinski, Marcy Collins, Hilary Powell, Jo Dawson, Judy Wagner, Kaela Stokes, Audrey McDonald, Robin Diebold, Sue Cleereman, Linda Dossett, Sharon Ford, Dalice Peterson, Michelle Cox, Gretchen Coon, and Sue Chatterjee. And a huge thank you to all the wonderful friends on FB who helped me pick the cover art and provided encouragement along the way.

CHAPTER ONE

Emsley

The first time I saw the blue box of mystery was the last time I talked with my grandmother face-to-face.

"If you want to murder that cheating boyfriend of yours, I'm in," she told me. "I thought about it, Emsley. I can't help you bury his body, or Diya's, but I can provide you with an alibi."

She adjusted her Monet-print silk robe, blue-green with a smattering of purple water lilies, until it draped over her frail body just so. *The goddess in repose.* Stroke or no, prop-up bed or no, she was still Violet Velar, the Artist, the Diva, the toast of New York.

The cloud of disinfectant that hovered throughout the care center like highland mist in a Robinson Hall painting didn't dare breach her room. Her perfume embraced me. *Spicy, unrestrained, bold.*

I plunked a stack of art magazines and auction catalogues on her nightstand. "We can let Trey live another day. He's allowed to have a relationship with Diya, if that's what they want. We're business partners. I'm prepared to stick out the rough spots."

"You could come back."

I kissed her cheek. "You know New York is my Camelot." The magical kingdom I always longed for. "But LA is my reality."

New York auction houses seemed to have a secret charter that required auctioneers to look like the host of a British documentary series. You had to sound like you went to Cambridge in the sixties to be allowed on the stage.

"I'm not of a *distinguished* age, and here, that matters. I don't have a stature that commands respect." I turned down the metal bars around Violet's bed that the new nurse liked to pop up for safety, but Violet hated. "And I'm not the preferred sex. I'm missing the dangly bits."

She growled at that.

My sentiments exactly. "You know what Henry Fullerton told me when I asked for a promotion?"

"Henry was always an ass."

"Expensive pieces of art are bought by the rich as an investment. A star auctioneer must be a person the CEO of a hedge fund would find trustworthy at a glance. Someone they could see themselves golfing with on a Sunday." Henry's exact words, his excuse for keeping me in a junior position year after year. "Anyway, if he wasn't an ass, I wouldn't have started looking at other opportunities." When I was in a generous mood, I could almost convince myself that Henry Fullerton had done me a favor. "I wouldn't have started my own business with Diya and Trey."

Violet's Valkyrie gaze softened with concern. "Are you sure you want to keep living with them?"

"It's not a matter of *want*. It's a matter of being unable to predict lottery numbers." I settled into the recliner next to her bed with my bag and teased my laptop from the mess of papers in there. "Believe me, I want to have my own place. And someday soon, I will. And then I'm going to buy Diya and Trey out of the business."

I wanted to reach a point where I was calling the shots, where I was my own woman, because I wanted to branch out into benefit auctions. I wanted the current business to be strong enough that I could do benefit auctions for free. My dream was to hand a million-dollar check to stroke research one day. I daydreamed about that research helping Violet. I wanted nothing more than to see my grandmother restored to her old self.

Our niche auction house, Ludington's, handled political fundraisers, focusing exclusively on Hollywood celebrity donors. I didn't miss stuffy New York estate auctions of boring paintings from dusty financiers whose collections were accumulated strictly as an investment. In LA, we dealt with actors or producers or directors who offered a weekend at their ranch, or art they'd created, or a dress from an

Oscar-winning role, down to smaller items like signed scripts. Our auctions were fun. They zinged.

"We're perfectly positioned to take advantage of Hollywood's political activism," I said, straight out of our standard proposal we gave to potential investors. "We're going to make serious money. Hopefully, soon."

I shouldn't have talked about work on my day off. My phone immediately pinged with a text.

Tonight at ten at the hotel?

Violet raised her head from her pillow. "Is that your mother?"

"Mark Selig. Junior congressman. We're about to sign him as a new client."

I'm in New York for the day. I texted back. *Monday morning at ten at the office?*

"Watch out for those." Violet wiggled her toes. "Men who come to power early tend to develop an awful sense of entitlement."

She wasn't wrong. "We need to figure out when we can meet up. I had a meeting with him yesterday that fell through." A noon intro session at Ludington's.

An hour before the meeting, he rescheduled for 10:00 p.m. at his hotel's restaurant. On arrival, the maître d' informed me that the meeting was moved to the gentleman's suite. I'd pretended that I had an emergency phone call and had to leave.

When something like this happened, I usually asked Trey to take the rescheduled meeting, but Selig had requested me specifically because he had concerns about our auction format, which was my area. I was going to have to deal with him.

"Oh, honey. Are you going to lose out because you came to visit me?"

"He's in LA for a few days. We'll meet when I get back." And that was as much time as I was willing to waste on talking about Selig. "Hey, guess what I had under the hammer this week?"

"Trey's face?"

Violet was still indignant on my behalf, and I loved her for that. "I auctioned off an A-list action star's sweat-stained jockstrap for a hundred grand."

"I hereby pronounce Old Hollywood glamour officially dead." She closed her eyes as if the idea pained her, or she was offering up a prayer for Hollywood's collective soul. Then, after a mournful moment, her eyes popped open. "Did it stink?"

"Didn't smell like roses at dusk." My laptop beeped. "Mom is calling."

"Remind me later that I want to give you something," Violet said quickly.

Then the call connected, and Mom ruled the screen from Florida, in all her tanned and teased glory.

"Why are you so close to the screen? Put that laptop somewhere so I can see the both of you," was her opening bid into the conversation.

Mom excelled at issuing orders and preferred all things orderly, in their place. If something wasn't the way she liked it, she made it that way. Born Johanna Velar, she'd changed her first name to Anna in high school. And then she married Philip Gregory Wilson right after graduation to divest herself of Velar, Violet's maiden name, a clear sign that my mother had been born out of wedlock. Johanna Velar—too exotic, people would think she was a foreigner, for heaven's sake. Anna Wilson—American, traditional, conservative, perfect for a dentist's wife. And then, when she finally had me, she named me Emily Wilson. Except, starting in kindergarten, I made everyone call me Emsley, Violet's nickname for me. Which drove my mother crazy.

Dad popped up behind her, golf bag over his shoulder. "Violet." Then to me, "Hi, dumpling." And then he kissed Mom on the cheek. "Why is my beer fridge in the garage full of face cream?"

"They discontinued Buti Balm." Other people would have to lose a limb to look that pained. "I had to stock up. Where are you going?"

"To beat the checkered pants off Bob." Dad waved at us, then disappeared from the frame.

Mom had adjusted her clip-on camera for my father's sake, so now she was off-center, only one eye showing, growing larger as she scooted closer to her computer. With her mascara running from the heat and humidity, I felt like the eye of Sauron was staring at me. "When did you get there?"

She wanted to know if we'd been talking behind her back.

"Barely walked through the door."

"How is your broken hip, Anna?" Violet asked her only child.

"Healing. I know better than to walk on the slippery pool deck barefooted." Mom huffed at her own carelessness. "We should have been back north a week ago."

My parents lived in Hartford, Connecticut for most of the year and usually drove down to the rehab center in New York when I visited each month. Two obligations with one stone, the pinnacle of practicality. Practicality and predictability were my mother's highest ideals. Forced changes to schedule threw her off track. She was not one to handle life's curveballs well.

I felt bad for her. "If Violet needs anything, I can help." Nobody should have to sit through a three-hour flight with a shattered hip.

"Thank you." She didn't wallow in gratitude, but moved straight on to "Now tell me you're back with Trey."

"Not if all the men were gone and all the batteries were dead." I'd read that in a book somewhere and saved it for this moment.

"Avery! How can you be so…" She wanted to say *vulgar*, but she thought the word *vulgar* was vulgar, so she delicately trailed off. "Think of your company. When you marry him, between the two of you, you'll be majority shareholders."

"I don't have time to date."

"Men aren't attracted to you because you always wear black. At least chuck the pants. Don't make that face. Men want to see women's legs."

"If I ever develop a sudden, burning need to

know what men want, I'll send out an online survey."

Mom sighed with the exasperation of mothers of disobedient daughters everywhere, as if my thorny impertinence was tearing out the stitches from the fabric of society. "Just pick a dress with sex appeal for that *Fast Business* interview tomorrow. You never know who'll see you."

"It's a business magazine, Anna." Violet stepped up to defend me. "Not a mail-order bride catalogue."

I loved my grandmother with the fire of a mega sun flare, the kind that knocked out the internet and messed up satellites in orbit.

Mom launched into her I'm-never-going-to-have-grandchildren routine with the crackling energy of a runaway auction. Then she slammed her signature why-do-I-even-bother look at me like a hammer and abruptly transitioned to "How is business?"

"Growing." I sent the hopeful thought out into the universe. Truth was, our survival depended on our next few contracts. "We're signing a new client."

My phone pinged. A text from Trey. *Contract fell through.*

Damn Selig. We offered an excellent service. He would have made money for his run with us. Why wasn't that enough? Why did my presence in his hotel room have to be part of the bargain?

We needed more new clients. We needed to spend more on PR and customer outreach. I texted that back to Trey, out of sight of the laptop camera. Failure was my mother's catnip.

Three little dots wiggled on my phone. Trey was typing. Then the dots went *poof* away. Nothing. He was thinking about my suggestion. That he'd never once taken my word for anything annoyed me, but I let the familiar aggravation go. Consideration was better than a knee-jerk *no*.

"I don't know how long you can possibly last." Mom rolled right along. "You built a company based on the whims of politics. How can you be so irresponsible?"

"Why don't I just open a cupcake shop? Do something feminine?" I stole her next line.

"People have to eat." She shot me a withering look, then trained her Sauron eye on Violet. "What did the doctor say yesterday?"

"I want to talk to you about something else." My grandmother smiled at me impishly, so I knew to brace. "I sold the house."

No! Shock yanked my spine straight. Violet's four-story brownstone in Greenwich Village had been the nest of my best childhood memories.

"What do you mean you sold the house?" Mom's voice shot up. "We did not discuss selling."

"It didn't need to be discussed," Violet said gently. "I've been behind on the bills here, and I don't like being behind."

She didn't need our agreement. She was right. The decision clearly made her happy. I wasn't going to tell her how hard the news hit me.

She read it on my face. "Our love for each other doesn't live in that house, honey. Our memories won't be included in the sale with the appliances."

"I don't think I'll ever be able to think of your home as just a pile of bricks."

"Think of it as I do. A place of great comfort, and lots of love, and blooming creativity. We were blessed by it for a long time. And now we release it with gratitude. May it delight all who enter the doors, for at least another hundred years."

And there she was, my grandmother, shifting the world with a handful of words.

"I'm glad you found a solution."

Her lopsided smile reappeared. "I also started a new NYU scholarship."

"Oh, here we go again." Sauron squinted with enough disapproval to give all of Mordor pause. But not Violet.

"Ninety-day settlement," my grandmother said. "I made Emsley my sole beneficiary. Other than the house, there's only the contents. You said you didn't want any of it, Anna. Bram is taking care of the details."

"Isn't Bram too old to still be working as an attorney?"

Violet dismissed Mom with a regal turn of her head. "You can donate what you don't want, Emsley. And then please arrange for cleaners."

My mother's huff held a wealth of meaning. *I can't believe I'm not being consulted. Decisions made in haste are repented at leisure. You will all regret this later. Don't come to me crying.*

"I don't care about the furniture," she said. "But for the record, I don't like this sudden sale. Now, tell me what the doctors said."

Violet summarized her latest tests that indicated a slight improvement. Then Mom signed off. Her bones hurt when she sat still too long.

I stashed away my laptop. "I'll sneak downstairs for some predinner sweets." And as I headed for the door, I told my grandmother what I always told her, "If I'm arrested, send bail money."

Out in the hallway, I bumped into Violet's neighbor. She'd reached the window at the end since she'd waved at me earlier, and was now negotiating the return trip.

"How are you, Mrs. Yang?"

"Out for a run. Boston Marathon is coming up," she deadpanned. She was another indomitable spirit.

She watched me for a few silent seconds as if deliberating whether to say more. I was pretty sure she'd go for it. She usually did.

"Do I look like I'm hiding something?"

I scanned her from her yellow daisy dress to her terrycloth slippers. "Are you?"

She reached into her bulging pocket that I'd thought held a wad of tissues. And with the flair of a magician, she produced a fuzzy yellow chick. "What do you think?"

"Poultry is an interesting choice for a healthcare facility. Is this sanitary?"

"Eh. We have therapy dogs twice a month."

"Where did you find it?"

"They took some of us on an enrichment bus trip to the Chinese Market."

"And you brought home a friend." Who was I to judge? Honestly, it was nothing Violet wouldn't have done if she were ambulatory. "What's her name?"

"Lai Fa." The two syllables slipped off Mrs. Yang's tongue as if whispered by a spring breeze. "It means beautiful flower in Chinese."

The chick did resemble a fluff of dandelion. "She looks very sweet."

Mrs. Yang slipped her secret companion back into her pocket with loving care. "Don't tell anyone?"

"Who would believe me?"

The downstairs kitchen brimmed with the aroma of baking lasagna. When I inquired after dessert, the woman doing dishes simply asked, "Mango pudding or maple ice cream?"

"Mango pudding, please."

I received twin bowls—no subterfuge needed. Violet and I made up the heist to keep life interesting.

I walked back into her room with "Quick. We must destroy the evidence as fast as we can."

The afternoon light hit the bed just so, diamond dust glittering in her silver hair. Her lively eyes sparkled. I half expected her to rise from the bed and declare that she was ready for her easel and her paints.

"Next time I come, I'll take you to the garden."

"Ooh, it's been forever since I've been out there." She swept aside the art magazine she'd been reading. "Anybody catch you?"

"Close call. They chased me down the hall, but I lost them in the elevator."

"That's my girl." We exchanged coconspirator grins, then settled in to savor our treats. We discussed art, then speculated about which of the staff members were having affairs with each other. We placed imaginary bets on who would elope.

"My money is on the PT guy and the blonde night nurse." I was about to explain why, but the clock on the bedstand caught my eye.

Have we been talking that long?

Half the afternoon had flown by.

"I have to go." I leaned in for a hug.

"Hold on, I told you I wanted to give you something. There's a box in the bottom of the wardrobe."

"What is it?"

"We'll talk after you've read through the contents."

The robin's-egg-blue box hid under Violet's robes and caftans, *Tiffany's* printed in silver on top. The sides were held together with strips of tape as if by the ribs of a corset. The once elegant, belle-of-the-ball box had aged into a disheveled old lady. Judging by the paint splatters that reminded me of makeup applied by failing eyes, the package must have sat in Violet's artist studio for some time.

The tight lid didn't want to open, but I managed. "Letters?"

I lifted out a handful of yellowed sheets from what had to be over a hundred pages, each covered with loopy cursive in fading ink. "I'll bring a bigger bag next time. I don't want to jam them into my laptop case and damage the paper."

"Take the diary, then." Violet was looking at the box, not at me. "The letters are in Dutch, anyway. The diary is in English."

I fished out the little green volume from the pile of loose papers.

"I'll read it on the plane." I sealed the lid and slid the box back into its hiding place. "Are you sure you're all right?" I returned to Violet for another hug. "I'll call you tomorrow. I love you."

"Love you more."

Her voice was too frail. I didn't like the tremble in it. I wasn't going to wait a whole month for another visit. I was going to make time in my schedule and come back next week.

And then we'd talk about her diary. Curiosity was killing me.

In an hour, I was at the airport, and an hour after that, I was settled in my seat for takeoff. I had the little green book on my lap, and I couldn't wait to jump in. I was about to meet Violet's scandalous past.

I cracked the cover open, but before I could read a single word of the loopy, handwritten cursive, my phone rang.

"Hey, Mom."

"You *cannot* hire a cleaning service," she said with a vehemence she usually reserved for things I did that kept me from *securing a man*. "I'd clean the house out myself if I could. And golfing is one thing, but your father's heart can't take carrying boxes down all those stairs. You can take time off from work. Give Trey a chance to miss you. Who knows what risqué pictures of Violet with her celebrity friends might be at the house. You know what tabloids pay these days for sordid secrets like that? Do you want our family splashed all over the papers?"

"I'll clean. Relax, Mom."

"I know you idolize your grandmother, but she wasn't so perfect when I was young. All the wild parties. Strangers at the house at all hours of the night. Or she'd drag me to a museum, then walk away, under the spell of some great new idea for her next work. I would be crying in the corner, surrounded by people I didn't know, lost and terrified."

"I'm sorry."

"At least you know who your father is. Imagine if I had so many lovers, I couldn't tell you where you came from. How would you like not knowing your father's name?"

"You know I love Dad. I can't even imagine how terrible it must have been for you. I love you both." And I loved Violet too. But I was willing to accept the possibility that the Violet I knew was different from the Violet my mother had lived with.

"Be nice to Trey. He'll realize what a fool he's been and come back to you, you'll see."

An announcement came through the speakers, the captain asking all passengers to turn off their electronic devices.

"We're taking off. I have to go. I'll call you tomorrow."

I didn't have a chance to put my phone away yet when it pinged—a text from Trey.

After all the time he'd taken to think about my suggestion, he must have seen my point. I expected him to respond with *Okay, we'll invest in marketing*. Instead, he wrote: *We need to shut down*.

The words slammed into me as if I'd been physically hit. Shock pinned me to my seat.

I was working on forgiving him for Diya, but if he messed with our business, the tiny baby auction house I spent every ounce of my life energy to birth and nurture...

I texted him back.

I don't quit.

We were going to have to talk as soon as I stepped off the plane.

To keep myself distracted until then, I opened Violet's diary at last. Only to discover that it wasn't Violet's diary.

CHAPTER TWO

Johanna

1887, Amsterdam, Netherlands

We were not expecting visitors when the doorbell rang in the middle of Friday afternoon.

Mama and the maid had emptied the kitchen cabinets, washed them out, and were waiting for them to dry in Amsterdam's summer heat. The back door stood open for the breeze. I was sitting at the table next to my sister Mien, scribbling in my journal and hoping to go unnoticed. Anke, a quiet village girl who was new to service, was using Mama's wedding ring to divine whether Mien would have boys or girls someday.

Mama's ring was suspended from a silk ribbon—it had to be red for the divination to work—over Mien's open palm. If the ring turned left, boy. If the ring turned right, girl.

"Oh, a boy, another boy!" Mama set down her embroidery, a pink flush of pleasure painting her cheeks.

Then the ring stopped and would turn no more.

"Ten children, just like me." Mama clapped. "Your turn, Jo."

I could see the crimson drops my heart bled onto the page in front of me as if they were real. "I don't care." I should have taken my journal and hidden upstairs. "I am not in a blessed state."

Neither was Mien, who, at twenty-nine, was old enough to leave childish games behind. Neither of us was married, although Mien, being four years older, would probably be marched to the altar before me. My dearest friend, Anna, should have been sitting at the table—at least she was engaged. Alas, Anna, always the lucky one, was in Scheveningen with her parents, on their annual vacation at the sea.

"Don't you want to know if you'll have a family?"

Mien's disapproval needled under my skin, but I swallowed a heated response. I had but a moment earlier promised my diary to be a better person, more patient in all things.

On the other hand, I had not pledged to be silent.

"I want to know why we are alive. I want to find my purpose." At the end of my life, I wanted to be able to look back and be proud of what I had accomplished. I wanted to leave behind...*something*.

Mien's groan was so unladylike that Mama tsked at her. Then she smiled at me. "Someday, you will meet the right man and marry, Jo."

"Or I shall be an independent woman."

"Heaven forbid. There is no reason to despair."

Anke lowered the ring to the table, in obvious discomfort at our bickering. "I'll see if the kitchen towels are dry on the line."

She grabbed the basket and escaped outside, laughter entering behind her. A horse-pulled *trekschuit* was passing by on the canal. The antique barge carried tourists to the Rijksmuseum built on our street the year before. I would much rather have been going there myself as well.

Since I was stuck in the kitchen, I had to distract Mama before she progressed from dreams of grandchildren to actual matchmaking.

"Do you think I shall ever accomplish anything?" I asked her. "Will history remember my name?"

"What nonsense. The purpose of a woman's life is to ensure that her husband is happy." Her tone tipped, gently lecturing as she picked up her embroidery again. "Women are like the canals, steady and calm, the supporters of life. Men are like barges traveling to the seaports, having adventures and collecting their treasures. Wives are to husbands what canals are to barges. *Important.* Life in Amsterdam wouldn't be possible without the canals."

She looked inordinately pleased with herself at having explained it all so neatly.

"You know how much I *want* to be important to Eduard."

Mien peeked at my journal over my shoulder.

"What did he tell you when you two went boating last week?"

I snapped the cover shut. "He has given me every encouragement."

"And has not returned since."

"Oh, my Jo." Mama patted my cheek. "How about Garrit? A widower, barely thirty and with five young children. He must marry soon. He asks about you every time I'm in his butcher shop. I wager he shall be visiting your papa with a special question before you know it. Then your purpose will be defined for you at last. Won't that be splendid?"

Splendid drudgery.

"I sent in an application for a teaching position at the girls' school in Utrecht." I'd been holding the news until Papa was home as well, not wanting to have to fight the battle twice, but Mien's needling pushed me too far.

Her smile bloomed syrupy sweet. "In the same town as Eduard's university. Isn't that a—"

Mama cut her off with a sharp glance. "Didn't you promise Sanne you would join her at the park and help with the little ones, Mien?"

"Yes, Mama." She snatched her hat from the table and hurried out the front door, just as Anke slipped in with the wicker basket of stiff linen through the back.

"You may start ironing." Mama picked up her ring and began to untie the ribbon, ready to go about her own business.

"Garrit smells like lard-fried onions," I mumbled

under my breath. What I wanted to know was whether Eduard's heart was truly mine. If the ring predicted children, they would be his. I held out my open palm to Mama. "All right. Please, show me."

Her smile had never been more approving. The golden ring spun on its red ribbon, scattering light around the kitchen. I didn't know which one of us was holding her breath the hardest.

"A boy first." She was no less thrilled for me than she'd been for Mien. "Now let's see about the rest of them."

Eduard loves me. He will marry me.

I waited, hypnotized, for the golden circle to turn again.

That was the moment when the doorbell rang.

The sound cut through me like the night train's lights through the dark, its sharp whistle jostling people from their dreams. My mouth, which had fallen open with wonder, snapped shut with irritation.

Mama palmed her ring. "I wonder who that is."

Someone with terrible timing. But *what if…* I shoved back my chair and cut in front of Anke. "I'll see to the visitor."

I patted down my hair and straightened my dress. I opened the door floating on wings of hope, then crashed to the ground of hard disappointment. "Oh, hello." *I must smile.* "What a lovely surprise. Please, come in." I called back to Mama, "Theo is here. Dries's friend from France."

He brought the not unpleasant scent of pipe

tobacco with him, his tan suit wrinkled from the long trip. My heart leapt with a new possibility.

"Where is my brother?" I glanced past Theo. Maybe Dries was paying the carriage driver.

"Mevrouw Bonger." Theo snapped off his hat. "I come alone." He was as breathless as I had been just a moment before, his blue eyes wild, his fingers twitching on the handle of his carpetbag, the man clearly in the grip of turmoil.

"Have you come from visiting your mother? Does she fare well?"

The first time my brother brought Theo to our home had been shortly after his father's death. Maybe he was back in the Netherlands because some ill had now befallen his last remaining parent.

"Her letters suggest her mood is improved." Theo's gaze jumped from our ebony hat rack to the vase of sunflowers, then to the picture of King William III next to the mirror—everywhere but me. "I haven't seen her in some months. I traveled straight here from Paris."

Worry wrapped around me between one breath and the next. "Is anything amiss with my brother?"

Theo's eyes briefly met mine at last. "Dries is quite well and sends his love."

Thank God.

Anke silently whisked away Theo's hat and bag, and then I showed him to the sofa, where he collapsed as if from nervous exhaustion, then jumped up again when he realized I had not yet sat.

Mama stepped from the kitchen, shooting me a questioning look.

I could give her nothing.

"What a lovely surprise." She ran her fingers over the old brown dress she'd put on for cleaning. She'd already shed her stained apron. "Theo, welcome." She glanced toward the door. "Has my Dries come with you?"

"Dries remains in Paris, in good health, Mevrouw Bonger." He kissed her hand a breath too late, and then straightened a breath too fast. "I apologize for the unannounced visit."

"Any friend of my son is always welcome in our home. Please sit. I'll ask Anke for refreshments." And with that, she turned right out of the room, leaving me alone with our visitor.

I perched in the armchair next to the piano and folded my hands on my lap, while Theo lowered himself back onto the sofa, with more decorum this time. I couldn't untangle the emotions that flickered across his face *Worry? Irritation? Fear?*

On his visit the year before—when Dries, Theo, and I had gone to the Rijksmuseum—Theo had been amusing, even brilliant with his knowledge of history and art, his eyes kind and encouraging. Now they burned with a disturbing intensity.

"Is all well with you, Johanna? And the family?"

"We are all well. Thank you. Papa and Henri are at work at the insurance company. Sanne walked the children over to the park, and Mien just went after them." I had already asked about his mother, so I had to ask about something else next. "How is work at the gallery? Goupil?"

"Ah, you remember." His smile sparked as if I'd given him a gift. "I am nudging them slowly toward progress. They are yet to allow me to display anyone but the artists of the Salon on the main level, but I finally have a few impressionists upstairs. Monet, Degas, Gauguin…"

More words pelted me, but my mind slipped into a daydream in which my Eduard appeared at the door to propose. I envisioned a wonderful life together: a home even finer than Papa and Mama's, a son, and endless, blissful contentment.

"And then there's Guillaumin." Theo's excited voice cut through my daydream. He was listing more artists he admired, some vaguely familiar.

"Dries has been writing me about the impressionists."

Theo launched into even more fervent praise.

Thank heavens, Mama soon arrived, followed by Anke with the tray.

Anke poured for all of us, the scent of strong black tea and bergamot filling the air.

"Please, try the boterkoek," Mama urged.

Theo ate the butter cake in haste and praised it even faster, then jumped to his feet again, which startled Mama so, her treasured Delft cup rattled against the matching saucer. "Might I take Jo for a walk along the canal?"

Mama held her saucer in both hands to avoid

further upset. "Of course. Finally, a sunny day after all that rain."

I nearly feigned a headache, but then thought of Dries. What if my brother had sent me a private message? Possibly concerning Annie, an aloof, boring, blonde English-type girl he had become secretly engaged to last May.

Intrigue at last. I sprang from my seat.

Theo ambled along the water in mysterious silence, then suddenly stopped and turned to me but still wouldn't say a word.

"Is Dries reconsidering his engagement?" I finally asked.

"Jo." Theo gave a little nod, not in response to my question but as if he'd just made a decision, as if he was committing himself to something. "You surely know how I feel about you. You must know that I want nothing more than to spend the rest of my life with you and put all my happiness into your hands."

I wasn't sure I'd understood him correctly, but I feared that I had, so I didn't ask him to repeat himself.

I could not have been more surprised if the ducks on the canal lined up on the water in the shape of a tulip and began singing the Dutch national anthem.

For a moment, I even considered that Dries had put Theo up to a prank, but the raw emotion in Theo's eyes and his earnest expression suggested my answer meant everything to him.

I hid my hands in the folds of my dress. "I don't understand."

"Would you do me the honor of becoming my wife, Johanna Bonger?" He waited with a solemn, reverent smile, his earlier nervousness gone, as if he could relax at last.

Would I...

"Why?" flew from my lips before I could hold back the startled response. "We've met twice in the past two years. You barely know me."

"Are you no longer free? Dries never mentioned anyone else. I ask him about you often. I hoped..."

"I am free."

"If your heart is not already engaged..."

"My heart is *very* much engaged."

Theo broke into a fast walk, then pivoted, shifting from one foot to the other rapidly as though he might jump into the canal.

I eased toward the house. "We should return to Mama."

Desolation shaded his face past ashen. Even the sky turned gray behind him, casting a dull gloom over the water. "Is there nothing I can say to convince you to consider my proposal?"

"I know well the suffering unrequited love can cause, but I cannot gift you the answer you wish for, Theo."

"At the Rijksmuseum with your brother, the three of us together. Do you remember what fun we had?" His entire body begged, from his eyebrows to his fingertips. "You were so full of inquiry and intelligence. You asked me question after question. I would be happy forever if I had a partner in life such as you."

I could not form a response beyond a desperate "Theo, I cannot."

He returned to walk grimly beside me. I feared he might cry. I feared I might yet break down myself from sheer sympathy.

"How is your brother?" I rushed to ask. "The painter." He had two brothers and three sisters. "How does he like Paris? You must be glad he finally decided to move there so you can be together again."

"Vincent is finally adding color and light to his paintings after much urging on my part. He needed Paris. He needed to experience the new spirit of the times. The dreariness of Antwerp wasn't beneficial to his health or his painting." Theo spoke haltingly, as if he hadn't fully left the pain of our previous subject behind, but was unable to resist telling me about his brother. His expression softened. Another woman, who was not already in love with a different man, would have found him handsome.

"Dries wrote about Vincent's terrible illness and other troubles last year." My brother was of the opinion that a lot of Vincent's problems were caused by his stubbornness. "He has fully recovered?"

"For the time being. Unfortunately, he is prone to relapses. I wish he would rest and eat more."

And drink less. Another tidbit I suddenly remembered from Dries.

"I must help him in any way I can." Theo looked

at me with a disconcerting longing, but he stayed on the topic of Vincent, thank heavens. "As young boys, we pledged our support and devotion to each other for the rest of our lives. We swore an oath."

I had my favorite among my siblings, Dries, so I appreciated the sentiment. "It must be liberating to find one's true calling."

And to be allowed to follow that calling.

"He first chose the church." Theo nearly smiled. "Did Dries tell you? Vincent ministered to the most wretched miners, down in the darkest shafts. He gifted away all his belongings. If he saw someone poorer than him, he gave the shirt off his own back."

"A shining example of his faith."

"The church expelled him for taking the teachings of the Bible to the extreme." Theo sighed with fraternal desperation. "His idealism is more suited to painting."

We reached my parents' yard. *Just a few more steps.* "Is his art popular in Paris?"

"He will have his first sale soon, I predict. You should see his *Tulip Fields*. A bridge between styles, his past and his future, a new direction with light. When I first saw it, I felt as if I were witnessing color being born…" He gushed on as we went in.

He had more brotherly love in him than water in Amsterdam's canals, and for that I liked him, but I could not love him.

"Had a pleasant walk?" Mama's expression promised a tidal wave of questions as soon as we were in private. She wasn't going to believe what I had to tell her. "More tea, Theo?"

"Thank you, Mevrouw Bonger, but I must take my leave. My own mother is waiting."

"I'll show Theo out," I offered before Anke could interfere. I owed him that much. And also, it allowed me to defer Mama's interrogation for a few more minutes. I had to present the proposal in such a way that she would see its absurdity instead of a grand offer I must throw myself on immediately.

Inside the front door, Theo picked up his carpet-bag. And then he just stood there, until I wished I'd let Anke see to him after all. Standing endlessly in the small, enclosed space with my jilted suitor was quickly turning torturous.

What more does he want?

"Johanna, can you not offer me any hope at all?"

Only a cruel woman would string him along. "I am sorry, Theo."

His sad smile could have made angels weep an entire spring's worth of rain. In the end, he could no longer maintain even that small smile. The corners of his mouth sank. He pushed his hat onto his head, over his dark-copper hair, with a grave finality. "Goodbye, Johanna Bonger."

"Goodbye, Theo van Gogh."

He descended our front steps, his feet halting on the pavement. "May I write?"

I couldn't say no again, not to such a small request. "Yes."

A single word. But, oh, how much power a single word could have.

I could not have fathomed that because of that one yes, in three years' time, two people I loved would be dead.

CHAPTER THREE

Emsley

"I'll tell you a secret, Emsley." Diya crossed our small break room at the Beverly Hills Four Seasons where I was hiding to conquer my pre-auction nerves. "Men want three things from women: stimulation, adoration, and nurturing. You have to know what to give them and when." She filled her cup with coffee, lowering her voice until I could barely hear her over the noise in the hallway. "And you have to give it to them wrapped in sex."

This was how far I'd fallen: I was listening to relationship advice from my ex-boyfriend's new girlfriend. My eyeballs felt as if they were rough carved from granite: stone dry and too heavy to roll. I'd slept too little on the plane from New York to LA, then dragged myself to the office straight from the airport. I'd showered at the gym on the building's top floor and changed into fresh clothes I kept at work in a garment bag. I might have been exhausted at the *Fast Business* interview, but at least I hadn't looked like someone had just pulled me out of the overhead luggage compartment.

"I don't have time for a man." I'd been saying that a lot lately, but nobody believed me. I hadn't even had time to catch up with Trey about his stupid text yet. "I had the magazine interview this morning, and then I've been here since, setting up tonight's auction."

I had minutes before the guests would be arriving, and I didn't want to spend those minutes with Diya, talking about men. When she'd walked in, I'd been about to call my grandmother to ask her about the green diary.

Diya sloshed soy milk into her coffee, careful of her shimmering turquoise dress. Designer wrap dresses were her uniform like mine were black suits. She dressed to fit in with the celebrity clients she handled. Trey dealt with the politicians. I was the auctioneer.

Diya checked the door over my shoulder as she moved to the food table. "How many new events did we sign this week?"

"Two." *Not enough.* "If we survive the next couple of months, the midterm elections might save us. We could be rolling in new contracts."

She picked up a plate, then put it back down, carefully *not* looking at me. "If we have to, I'm okay with dissolving the business."

Ah. Trey had already talked to her. Of course, he had. They'd been together while I'd been in New York. I tried my best not to feel as if they'd banded together against me. I tamped down my resentment.

"I don't want to dissolve." I mentally choked the idea with both hands. "We can fix our problems." I backed toward the door. "I have to go and greet guests." A successful auction house was built on relationships and referrals.

Diya glanced past me again, and from the relief in her eyes, I knew what was coming. "Trey!"

Trey dropped a kiss on Diya and gave her a raspy, chick-flick-movie-quality "Hey." He barely spared me a glance. "Emsley."

I refused to let it hurt.

He was California tousled-blond, tall and lanky, preppy geek in all the right ways. Used to be mine. But while my head was always in the business, Diya paid attention to people. And Trey liked attention.

I refused to let it hurt.

I led an organized life divided into two columns: Building the Business and Time Away from Business. TAFB.

All things TAFB were to be avoided.

And then another girl snagged my guy. *Surprise.*

I refused to let it hurt.

"Everything ready?" Trey inhaled the aroma wafting off our cups. "Let me grab some black gold."

I didn't tell him that *black gold* was a reference to crude oil. The less we talked pre-auction, the less he'd get on my last nerve.

"It doesn't have to be awkward. Right, Em?" Diya picked up a plate again and piled it with his favorites: crab cakes and mini quiches. "We're all friends. I know you want us to be happy."

By *us*, she meant the two of them. I'd been lost between her two sentences like the Brazilian cheese puff she accidentally knocked off the table.

"Everybody deserves happiness." For me, right then, that meant staying in business.

I swiveled to Trey and put in my preemptive bid. "I don't want to shut down. If you two want out, that's fine. But I'm not letting Ludington's go."

We walked out of the break room together.

"Would you prefer a month of emergency meetings first?" Trey's tone had a sarcastic, belittling edge. *Did he do that before? Did I just not notice?* "This isn't the time for a meandering hike up Mount Denial, Emsley. Mark Selig flew back to DC because you couldn't accommodate him. Anyway, nobody said we should throw away what we have. I looked into political polling. That's where the money is. I want us to go in the direction of profit."

Diya shifted closer to him so they were walking shoulder to shoulder, a single unit. "Polling is a growing field."

I didn't have time to smother two people, even if I conveniently tripped over a stray chair cushion. "Ludington's is an *auction house*. And, I'm sorry, Trey, but you don't get to pick the direction. I'm the face of the business, and I'm an auctioneer. I came up with the idea because this is what I want to do. I'm not a pollster. I like what we're doing."

"So it's all about you? It's a freaking ego thing?" Ego he understood.

"It's a perseverance thing."

My earliest memory of my grandmother was her visiting us in Connecticut—a surprise visit. She didn't do any other kind. I had asked her how she'd gotten to be so famous. Violet Velar looked her only grandchild in the eyes and said, *"You succeed by not failing."*

Even at age seven, the advice had struck me as a profound truth of life.

I wasn't going to cut and bail. I refused to be that kind of a person.

Diya soothed Trey with a smile, then glanced at me. "Trey is right. We have to make money."

For her, Ludington's had always been a job. She wasn't emotionally attached to the company. But she *was* emotionally attached to Trey.

"If you think Ludington's is going under and you want to quit, quit. You can sign your shares over to me." *Always ask for what you want. If you want to participate in the auction, you have to bid.*

Diya owned twenty percent of Ludington's, while Trey and I owned forty percent each, in proportion of what each of us had brought in, cash and intangibles combined.

She blinked at me. "For free?"

"What's the difference between us shutting down

and you walking away with nothing, and you walking away with nothing and letting me keep trying to save the business? You'll have no further liability. If I'm sued, it won't touch you. If I go bankrupt, it doesn't go on your record. We all get what we want." *Please.* "Trey?"

"Like I said, I'm not talking about a complete shutdown. If you hate the idea of polling so much, you quit. I'll buy you out. How does two hundred grand sound? You get back what you put in."

"No."

"Then you buy me out. A million dollars."

"There's no million dollars."

"I put in a million. Ludington's couldn't have happened without me."

"As it couldn't have happened without Diya." Who brought in her finance degree and kept us afloat all this time, in addition to having a singular ability to corral celebrities. "As it couldn't have happened without me." My knowledge of the industry and the original client base I'd brought with me, and my starting stake. "But fine. I'll buy your shares."

I'd fantasized about saying those words. Ideally, in a distant future where I actually had money. This confrontation with my partners was coming way too soon. I wasn't ready.

"If we're shutting down, time is of the essence." Diya was the first to recover. She knew I'd spoken on impulse, and so she passed right by my unrealistic offer. "If we keep going with the office rent and payroll expenses, we'll be even further in the red. We don't want to go bankrupt. We don't want to be known as a complete and utter financial disaster."

"Thirty days to buy me out." Trey watched me with that blandly pleasant look that meant he was in future-billionaire mode, baiting a hook. "I sign my shares over to you if you pay me a million dollars within thirty days."

We stopped. The silence was complete until a passing hotel employee dropped a plate from her tray. The china smashed onto hard tile, the sound of my dreams shattering.

"She can't pay you." Diya remained the voice of reason.

"If she can't buy me out, she agrees that I buy her out." Trey was on a roll. He was also too close. Almost a foot taller than me, he had a habit of standing over me with his head bent, looming. It always made me feel even shorter than I was. Diya had once asked, *"Don't you just love the way he makes you feel dainty?"*

He didn't make me feel dainty. He made me feel overshadowed.

I stood my ground. Ludington's had been my idea. *My dream.* He'd own it over my dead body. "Deal."

Diya fretted. "You're both making a mistake."

"So be it. I'm entitled to make mistakes. You'll have each other, and I'll have the company."

"Fine. If Trey wants a million, I want five hundred thousand."

"We'll talk about it later." When she stopped

pulling numbers out of her... "I have to go greet guests."

I hurried away from them, willing the night to be a sparkling success.

I'd arranged for finger food catered by André Milano, LA's newest celebrity chef. There'd be clinking crystal and glinting diamonds, stars in designer gowns. I'd planned for a Violet's kind of event.

I called her on my way to the front of the hotel. "I miss you already."

"I miss you too, honey. How was the interview?"

"Positive. But they brought up your stroke. I'm sorry. I don't know if they'll put you in their article. I wanted to give you a heads-up."

"Did they ask about my sordid past?"

"Is the media a den of vipers? Lucky I'm a ninja-level expert at deflecting personal questions." I didn't want her to worry. "Any proposals today?"

"One of the second-floor patients, Louis, has potential. Cuban jazz musician. He gave a concert at lunchtime out in the hallway. He plays the saxophone like a dream, *and* he's a decent poker player."

"Strip poker?"

"Would you disapprove?"

"Only if he wears tighty-whities."

Violet laughed. "It's nice to have support from one's family."

"Talking about family..." As soon as I started the sentence, I regretted it, but at that point, I had no way to go except forging ahead. "Did you ever lose Mom when she was a child?"

"Don't be silly. Of course not. Did she say I did?"

"Like, in a museum?" I went around the corner and almost ran headfirst into an overpacked luggage cart.

"I let her wander so she could discover what she liked. Some parents drag their kids around, telling them what each painting means. Make them memorize artists and titles and, for heaven's sake, dates, instead of letting art speak to those open young hearts. I wanted your mother to think that the Met and MoMA were her playgrounds. We went there to visit friends, to have fun. I let her explore. I hope she did the same for you."

"Mom held my hand wherever we went until I was ten. I had more fun when I was with you. Remember when you took me to the Met in fifth grade? The staff recognized you, and they treated us as if we were rock stars." I'd wanted to be just like her when I grew up.

"Remember the Guggenheim?"

Oh yes. "I wrote in the visitors' book that I was disappointed they didn't have your paintings."

"And you signed it Princess Lilian of Lichtenstein."

"I wanted to give my words weight."

Instead of laughter on the other end came "What other terrible tales did you mother tell you about me?"

"Nothing." I wanted to ask about my grandfather,

but I'd asked once in middle school, with the innocence of a child not knowing she was treading on sensitive ground. The deep hurt on my grandmother's face made me wish I could take the question back. I'd been relieved when she'd changed the subject.

When I was twelve, I'd spent the entire summer poring through pictures of celebrities on the internet. Considering the circles Violet had run in, I'd been convinced her lover had been someone famous. My mother had a cleft chin. I googled images of Kirk Douglas, but then settled on Timothy Dalton. I daydreamed about him showing up to take me to the Oscars, how he would introduce me on the red carpet as his granddaughter.

He never did come for me, but at least I won the grandmother lottery. "I loved all our outings. You're going to recover." I crossed the resplendent lobby, discarding my empty cup on a coffee table, dodging hotel guests who were checking in. "And then we'll go on new adventures together."

"Damn right we will. I might not run with the bulls in Pamplona, but I wouldn't mind a last flamenco in Andalusia with a handsome Spaniard. We'll find us a pair of them."

Now *that* sounded like the Violet I knew.

"Talking about looking irresistible," she said. "One of the nurses makes jewelry. Next time you come, remind me that I ordered you a pair of earrings. Sunflowers. You know why?"

"Van Gogh?"

"That's where my interest was born, but then I started liking them for themselves. Sunflowers are adaptable, for one. Seventy species. You plant them somewhere, and they'll figure out how to grow. They'll come up in the rich loam of rivers as easily as in arid, poor dirt. The worse the soil, the bigger they flower. They're scrappy as hell, but they always look like stars."

I was almost at the front door, out of time. I'd bring up my grandfather in person the next time I flew to New York. I wanted to use the few seconds I left on a different question.

"Who wrote the green diary you gave me? I thought it was yours, but now that I'm reading it..." I'd only managed the first entry on the plane. "In the front of the book, someone wrote the name Clara. But inside the diary, she calls herself Jo. She lived in the Netherlands a hundred years ago. How did her diary end up in New York? Why is it in English? And, most importantly, why do you have it? Wouldn't something like this stay in the family? Are we related to Vincent van Gogh?"

For most of my life, I've been trying to figure out who my grandfather was. Was Violet telling me who my great-great-great-grandfather was instead?

Johanna Bonger married Theo van Gogh. I looked it up on the internet. They had one son. His descendants are well-documented. My ancestors weren't among them.

Yet Violet had the diary.

If I wasn't Jo and Theo's great-great-etc-granddaughter, could I be Vincent's? The theory gripped me, filled me with a wild thrill. Vincent never married, never had children. On the record. He did frequent houses of prostitution, however. He lived across the street from one when he lived in the famous Yellow House he painted in Arles. When he cut off his ear, he gifted it to one of those prostitutes across the street.

My next thought would kill my mother if I ever spoke it out loud, but...

Was one of our ancestors the love child of a French whore and Vincent van Gogh?

CHAPTER FOUR

CHAPTER FOUR

Johanna

    1888, June, Scheveningen, Netherlands

"Did you have a tragic love affair in Utrecht? Is that why you fell so sick? Did Theo van Gogh visit?" My best friend, Anna, kept pestering me as we hurried along the beach. She was driven by fear that her mother was going to be frightfully cross with us if we arrived late for lunch again. I was staying with her family at a resort in Scheveningen. "Did Theo and Eduard duel over your heart?"

"No. Because my life is not a Shakespeare drama." I kept up with her, driven by hope that the letter the postman mentioned when our paths crossed on the way out was from the man I loved. I would have turned around right then and there to claim and read the missive, but I'd wished to escape Anna's chiding about being obsessed with Eduard. "I haven't seen Theo since he proposed."

The wind whipped our white linen skirts like fishing boat sails, and when it failed to blow us off course, it went after our wide-brimmed straw hats. As we fought the gusts, our heels sank into the soft sand. We struggled on, undeterred, regardless.

"There had to be heartbreak involved." Anna's voice carried a measure of hurt. She thought I was keeping secrets from her. "A third man? Was he *maddeningly* handsome?"

"*You* are maddeningly mistaken. Utrecht was..." *Impossible to explain, other than to say that my first attempt at independence had utterly failed.* "I felt like the city sat on my chest like an enormous black bird. I couldn't breathe. At night, I couldn't sleep. I had dark, shivering premonitions of something terrible happening, and I could almost see..." I swallowed the rest. "I sound more melodramatic than the schoolgirls I taught."

"Did you see Heathcliff in the mist?" Anna threaded her arm through mine, a gesture of acceptance. She finally believed me that I was holding nothing back. "You shouldn't read those gothic novels."

"You sound like the school doctor. *Reading adversely affects young women's mental state and causes melancholia.* He was convinced that romantic novels were the root of all evil. He also thought that independent minded, when applied to a woman, was a synonym for addlebrained."

"What kind of powder did he give you for excessive reading?"

"Something vile that I sprinkled on the geraniums in the window. He also prescribed horseback riding to rattle everything back into proper position in my brain."

"How smart. I wouldn't have thought of that. Did it help?"

"No." I'd remained lost in a sea of sadness. "I could barely rise from bed. I kept waiting for Eduard to visit. He knew I was there, yet he never came."

The wind made my confession easier, snatching every other word. I felt as if I were confessing to the sea that stretched immense and benevolent to the horizon, offering no judgment.

Anna heard enough to respond with "I'm glad you're here now. The sea air and Dr. Hollinger's special diet at the *Kurhause* will set everything aright."

If I have to eat another bowl of the resort doctor's onion, cabbage, and beetroot soup... My heart was sick with longing. As Eduard was the source of my malady, only he could be its cure. I couldn't wait to read what he'd written. It might even be a proposal. They could come on quite suddenly and without warning, as Theo van Gogh had taught me.

"I wish I could reclaim the months I spent at Utrecht." So much time wasted. "Dries wrote me about something curious." A word from my brother's last letter bobbed in my mind like a seal on the sea. "*El anacronópete*. A book by the Spanish writer, Enrique Gaspar, about a machine that can fly you back through time."

Anna was wide-eyed astonished. "For what purpose?"

"To correct the mistakes of the past."

A wave splashed too close to us, and we jumped away, but soon went back to walking as near the water as we dared.

"It's only that…" Thoughts that broke my heart were always fiendishly difficult to articulate. They lodged themselves inside my chest. That my corset scarcely allowed me a full breath did not help. "I wanted to make a difference. I thought I would leave my mark on my students' lives and that would be my legacy. But I'm not the person I thought I was."

There, the core of the matter. The horrible, disappointing truth.

"How so?"

"I wanted to be independent. I thought I was ready to be independent. That I *was* independent, an adult woman. I should have been able to manage in Utrecht. Dries moved to Paris, a whole other country, and he is managing."

"The whole world is set up for men to manage."

She wasn't wrong. My brothers could go anywhere at any time, talk to anyone. Their opinions were heard and considered. In Utrecht, as an unmarried woman, I had not been able to dine at a restaurant alone, or walk in the park, or visit the museum.

Unless I could find a chaperone to accompany me, in my free time I'd been trapped in my room. And all my suggestions to improve my students' education and their circumstances in the dormitory had been summarily dismissed by the director of the institute.

Ahead of us, a young woman darted from a yellow-striped cabana with a squeal.

Anna whispered, "Goodness, she is naked."

We slowed and stared.

The blonde woman wore absolutely nothing but ankle-high swimming shoes, blue cotton stockings with matching bloomers that ended just below her knees, a matching swimming dress, and a hat. Her arms below the elbows were *entirely* bare.

She crossed the sand and ran into the sea, then disappeared in the waves. She resurfaced in a spray of water, faced the sun, and laughed.

Soon, three others darted after her from their cabanas, all similarly undressed, all similarly reckless.

Anna's nostrils trembled. "The freckles!"

Yet the sisters—they looked alike—weren't bothered by the sun or the curious eyes that followed them.

I couldn't make myself turn away either. "Who are they?"

"The Newhouse girls. *Americans.* Their father is Gordon Newhouse, the shipping magnate. His wife is Dutch, and she brings her daughters to the Netherlands every summer. Mama met them on our first day here, at lunch, before you arrived."

Another gust of sea breeze hit us. We hurried along.

"Did I tell you…" Anna pressed her hat onto her head. "That the stove we ordered for the summer kitchen will be delivered this week? Only one more month, and my true happiness begins. Something only marriage can give a woman."

I didn't bring up my brother Dries and his bride, both miserable, their marriage certainly no start to any joyful life. "Jan loves you."

"And I shall endeavor to love him."

She made it sound easy. "But what if you can't?"

"We have enough in common. I studied at art school. He is an artist."

"A union of kindred spirits, true harmony, is very much my idea of a good marriage. But above all, I wish for true love."

"Love can also bring a person to ruin, or heartache." She meant Eduard. When I bristled, she quickly changed the subject. "My aunt is gifting us two down comforters and four down pillows." Her fingers fluttered in the air as if she was fluffing the pillows already. "Mama is giving me another double set for when we shall have guests staying with us. Do you think that will be enough?"

"Mmm." A man and a woman descended the steps of our resort, distracting me. They cut across the sand to the water's edge. They stood in place for a few seconds, the man with his hands on his hips, the woman straight backed and holding a parasol, as if conducting an inspection. Then they marched back.

"On a day visit, with 'see the sea' on their calendar, checked," I speculated, then felt a flash of shame at ridiculing them. *Judge not, so you yourself shall not be judged.* "Perhaps I am the same. Finish school, pass exams, gain teaching certificate—all checked, one after the other. Be patient until Eduard's proposal. Except, I've never had patience. And now I'm losing even hope. Will I ever know happiness?"

"I imagine happiness like needlepoint. Dots of color, precious moments placed next to each other as time passes, small joys doled out over a lifetime." A dreamy smile stretched Anna's enviable, fashionably thin lips. "You look back, after forty or fifty years, and you see the most beautiful picture."

"I'd take a year of pure joy over small moments spread out over a lifetime." I'd been gathering those *moments* for years. A glimpse. A smile. A flower gifted. They stubbornly refused to add up to a proposal. Eduard's small gestures were too few and too far between, leaving me starved. "I would prefer unbridled passion."

We reached the steps and hurried up, cutting across the wooden walkway. *Thump, thump, thump,* our shoes tapped out a rhythm, a strange heartbeat.

The porter opened the Kurhause's front door for us. "Mevrouw Bonger. Mevrouw Dirk."

We crossed the high-ceilinged lobby, leaving a light dusting of sand on the marble floor in our wake.

Anna careened around an assistant who pushed a cart of vitamin water. "Mama will be in a mood if we made her wait."

We marched past another assistant who was helping an older gentleman to his feet, then we burst into the apartment, Anna first.

Nobody was waiting for us.

"We're not late." She was breathless with relief.

I simmered with impatience. She stood between me and the hall table. "The mail?"

"Oh. Here. Two for you. One from Dries, and one from Theo." She handed me the letters. "The rest are all for Papa."

Crestfallen, I scanned my brother's letter first.

"Dries says Theo has thrown himself completely into the Bohemian lifestyle." I summarized as I read. "He's running around with his young painter friends and ruining his health. He avoids Dries's company." Cutting guilt had me lowering the page. "I fear it might have to do with my rejection of him last year. I feel responsible. Dries has been lonely in Paris. And now I've ruined even this friendship for him."

"And what does Theo have to say?" Anna removed her hat and held her hand out for mine to hang them both. "I can't believe he still writes you."

"Frequently. I am even corresponding with one of his sisters, Wilhelmina. We share a love of literature. Theo encouraged her to reach out to me."

"Leave it to you to make a new friend just to talk about books." Anna's laugh was indulgent. "Does Theo still profess his love?"

"He writes about art and politics for the most part. And books," I added, knowing it would elicit a groan from Anna. It did. "He challenges my views.

His friendship might be good for me. Dries always says being challenged is the only way to grow." I finished Dries's letter and looked up. "Does Jan challenge you?"

"Goodness no. And neither should he. I wish for nothing but peace and harmony in my marriage. I should not like to be put out by wild ideas."

I cut Theo's letter open. He and I had been discussing the institution of marriage, and he continued where he last left off. "You know, Theo believes as you do, that love and deep affection in a marriage is built day by day."

"While you wish for passion described in those silly novels." Anna's indulgent smile widened. "You are supposed to enjoy them, Jo, not believe them."

"I think a couple should be in love before saying their vows."

"Have something like you have with Eduard?"

Just hearing his name on Anna's lips made my soul ache. I silently nodded.

"But do you, Jo?" Distress clouded Anna's bright eyes. "Do you truly have anything with him?"

I had to grit my teeth so I wouldn't say anything that would offend my oldest friend.

Easy for her to belittle my thwarted love when she was so close to matrimony. What did she know about the *agony* of endlessly waiting and hoping? Resentment lodged in my throat like one of Dr. Hollinger's dry, course-ground peasant rolls. I had to work to swallow it all down.

I escaped to the window with my letters and

stared out at the sea, feeling as if the gray waves were churning inside me.

Anna came to lay her narrow hand gently on my arm. "I didn't mean to vex you."

"I must hold on to hope."

"Are you in love with Eduard, or with the idea of him, the idea of love? Are you holding on to hope, or are you holding on to misery?"

"Eduard is the kindest, most dependable—"

"So kind and dependable that he never visited you in Utrecht? And he hasn't written in ages."

"He is busy with his studies. You know how sweet he's been before. He escorted me everywhere. He brought flowers. He took me on boat rides. Last summer, whenever we were alone, he drew me so close… I might as well have been sitting on his lap," I whispered. "He's giving me time to adjust to such a major change in my life as marriage before he would confess love. There's an understanding between us. An understanding between our families."

"And Theo?"

"He barely knows me."

"Yet Theo has given you careful consideration. And you must have grown to know each other better through your letters. He encourages your fondness for books. He even provided you with the perfect corresponding partner in his sister. He knows what he wants, and he wants you. He is not afraid of declaring either his feelings or his intentions."

If I only loved Theo.

I had his letter in one hand and my brother's in

the other. "Dries is asking me to visit him in Paris for Christmas."

"You must go and save Theo from absinth and French women. Look at it as an adventure."

"Because Utrecht went so well? I—"

Anna's parents, Meneer and Mevrouw Dirk, strode through the door, cutting off the rest of my argument.

"You are here." Mevrouw Dirk's head was uncovered, her hair a teetering haystack. The wind must have stolen her hat. "Good. I was hoping we could present ourselves at lunch on time today."

Meneer Dirk caught the letters in my hand and headed straight for his own small pile of envelopes. "Treasure your correspondence, Mevrouw Bonger," he said as he sorted through his mail. "I predict that with that infernal telephone device spreading, letter writing will soon become a lost skill."

Mevrouw Dirk tugged off her lace summer gloves. "I am sure it won't come to that."

His wife's words did not calm Anna's father. He tended to take any opposition as an attack. "No more carefully constructed sentences." His tone elevated. "People will call with the most trifling matters the moment the fancy strikes them. My dear, I expect your mother, to call me in the middle of reading my morning papers to tell me what she had for breakfast." He chopped through the air with the envelope he held. "Mark my words, ladies. Part of civilization itself will be lost."

Anna pressed a hand to her chest. "Papa. Not the epistolary arts!"

She shot me a quick glance of mirth.

I kept a straight face, but was laughing inside, our argument forgotten.

"Where is the maid? Brechtje!" Anna's mother called, giving up on soothing her husband. And when the girl they'd brought with them ran from the back, Mevrouw Dirk gestured to her hair. "You must fix this frightful mess. I can't walk into the lunch room looking like a…"

"Sea monster?" Anna's father suggested.

"Arnold!"

I turned back to the window, so they wouldn't see my smile. The four American girls were still frolicking in the North Sea. They were undaunted by the occasional wave that knocked them over.

Everyone else kept safely to the beach.

Mevrouw Dirk passed by me on her way to her dressing table and glanced out. "How foolish."

How free. How brave.

"You should go to Paris," Anna said quietly, then walked to her room to see to her own appearance.

She was right. I had no time machine to reclaim the miserable months I spent at Utrecht. I had to move forward. I would go to France. I would brave the trip.

And if I was thrust into Theo van Gogh's company while I was there… I would cross that particular footbridge on that specific canal when I came to it.

CHAPTER FIVE

Emsley

A soft sound whispered through the line, the air rushing out of Violet's lungs. "Let's talk about this after you've gone through the whole box," she said instead of addressing my question about our family's connection to Vincent van Gogh. *Does she sound distressed? Why would she sound distressed?* While I worried, she said, "You have a great event tonight. I hope it brings you new contracts."

"I hope you win at strip poker."

"You do strip poker right, and there are no losers."

How could I not laugh? "I love you."

"Love you more. How many guests are you expecting?"

I stepped outside into the balmy, honeysuckle-scented evening. "About two dozen A-list celebrities, along with as many politicians and a hundred of their wealthiest supporters. Not that I'm nervous."

I had to make tonight a resounding success. If I didn't, all would be lost. I kept that to myself. I didn't want my grandmother to know how desperate the situation was, how close I stood to the abyss of utter failure.

"You let your smile shine from your soul." Violet's love-laden voice wrapped around me. "You let courage beam from your heart. The night is yours, honey. You drive this auction like it's a Lamborghini.

Drive it like a Lamborghini. Drive it like a Lamborghini. Right.

Nobody must suspect that my company was falling apart.

Under no circumstances could I allow any stress to show on my face. To be successful, I had to radiate success. I had to focus on nothing but the positive.

I elbowed Diya. "Arthur Zigler is here with his mistress."

We stood by the steps of the auction stage. Over a hundred VIPs filled the Beverly Hills Four Seasons' Culina Caffè, a sea of pre-auction buzz surrounding us.

Diya searched the crowd for the sixty-something ex-wrestler who owned a string of luxury car dealerships in Cali. "Anastasia?"

"New one." The night was looking better by the minute, and I focused on that. I couldn't think about my deal with Trey and Diya to buy them out, or I'd panic. Further discussion, and saner numbers, would have to wait until we were at home tonight. A whole other battle for which I had to gird myself.

Diya finally found Zigler's table. "You think someday he'll graduate to women old enough so they don't have to buy their drinks with a fake ID?"

"I'm just glad he brought her." Zigler always bid more when he had a mistress on his arm. And he bid the most when the mistress was new. "Maybe he's a Charlie Chaplin fan and he'll go for the set of original movie reels."

"Remember when he dropped a hundred grand on that guillotine?"

A *working* guillotine, from the set of a surprisingly popular French arthouse film. "I almost fell off the stage."

I signaled to our sound guy, and he switched the music from sedate jazz to a brain-pounding rendition of *Start Me Up* from the Rolling Stones. Everyone fell silent, simply because they couldn't talk over the beat.

I conquered the steps.

This is my auction.

I am in control of my room.

I strode forward.

The stage, my red auction hammer, and the five-inch heels on my red pumps lent me authority. At five-five, I wasn't given an imposing stature, but I had excellent balance. I could have walked across those planks in stilts. The universe giveth, and the universe taketh away.

Another discreet hand signal, and the music faded. Into the sudden silence, I said, "Welcome, distinguished ladies and gentlemen. We're all here today to support Senator Rutger's campaign. Bid early, bid often. Don't be shy."

Most of our guests put down their glasses. They were ready to roll. I could deal with the few who weren't. We always had a certain percentage who only came for the entertainment—nobody liked free-bies more than the rich. The auction was of the champagne-and-canapés format. I didn't do elaborate dinners where participants focused too much on their food. I didn't like having to fight for their attention.

"I'm sure you already have your favorites picked out in today's catalogue." I zipped along before anyone could become distracted. "But I'm happy to announce that we have a handful of surprise items that will make you giddy. So let's start with one of those."

I gestured at the screen behind me with my red power hammer, while I clicked the remote in my other hand. A hillside with endless rows of grapevines appeared. "A weekend at nine-time Oscar winner Francis Copland's vineyard in Napa Valley, a guided tour of the wine cellars by our generous donor, and two cases of wines of your choice to take home."

The audience clapped.

"The perfect date, the perfect surprise present, the

perfect getaway. Because you're the type of person who wants to put a smile on the face of the one you love." I gave them something they could visualize. "After the past couple of years, you deserve a break." In case anyone needed justification.

I paused to create suspense, then said, "The bid starts at ten thousand dollars."

Two dozen hands shot into the air.

"Do I hear eleven? Imagine strolling through the vineyard at sunset, holding hands. You work hard. Success requires many personal sacrifices. So how about the perfect weekend to reconnect, to show that you care, to fall in love all over again." Always tell a story. Stories sell.

The hands were back, even higher.

In the end, the weekend went to a Silicon Valley venture capitalist at the solid bang of my red hammer. "Sold to the gentleman in the spectacular green bow tie for nineteen thousand dollars."

His wife kissed him on the cheek and shot me a look of pure gratitude. In her sixties, she resembled Audrey Hepburn at that age, showing off a shimmering silver gown fit for a Hollywood icon.

Here was another reason for my simple black outfits. I wanted my clients to be the stars. I wanted them to feel like they were in the limelight, that the women were the princesses of the ball.

I clicked my remote, and a life-size painting appeared on the screen behind me. At the same time, two white-gloved assistants brought the original on stage and placed it on the waiting easel.

"Lydia Lawrence, three-time Oscar winner. Self-portrait." Lawrence wore a navy-blue suit with a red shirt and stood on the roof of a high rise in a power pose as if about to take flight. "The first actress to have successfully fought to be paid the same as her male costar in a major action production. The founder of StarRise." A small studio that focused on underrepresented stories. "And a talented artist." Her works were just becoming collectible.

A gratifying number of hands went up.

The painting found a home with Meredith Meyer, the studio head who'd been Lawrence's mentor back in the day. "To the lady in the best tiara I've ever seen, for fifty thousand dollars."

Tiaras and elaborate ball gowns were Meyer's trademark look. She was a queen, and she didn't mind if everybody knew it.

I moved on to a custom-designed day at Universal Studios. The next expected megahit. An all-star cast.

The spectacular set visit went for a hundred grand to a nineteen-year-old social media influencer who would probably gain another million followers when she livestreamed her day. I was proud of her for not taking the easy way like one of her online rivals who'd recently leaked a sex tape.

By the time I retired my hammer at the end of the auction, Ludington's had raised close to a million dollars for Senator Rutger. Our commission would be fifteen percent of that. Someday soon, I was going to hold an event like this for stroke research, and I was going to wave the fee.

Diya beamed as I came off the stage. "The night's a win."

Trey stood next to her, his hands in his pockets. "Not enough. To make it, we'd need to bring in this much every single week."

"I'll keep that in mind going forward. I was serious about the buyout. Let's talk some realistic numbers." I would come up with the money some-how. "Then we can sign papers." I wanted every-thing in writing before he changed his mind.

He opened his mouth to respond, then snapped it shut and took off for some last-chance schmoozing with the senator, who was leaving.

Diya flashed me an apologetic smile, then scur-ried after him.

I'd been the first to arrive, and I was the last one to leave, two hours after the auction ended. Diya and Trey were long gone. They left with the senator, who offered them a ride in his limousine. I made sure nothing was left behind at the hotel before I called an Uber.

The plain yellow house Trey, Diya and I rented on a narrow, one-way street was a century younger than its neighbors, squeezed between two regular-size homes by a sharp-eyed developer. When we'd first moved in, I'd thought the barebones style was cute, my first adult digs. Now the narrow house looked stuck and out of place, wedged in there, trapped.

Trey was wrapped around Diya on the living room couch when I walked in.

They'd rushed home to be together. Because they were a couple. I hated that it hurt. "Hey."

Diya untangled herself and offered me the bowl of popcorn. "ABC is running a horror marathon. Want to hang out?"

We had to talk, but I had nothing left, no energy to pretend that we were all great friends. No energy to renegotiate business. "I'm beat. Could we have a meeting first thing in the morning?"

Tomorrow was another day.

I climbed the steps upstairs. Stopped at the top of the landing. "I'm giving you guys notice. I'm moving out as soon as I find my own place."

It was long past time. Violet was right.

Diya half came off the couch. "Em…"

"We'll talk about it in the morning. I need sleep."

I headed to the back room and closed the door behind me.

Diya used to live in the back room, Trey and I in the front one, and we used the third room for storage. Then Trey and I had broken up, and a few days later, Diya and I switched places. Like replacing a plug-in air freshener when you wanted a different scent.

I was too tired to think about it.

I was tired of thinking about it.

I soaked in a long shower, then collapsed onto my wrinkled cotton sheets.

I woke five criminally short hours later to my phone ringing.

"Your grandmother's doctor just called." My mother sounded squeaky, and before my brain processed her words, I thought the sound was weird because my battery was dying. But then my brain caught up, and my heart went squeaky next. Nothing good ever started with *The doctor called*. I braced.

"Violet had another stroke overnight. I can't sit through the plane ride. Can you fly back to New York?"

"I'll book the first flight." I scrambled off the bed and tripped over my shoes. "Did you talk to her? What did she say? How is she?"

"She's not conscious. When you get there, talk to Dr. Gonzales," Mom told me.

Dr. Gonzales had no encouraging news I could pass on to Mom when I called her from the elevator on my way to the third floor. She asked a dozen questions, but I could only tell her what I'd been told down-stairs. "No significant change."

Violet's room had been transformed into a hospital room, with a high-tech hospital bed and monitors and IV stands. Machines beeped around her, like robots communicating with each other. It didn't sound like they had anything good to say.

I moved closer to the bed. With the tubes and wires and mask, I could hardly tell it was Violet. My chest hurt, as if I were breathing in crushed razor blades with every breath.

The stupid guardrail was up. I turned it down and sat on the edge of the mattress. "It's me. I'm here. If you open your eyes, I'll bring you mango pudding."

I took her hand, pictured the trauma in her brain, and willed the cells to repair themselves. "You can't leave me." I caressed her blue veins with my thumb. "I told Diya and Trey I was moving out. The business might go under. I want your advice on a hundred issues." I was trying to outbid Death, which one of us needed her more. "Probably two hundred. And you need to tell me about Van Gogh."

Movement at the door caught my eye. "Mrs. Yang."

"Oh, Emsley." She inched in, half slumped over her walker, moving even more slowly than usual. When she reached me, she gave me a one-armed hug.

We struggled to work up a smile for each other's sake, but neither of us succeeded. I took my bag off the recliner so she could sit.

She didn't. "Can't stay. PT guy will spank me if I don't do my laps."

"Is that a worry or a hope?"

Any other time, we would have laughed together. Now her lips trembled.

If she started to cry, I would too. Best not to give either of us the chance. "How is Lai Fa?"

She patted her pocket. "Want to hold her for a minute?"

"Oh, sure. Let me be the one who gets busted with a smuggled farm animal at a healthcare center." But I couldn't resist.

Lai Fa was all warm and soft, a fluff of comfort. She offered the sweetest chirp, looking at me with black apple-seed eyes as if asking, *Are you my mommy?*

Footsteps sounded in the hallway.

Mrs. Yang slipped the contraband chick back into her pocket. "How long do you think before Violet comes back to us?"

"Soon." The footsteps went past. "Do you think she can hear what we say to her?"

"I hope she can." Mrs. Yang reached over and patted Violet's knee. "You know I love you as if you were my own sister, but if you don't wake up, I'm going after Louis." Then she turned, slowly, painfully. "I'll be back on the next lap."

She shuffled out.

I adjusted Violet's blanket.

"I think she meant it. You don't want to miss strip poker. I've been looking forward to hearing the details afterwards. Do you really want Mrs. Yang to take your seat at the table?"

Violet didn't open her eyes. Her lips didn't stretch into a lopsided smile. Her fingers didn't squeeze mine.

"Your doctor said we're in the wait-and-see phase. I'd appreciate if you didn't make us wait too long. I'd like to *see* you recovered."

She'd had a near full recovery from the first stroke

and partial recovery from the second. She could do it again. She was Violet Velar.

A silver-haired man rolled in with a saxophone, maneuvering his wheelchair around the cables on the floor. *A knight on his horse, with his sword.*

"I'm Louis. You must be Emsley." He had a soft Cuban accent. His neatly trimmed pencil mustache drooped. He couldn't take his eyes off Violet. "It's my fault. I'm so sorry."

"It's a stroke. It's nobody's fault."

"Violet—" Louis choked up. "She wanted to sneak over to the hot tub in the PT room in the east wing. She talked me into giving her a ride."

For a moment, I was confused, then I realized a ride *on his lap.*

"I told her we should ask the nurse. But you can't say no to Violet."

My brain glitched out. "She had a stroke in the hot tub?"

"After we came back."

"Do the doctors know about this?"

Nod. "I am on probation."

"Hold on for a sec." I texted my mother. *Did you know about the hot tub?*

She texted back. *Just found out. I'm discussing it with our lawyer.*

I wished she'd talked to me before she talked to her attorney.

"I am so sorry." Louis shrank, collapsing in on himself.

Maybe the hot water caused my grandmother's

stroke, maybe it hadn't. "Honestly, sneaking off to the hot tub is so quintessential Violet. She always lived life on her own terms. Really, the only surprise is that something like this hasn't happened sooner."

Louis teared up. He lifted his saxophone. "Mind if I play for her?"

"Go ahead."

He touched the instrument to his lips that drooped almost exactly like my grandmother's, then he played a meandering jazz piece, tenderness turned into melody.

By the time he finished, I was blinking back tears. "Are you a professional musician?"

"I've been a lot of things." For a second, he seemed to be content to leave it at that. Then he looked from Violet to me. "I floated over from Cuba to Florida on an inner tube when I was ten. Back then, if your feet touched US soil, you were granted asylum. I stayed with an uncle who owned a restaurant in Miami."

His gnarled fingers caressed his saxophone. "Couldn't cook. Burned everything. Wasn't any better as a waiter either. Lost my uncle more money in broken plates than my work was worth. If I couldn't work in the kitchen and couldn't work the floor, I had to entertain. I played the saxophone a little already, so I learned to play better. Soon, people came into the restaurant just to listen to me. Ended up cutting three records. Had my fifteen minutes of fame."

He stayed for the better part of an hour, soothing my soul. I hoped Violet could hear him.

After Louis left, I laid my head on Violet's pillow. "I couldn't love you more if you were an oil baron bidding a million dollars on a Broadway ticket at my auction."

She didn't say *I love you* back, but I could feel it anyway. Like when you were near water, and you closed your eyes, and you still knew you were near water because the air was different. Her love clung to my skin, my hair, my heart.

I stayed like that until my neck hurt almost as much as my soul, and then I walked around the room. I had brought my laptop with me, but I wasn't in the right mind for work. I had the little green diary too, but I couldn't focus on that either. Jo's hopeless crush on Eduard would have to wait.

Diya called. "How is she?"

"The same."

"I'm so sorry, Em."

"She'll wake up soon. Her brain just shut the noise down while it's recovering."

Silence. Followed by "I'm calling to tell you, and I know this is horrible timing…" She trailed off.

Trey said something in the background. Words I couldn't quite catch.

Then Diya recovered. "I wanted you to hear it from me. We're friends, but I have to do what's best for me. I'm sorry. You can't raise the money for a buyout. We both know it."

I stopped by the window and beheld the black

night, feeling as if all that darkness was sucking me through the glass. I knew what she was going to say. "You sold your shares to Trey." My stomach cramped. "He borrowed half a mil from his father? Why didn't he borrow it to keep us afloat?"

"Trey and I agreed on two hundred thousand. Look, it was two hundred or nothing. Now I can pay off my student loans. Do you hate me?"

I didn't have it in me to manage her guilt. "I don't have the bandwidth to think about this right now. I have to go."

"I'm sorry, Em. Give Violet a hug for me."

I hung up, anger popping in my stomach like popcorn, burnt and bitter. Trey now owned sixty percent of the business we had built on *my* idea, with clients from *my* contact list.

The thought of losing Ludington's to Trey made me want to run screaming down the hallway. It'd been a mistake all these months to plaster over the tensions between us for business's sake.

I wanted to bang my head into the window. I didn't. I was afraid I'd do it too hard and crack the glass.

I could not fall apart. I was here for Violet.

"You have to wake up to help me figure this mess out," I pleaded as I turned.

Her monitors beeped a steady, reassuring rhythm.

"I know you'll wake up. In a few days, we'll be joking about this. We'll be eating pudding and talking about why you wanted me to read that old diary."

I walked to her wardrobe for the paint-splattered box and carried it to her bed. I riffled through the Dutch letters, all written by Johanna Bonger to the same woman. "Who is Clara? Why do you have Johanna Bonger's letters and her diary?"

Now that I've read the first two entries, I couldn't wait for more. I couldn't believe I was reading the words of a woman from a hundred years ago. A woman who'd known Vincent van Gogh. *If*, the little green book was a diary.

"To be honest, it might be a biography, written by the mysterious Clara." Here and there, there were notes in the margins that reminded me of editing notes on movie scripts I'd auctioned off over the years.

I reached the bottom of the robin's-egg-blue box, and my fingers brushed against a painting in a simple wood frame, the size of my two open palms side-by-side. My heart leaped. "What's this?"

No signature. The canvas was frayed in the back, the strange little painting grimy and crackled. The artist had painted a swaddled baby in the middle of his parents' bed. The image was too dirty to make out the details, but I could tell I wasn't holding a masterpiece—the colors off, the brushwork stiff. *Not Vincent's.* All my wild hopes crashed. I wouldn't have bought the piece if I had come across it in a Goodwill bin.

Johanna might have painted it. Weren't young ladies required to learn music and art back then?

They had *drawing rooms*, didn't they? Or was that Regency England?

Johanna did have a baby at one point. I couldn't wait to read how Theo won her over.

I held the uninspiring piece up for Violet. "Do you know who this is?"

CHAPTER SIX

Johanna
    1888, December, Paris, France

I was stalking Theo in Paris.

I'd meant to avoid him, but then I realized I could never forgive myself if I ruined his and Dries's friendship. I wanted to erase any tensions between the two of them, if I could. To achieve this, I had to talk to Theo—without giving him false hope that I sought him out because I'd reconsidered his proposal. And without letting him see that I was on the brink of falling apart from heartbreak.

I strolled along the Boulevard Montmartre and admired the shops decorated for Christmas. Unfortunately, when I finally reached the Galerie Goupil, I couldn't peek past the paintings in the window. The largest one in the middle—dancers on a stage—was enough to block most of the gallery's interior. The signature said Degas, a name unfamiliar to me.

The cold crept through the bottom of my boots and made it impossible to stand still for too long. I had to move along, if only to generate heat.

"*Excusez-moi, mademoiselle.*"

"*Pardonnez-moi, monsieur.*"

In Paris, nobody looked at me twice for walking alone. The French had a relaxed view of propriety. Or maybe I escaped attention because I was the least fashionably dressed woman on the street. Paris's sparkling flair overshadowed Amsterdam's Protestant modesty that my plain clothes reflected. I felt invisible in the visual feast that surrounded me, like a sad pigeon among dazzling parrots.

I strolled to Rue de Richelieu and stopped to allow a couple of hansom cabs to pass by, the clopping of horseshoes on cobblestones giving rhythm to the music of the city.

The wind blowing around the corner had me tucking my neck into the collar of my old brown coat. Instead of crossing the street, I turned around to go back to Goupil's for another look.

This time, fate favored me.

"Johanna Bonger!" Theo flew through the gold-lettered glass door, more robust than the last time I'd seen him, more color in his cheeks. He didn't look like a man wasting away from absinth or night-long carousing. He must have reformed since Dries had reported on him.

He lifted the smart derby hat he wore with his

Chesterfield overcoat, a rather dashing gentleman. "I didn't realize you were coming to Paris. Have you just arrived? Dries should have told me you were coming." When he moved to the side so as not to block the door, the painting of the graceful dancers caught my eye again, and he noticed. "Would you like to see more? Edgar is a friend of mine. We also have some of his sculptures."

Now that the large painting wasn't frustrating my efforts, I could appreciate the art. "His dancers make me think of fairies. One expects them to float off the canvas."

Theo gestured toward the door. "May I show you inside?"

I wasn't ready to be introduced to the people he worked with. I didn't want false assumptions to be made. "I am on my way to Le Palais Garnier." I wasn't lying. I'd hoped to go there next. "I wish to see the city's famous opera house that Napoleon III built."

"Le Palais is not much farther. Might I escort you?" He offered his arm, easily and smoothly, with the confidence of a man who was on his street, in his city, in his element.

I hadn't meant to spend quite that much time with him, but I could not refuse without being unnecessarily rude. "Thank you. Mama would approve an escort. The newspapers have been nothing short of hysterical for months and months about Jack the Ripper."

"Does she realize you're in Paris, not London?"

Theo walked on my left and sheltered me from the wind, a small kindness I couldn't help but appreciate.

"She thinks the killer could travel here just as easily as I have." She made me promise that I would write her daily.

"How long are you staying?"

Theo's voice was no longer that of a stranger, but intimately familiar. I had been reading his letters in my head in his voice all this time, I realized. "Two more weeks."

His eyes sparked. I had the impression he was holding himself back from bursting forward like carriage horses when they hear the starting click of a tongue. "Would you allow me the honor of showing you the city?"

I'd had no plans for the two of us beyond this "chance" encounter, but... Dries was always at the office, and I found little common ground with his reserved wife, Annie. "You must have a lot of work."

"For you, I will clear my schedule."

As expediently as that? The thrill flashing in his eyes flattered me. I couldn't remember the last time Eduard had been this happy to see me. He no longer visited, no longer brought gifts. We no longer talked about our future. We no longer talked about anything. The last time I ran into him, after returning home from my vacation at the sea with Anna and her family, I'd been stopping by to call on his mother.

"*Johanna.*" He'd been grabbing his hat. "*Regretfully, I cannot stay. I am meeting some friends.*"

As if we were nothing to each other. Even his

mother had been shocked. She apologized on her son's behalf after he had left.

Theo smiled at me, and I caught myself.

I will not think of Eduard while in Paris. My foremost resolution for the trip.

Eduard had openly courted me for three years, in front of his parents and mine, in front of our friends, then he inexplicably turned away. It'd become clear, even to me, that no proposal was coming. He was pretending that we'd been merely friends and he'd meant nothing by his attentions—which had been decidedly romantic! I was finished with being heartsick for him, heartbroken over him, letting him leave my emotions in tatters. *Finished.*

Theo just about pranced as we walked. "I cannot tell you how delighted I am by our meeting."

His disarming sincerity made me want to be more sincere myself. Our letters had made a difference. Thanks to our long-distance conversations on paper, we were no longer strangers.

"I have a confession to make. I did not run into you by coincidence."

He looked as happy as the boy pointing at the toy train in the shop window we just passed.

I glanced away from Theo's hopeful eyes, the exact color of the Paris sky. "I wish to talk to you about Dries. He mentioned that you two no longer spend time together." Theo had been my brother's closest friend in Paris, and Dries needed the support. His miserable marriage grew worse by the day. "I wish he were not so lonely here. If I am the cause of the rift between you two… Maybe you no longer seek his company because I…" How did one diplomatically refer to a refused proposal?

Theo understood my unsaid words and stumbled in shock. "I've neglected Dries. You're right. I treasure my friendship with your brother, Jo. It's only that I received more responsibility at the gallery. And Vincent…"

"How is he? Painting? You last wrote that he moved to Arles and was happy there."

"He's had trouble with his neighbors. And disagreements with Gauguin. They share a house. Did I tell you?" Exasperation twisted Theo's features for a second before he shook it off. "But you should see the colors in his *Bridge of Langlois*, how he suffused his work with life and light." Passion shone on his face once again, and his voice filled with exhilaration.

I kept thinking I barely knew him, yet I knew *this* was the true Theo. Here was a man showing me his true heart. Love for his brother. Love for art. Love for life. "Then you think success is at hand?"

"If only he wouldn't lose himself to dark thoughts." Frustration flooded back. "I am in constant worry about him. Mere talent is insufficient to succeed these days. One must have flair and charisma, and the ability to make friends easily. One must be able to manufacture the appearance of fame, even if one must resort to self-praise. And Vincent… It's not how our father raised us, you understand."

Their father had been a minister.

"Do you feel lonely without your brother?"

He gave a sad little nod. "I have taken in another lodger, for economy's sake."

When Vincent had moved to Paris, Theo rented a larger apartment. No opulent lodgings, according to Dries, just the two bedrooms, and a bathroom in the hall, shared with other tenants. Rents in Paris were astronomical. Vincent's departure had to have left Theo in a bind, but he was too much of a loving brother to tell me that.

He asked me about my family instead, and we talked about them all the way to the square, the time passing far more pleasantly than I'd expected.

Directly ahead, the opera house was a towering palace with its magnificent arches, majestic dome, and golden statues on the roof. The skill of the creators set my imagination soaring. "Do you think there are buildings in heaven?"

"If there are, this is what they look like. Should we go inside? Perhaps I could convince the guard to allow a quick tour?"

I didn't wish to be that much trouble. "Another time? I think I'd rather enjoy this rare moment of winter sunshine."

Out in the open square, the tall buildings no longer cast their shade over us. Even the wind that had raced down the boulevard without care for anyone's comfort was kinder here, as if halting to admire the glorious structure along with the tourists.

"Monsieur Degas!" Theo greeted a man who was hurrying in the opposite direction with a large camera under his arm. "I was hoping to run into you today to tell you we might have a buyer for one of your pastels." He shook the man's hand. "May I introduce a good friend from Amsterdam? This is Mademoiselle Bonger."

"*C'est un plaisir de vous rencontrer.*" Monsieur Degas kissed my hand. He was at least two decades older than Theo, and the way he squinted made me wonder if he had trouble with his eyesight. "Any relation to Andries Bonger?"

"A pleasure to meet you as well, monsieur. Dries is my brother." The name *Degas* tugged at my memory. "I've just seen your painting of dancers in Goupil's window. It's absolutely splendid."

If he was pleased that I liked his art, he didn't show it.

"Photography is my new passion. It's the art of the future." He gestured at his camera. Then he regarded Theo again. "An art I could not afford if monsieur here hadn't talked Goupil into representing me and selling my works. He is a good friend and an honorable gentleman."

Enough surprise flashed in Theo's eyes that I suspected Monsieur Degas did not often offer gratitude or compliments.

"Are you one of the impressionists?" I ventured to ask.

Degas's spine snapped rigid. "Certainly not." Every scintilla of warmth he had shown a moment before evaporated. "I don't understand the obsession with working outside. Artists who paint *en plein air* should be shot with bird shot."

His violent outburst rendered me speechless.

He executed a curt bow. "Mademoiselle." And then he marched on with his camera, calling back to Theo, "You may visit me at my studio tomorrow about that pastel."

I looked after him, committing his image to memory so I might accurately describe him in my diary. He was quite a character.

"I apologize for his brusque manner," Theo said as we moved on. "He prefers not to be called an impressionist."

"I gathered as much." My wry tone had him smiling, and then we were both fighting laughter. "What does he call himself?"

"A realist. And he's a good one. He has a painting in a *museum* already. At Pau. *A Cotton Office in New Orleans.*"

"New Orleans? It's an American painting?"

"He lived there for years. His mother was a Creole from New Orleans. His grandfather was from Haiti."

Theo regaled me with tales about some of his other artists next. Then we discussed opera. Then we talked about my preference for the theatre, and a play I had recently seen. I only realized it must be noon when people began sitting down for lunch at the restaurants around the square.

I stopped, startled by how swiftly the morning had flown by. "Thank you for walking with me. But you must have important matters waiting for you at work."

Theo took my hands. "There's nothing more important to me than being with you." His fingers warmed mine through my gloves. "My feelings have not changed since my visit to Amsterdam."

I glanced away, embarrassed by his open admiration. Heat crept across my face. A second passed before I could look him in the eye again. I felt as if I were seeing him for the first time.

Kind. Steadfast. Loyal. He cared about his family very much. Even Degas, who appeared to be a grumpy sort of man, praised Theo and considered him a friend.

"Might I show you Goupil tomorrow morning?" he asked. "We rarely have customers right after opening. And may I call on you the day after tomorrow at Dries's apartment?"

His unabashed eagerness made it impossible not to smile. "You might grow tired of me by then."

"Sunflowers will tire of the sun before I tire of you, Johanna Bonger."

I considered the man, the expectant smile on his lips and the hopeful light in his eyes.

I'd accomplished the purpose of our encounter. I'd talked to him about Dries.

Dare I step further?
Dare I risk my heart again?

CHAPTER SEVEN

Emsley

When I had first arrived at the stroke center on Monday, the doctors and nurses had been all sunny optimism. *She could wake up any minute.*

Tuesday, they were still encouraging. *We see a positive outcome for most of these cases.*

By Wednesday, the nurse who came to check Violet's vitals simply said, "She's in God's hands."

My brain was loopy from sleep deprivation. I had no new questions to ask. I'd been researching stroke and coma on the internet, and spent three days and nights reading medical literature. I could have written a doctoral dissertation on the subject, but none of my new knowledge helped.

I hung out on forums. Chatted with survivors.

Be patient, they said.

I had my own bed in the room. The loaner foldaway wasn't any more comfortable than the recliner, but at least it afforded a chance to be horizontal, even if I couldn't sleep more than minutes at a time. By Thursday, I was a desperate mess.

"I'd like to be roommates with you under different circumstances. How about you wake up and we go on a cruise?"

Violet remained silent.

"Hey, I read another entry from Johanna's diary. We need to talk about her. I have a lot of questions."

No response.

"I'm turning the company around. We just had a great auction. I'm going to buy out Trey. Then I'm going to branch out into benefit auctions. I'm going to raise a shit ton of money for stroke research that will help you walk out of this place."

She said nothing.

"All right. You know what? Let's play favorites." A game we had when I was a kid.

"My favorite thing about you is that all your life, you always went for what you wanted. Remember what you told me? *The meaning of life is to live it.*"

The rule was to take turns, but I went again.

"My favorite thing about you is that you always help everyone you can."

She was so small in the middle of the bed, as if she'd shrunk while I'd been in LA. I lay down next to her and closed my eyes.

"My favorite thing about you is that you didn't let obstacles stop you. You demanded to be seen, even if the art world considered you *just a woman.* You didn't stop to count broken bones while busting through the barricades. And you showed your students how to fight too."

When I'd been young and run out of *favorites*, Violet would go on and on about her favorite things about me. I was in college by the time I figured out that the game had been her way of building my self-esteem, an attempt to counteract my father's absent-minded inattention and my mother's frequent criticism.

"My favorite thing about you is that you never give up, so I *know* you're going to wake up and come back to me. Forget the mango pudding downstairs. Open your eyes, and I'll pull a heist at the Cheese-cake Factory."

We lay next to each other, like when I'd been a scared child and fled to her bed in the middle of the night. She used to have an old honey locust tree in front of her house, and when the wind blew, its branches scratched against the window my daybed was under. At the first crack of a storm, the first hard gust of wind, I'd be out from under my blankets and under Violet's so fast, I swear my feet didn't touch the floor. They say love gives you wings, but so does fear.

I counted Violet's slow heartbeats. True fear lived in the pauses. Fear that I wouldn't hear another *thump*.

As I listened, I dozed a little, until beeping moni-tors startled me awake. I scampered out of the bed, disoriented.

A nurse rushed in, one of the young new ones, Juliet. "Please step back."

Then more people crowded in, until I could no longer see Violet's face. My heart twisted and tripped. I stumbled to the window and stared out into the rainy afternoon.

I prayed.

I cried.

I prayed again.

She had to make it. She had to live. I couldn't imagine a world without Violet.

I prayed.

I cried.

I prayed again.

Juliet appeared at my shoulder. "I'm sorry, Emsley. So sorry."

Her words were like hard fingers at my back, shoving me onto subway tracks. I fell, then crashed, hard, and the black beast of grief ran me over.

Where were my legs? Where was the air from my lungs? Where were my words?

"No." I had to fight for the single syllable, and the rest didn't come any easier. "Please, you have to save her."

"We've tried. I'm sorry. You can say goodbye now, if you'd like. Take as long as you need."

Before I could process what had just happened, I was alone in the room with Violet. Everything happened so fast, I couldn't catch my breath. I just stared at her, disoriented.

The wires and tubes were disconnected, her

blanket pulled to her chin. She looked asleep, still regal, if disheveled. A queen resting after battle.

I wiped my eyes on the back of my hands. "Please wake up. Please talk to me. I'm not ready to lose you. I love you."

But for once, she didn't prove everyone wrong.

"I'm going to miss you so much."

I stood there and cried. When I felt I could string coherent sentences together, I called Mom. And a minute after we hung up, I could no longer remember what either of us said.

"Miss Wilson?" Juliet stood in the doorway. "Just wanted to remind you that there's paperwork for you in the office when you're ready." She came in and gave me a small box from her pocket. "In case I don't see you again. Your grandmother ordered these for you."

I opened the box on autopilot, numb. "The sunflower earrings." Stars on a black sky. Seconds ticked by before I could say, "Thank you." I didn't even bother wiping my eyes anymore, just let the tears fall. "They're…"

"She said you would like them." Juliet was crying too as she backed out. "Don't forget the office."

I slipped on the earrings. "I'll treasure them, always."

Sunflowers are adaptable, Violet had told me not long ago. *You plant them somewhere, and they'll figure out how to grow. They'll come up in the rich loam of rivers as easily as in arid, poor dirt. The worse the soil, the bigger they flower. They're scrappy as hell.*

I kissed her cheek. "Thank you, Violet." I straightened her blanket. "I know this is not the end. You've just gone ahead to the next party. Save me some champagne."

A sea of darkness and grief, paperwork, then a car. When I stumbled out in front of Violet's house at last, hours after her death, I couldn't remember how I'd gotten there. A search party with dogs and flashlights couldn't have found an ounce of energy inside me. I was shattered and exhausted.

The driver dropped two suitcases next to me on the sidewalk, one mine, one Violet's belongings from the center. I didn't notice when the car left. I couldn't see past the pain. I didn't see the people going around me. If anyone said anything—*excuse me*, or *are you okay*—I didn't hear them.

I stood in front of Violet's four-story brownstone in Greenwich Village and couldn't think past the hurt. A staticky screen flashed *system failure* in the middle of my brain.

A red FOR SALE sign ruined the window, a wound on the building's forehead. A smaller SOLD sign clung to the bottom like a leech.

The thought that I would never spend a weekend here with Violet demolished me. I raged against the unfairness of fate. Part of me would rather have set the building on fire than let strangers take over. Was anger one of the stages of grief? I couldn't remember.

My phone rang.

"I just saw your text." Diya. "I'm so sorry. Why didn't you call me? Trey sends his condolences. What can we do to help? When are you coming back?"

I couldn't face the house we shared. Or the office. "I'll be staying here for a while."

"Of course. For the funeral. We'll come. When is it?"

"On Tuesday. But I'll be staying longer."

"I can run Sunday's auction for you. Wait. Are you moving to New York?" Shock kicked Diya's voice into a higher register. "What about Ludington's? What— Did Violet leave you her home?"

"She sold it. Stroke care could bankrupt Bill Gates." True story. "I need to take care of things here before I go back to LA."

"I hate thinking about you there all alone."

Shouldn't have stolen my boyfriend. "I'll be busy. I have to clean out the house."

"Because your mom won't let strangers in there?"

Diya understood my family, understood me. I was going to miss having that in my life. I doubted I would see her and Trey much, moving forward. The hardest part about losing old friends was that you couldn't just replace them with new ones. The decade of history we shared—our college years, moving to LA, starting a business—were irreplaceable. I wasn't just losing Diya and Trey. I was losing the half sentences that would bring up a shared memory and have us break out laughing. Yet I could deal with losing that; I'd adjust. But I couldn't deal with losing Violet.

"How are you going to raise the money for Trey?" Diya asked.

I could not have cared less about money at that moment.

"I don't know. I can't think right now." I looked forward to being alone, having a huge house to myself, for days and days. Grief needed room. I needed time to mourn, to say goodbye to Violet. Maybe I'd find *her* diaries and discover who she'd really been, more than the scandalous stories in the society pages. I still had so many questions. How tragically stupid I'd been not to ask them while I'd had the chance.

I felt sick and achy, as if coming down with the flu, but instead of a virus, the dark sludge of grief was coursing through my veins. "I have to go."

I tapped away the call and fished the keys out of my pocket.

The front door at the top of the stairs was a piece of art, a gift from a prominent artist, one of Violet's many admirers. Carved waterlilies decorated the heavy wood. The door handle was a bronze mermaid. It was the kind of door you'd see in *Architectural Digest* "salvaged" now used as the headboard for a celebrity.

I stepped from the sunlight into the quiet shade of the foyer, entering a magical kingdom. *Queendom*, really. *This* was what I remembered from my infrequent visits.

Violet's house was a place where anything could happen and had: love affairs, fights, scandals. Many of New York's luminaries had walked the worn black-and-white marble under my feet. Some had behaved badly. There were rumors of a stabbing.

I set the luggage down and closed the door behind me. I should have been thinking: *perfect silence, perfect peace.* But all I could think was: *emptiness, loneliness.*

My phone rang.

Bram Dekker. Violet's estate attorney. I'd called him when I left the stroke center.

"I'm not going to be able to make it today," he said. "I apologize. I'm in court with a client, and there's one delay after the other. Could we meet tomorrow morning?"

"I'll be here. Stop by any time."

I walked past the grand staircase, into the room that had originally been the front parlor. As far back as I could remember, the entire first floor had been a gallery, most of the walls knocked down. *Nothing to constrict the imagination,* according to Violet.

The ghostly walls had once held vibrant paintings. Now the rooms stood empty. The soul had left the building.

I opened the basement door. *Dark basement. Abandoned house. That'd be a no for me.* I closed the door. I'd tackle the dungeon later.

Bran had said something, I realized. "I'm sorry. I missed that."

"I have to go. I'll see you tomorrow at ten?"

A headache pounded to life at my temple. "See you then."

The delay would give me a chance to reorient myself, an opportunity to recalibrate. I had to somehow swallow down the first taste of grief that filled my mouth and made it hard to breathe.

The wooden sign that used to hang outside, THE GALLERY VELAR, leaned against the wall. I caressed the letters. I was definitely going to keep it.

My mother called as I climbed the stairs with my carry-on to the second floor that was the continuation of the first-floor gallery, its condition pretty much the same.

"Are you there yet?"

"Checking the rooms."

"You haven't called any cleaners, have you?"

"I promised I wouldn't. It doesn't look too bad. The first two floors are empty."

On the third floor, Violet's perfume still lingered. I paused on the landing to fight back tears. I drew a deep breath and carried her with me. "The living quarters will need the most work."

"There used to be three bedrooms and a bathroom up there. Your great-grandfather had one of the original guest rooms converted into an office. He could step over and work when he couldn't sleep at night, without having to stomp up and down the stairs."

Violet had kept the room as her own office, with some minor changes.

"I like that there's a fully functioning kitchen up here."

"Made from the smallest bedroom. Violet had that

done when she'd converted the two bottom floors into a gallery."

I could see why Violet needed the upstairs kitchen. The kitchenette on the ground floor offered nothing more than a place for the caterers to wash their hands and toss away their trash.

Her bedroom was straight out of an opera, the Phantom's living quarters. The crimson velvet draperies and floor-to-ceiling gilded mirrors were the definition of high drama. A decadent crystal chandelier hung above the bed.

"You think you can get it all done?"

"I think I can manage putting stuff into boxes." I walked into the bathroom—golden clawfoot tub, large enough for two, pink marble tile. Echoes of my grandmother's presence filled every inch of space. "If I can't finish on this trip, I'll come back."

"How long can you stay?"

"Four days? Five, if I reschedule a few meetings. Diya volunteered to wield the hammer at Sunday's auction."

"Make sure you clear out everything.

You can donate furniture, but do not donate anything paper. If you donate clothes, check the pockets first."

"Want me to check if there are secret messages sewn into the seams?" I closed my eyes. "Sorry. I'm tired." And the headache was banging.

After Mom and I clicked off, I grabbed two painkillers, then ran the water in the bathroom sink for a minute before I drank from my cupped hands.

I wanted to lie down. I walked past my open suitcase, my clothes crowded to one side by Violet's robin's-egg-blue box. In my search for the pills, I had knocked off the top. The badly painted mystery baby lay with his eyes closed on his grimy canvas.

I would never know who he was or who painted him. Johanna Bonger? Or Anna Dirk, Johanna's friend? The diary did say that Anna studied art. Or the mysterious Clara, who'd carried on a correspondence with Johanna in Dutch and was possibly writing Jo's biography?

The ugly little painting was a symbol of all the questions I wouldn't be able to ask Violet, all the conversations we would never have—about the diary, the letters, my grandfather even.

I wanted to trash it. Instead, I held it up, as if my grandmother was floating invisibly just below the ceiling.

"What am I supposed to do with this?" I demanded from Violet's silent, lingering spirit.

CHAPTER EIGHT

Johanna
　　1888, December 24, Paris, France

I knew I was falling in love with Theo when I said, "I like the confident line work."

We stood in front of the fireplace in Dries's apartment, discussing the new painting my brother had bought from an artist friend and hung above the mantel. The painting depicted a man and a woman on a boat on the Seine, their faces reflecting a quiet and radiant joy, the whole world turning rose hued around them.

I'd come to Paris desperately hoping Theo would not bring up his ill-conceived proposal. I'd planned on talking to him about Dries, then going on my way. But now I wanted our conversations to continue. I wanted my last few days in Paris, with Theo, to last forever.

Say you'll visit me in Amsterdam again. Say you haven't given up. Ask me to reconsider.

Frustration that I could not broach the subject had me nearly dancing in place. But of course, initiating courtship was at the will of men. I was expected to stand there serene and demure. *Ladylike.* An expression I hated more than pickled eels. Ladylike meant do nothing, say nothing, even feel nothing if possible. To be ladylike required no less than to become the Mona Lisa. Since I wasn't a portrait of serene, mysterious feminine beauty, I had to offer something else.

Confident linework was an expression I had heard from Dries. My use of it told me how much I wanted to impress Theo, how much I didn't want him to think of me as a silly, know-nothing young woman. Over the past two weeks, while he'd shown me Paris, introducing me to the city's culture and art, his opinion of me had become important.

"Do you know the title?" If Dries had mentioned it, I couldn't remember.

"What do you think?" Theo examined me as carefully as he'd been examining the brushstrokes on the canvas. He always gifted me with his full attention. He offered the benefit of his knowledge and experience of art and life. And he challenged me to dig deeper for my thoughts and opinions. "What would you title it?"

We were alone in the room. The scent of Christmas filled the air: pine boughs and cinnamon. A yule log burned in the fireplace.

"*Courtship*?" The heat of a blush tingled over my cheeks.

"Or," Theo said, "*The Pleasures of Marriage.*"

I blushed even hotter.

"Matrimony holds many pleasures," he said softly. "A man and a woman discovering who each other are. Falling in love, based on the sure knowledge of each other, instead of wild hopes and fantasies." He took my hands. "Then growing together."

I couldn't look away from his eyes. Life was opening up before me like rose petals, in mesmerizing, mysterious whirls.

"My dearest Johanna, would you reconsider my proposal?" The words came on a soft breath, as if straight from Theo's soul. "Vincent says, *If you hear a voice within say you cannot do something, then by all means do that thing, and that voice will be silenced.* And so, I must ask." Theo moved half a step closer. "Would you, Johanna Bonger, do me the honor of becoming my wife?"

The gaslights flickered in their sconces. The room was holding its breath. I had nothing to hold, because with each word he'd uttered, a small puff of air had left my lungs, until they were empty.

I'd always thought love was a mad rush, a desperate burning, an instant cry of the heart for another. But during my stay in Paris, love had misted over me in slow sparkling drops like a soft summer rain. "Yes."

He slowly bent his head.

The reality of the kiss was altogether different from reading about the experience in what my best friend, Anna, called my silly novels. The heat that'd been tingling on my cheeks now tingled where our lips met. Warmth infused me, but not like the fire in the grate that I would no longer feel the second I stepped away. This warmth seeped into my heart, into my bones, and settled in.

For the first time in my life, I felt as if I were standing on the precipice of the passion my books had promised. I swayed toward Theo until I was leaning against him, grasping his arms.

Then Dries's shoes scuffed on the floor in the hallway, and we startled apart.

Theo used our last second alone to whisper, "Would you mind saying it again?"

The room spun with me. "Yes."

Dries paused in the doorway, glancing from the irrepressible smile on my face to the one on Theo's, while he remained subdued. "Congratulations."

Could he not manage better than that flat tone?

Theo didn't seem to notice. His smile only grew. He held on to my hands. "I asked for your brother's permission, and I also told Vincent what I planned."

Of course. This was why everyone had left us alone so suddenly.

Summoned by my thoughts, Annie appeared in the kitchen door. Her blonde hair was twisted into a severe bun, her dress a nondescript brown, with added material in the front to mask that she was expecting. "Best wishes to you both."

Her pregnancy had brought her no joy, and neither did our news. Her tone was closer to grim than felicitous.

I told myself to let go of all frustration and hurt at the lackluster response. My brother and his wife regretted their marriage, and neither wished the same fate on me.

I beamed all the brighter. "Thank you, Annie."

Then Dries dropped the wood he'd brought in on the hearth and shook Theo's hand briefly before he embraced me. "I do wish you all the happiness in the world, Jo."

Annie ducked back into the kitchen, calling over her shoulder, "We must leave if we are not to be late for church."

No time for a celebration.

Not even a toast.

I chose not to mind. I was engaged to a *good* man. My future had been decided at last, all the uncertainty over. Now all my questions about the meaning of life would be answered.

A thrill propelled me forward. I could not stand still. I nearly ran to the foyer for my hat.

Dries followed me. "Are you certain?" he asked in a hushed tone. "Or is it that you are desperate for a new city where everything doesn't remind you of Eduard?"

I shot him a forbidding look. "If you ruin this for me, I shall be most cross with you. I have left the past behind. Eduard was the infatuation of a witless young girl. He was a daydream. Theo is real."

While my *fiancé* stepped to the dining table and finished his wine, Dries quirked an eyebrow. "I know Theo is in love with you, but do you truly love him, Jo? Do you believe that you can make each other happy? It's not as easy as we naively think. I want you to be joyful in your marriage."

"I will be. I promise." I dropped my voice to a whisper, because Theo was coming over. "I wish you would believe me."

Dries walked away, granting us privacy.

"My dearest Jo." Theo's smile outshone the gaslights, as if all his worries about life had lifted like the morning mist from the Seine. "You have made me the happiest of men. How soon can we marry? I refuse to be engaged for two endless years like Dries. The sooner the better."

"What would people think?" Common sense broke into the dream where I floated. "Heavens, the gossip that follows quick marriages."

"I knew that I loved you three years ago when we first met. Must I wait for you longer still?"

"You will have to ask my parents for my hand first. Then, if they agree, we must have an official engagement, with a party at my parents' house. Mama would never forgive me otherwise."

"Next month?"

Could that be possible? A daring thrill ran through me. "If it can be arranged that quickly."

"And the wedding?"

His impatience infected me completely. "Once the

weather turns warmer. April? And we move to Paris immediately after?"

"As soon as we've said our wedding wows, we shall be on the train," he promised.

I wanted to return in time for the opening of the World Fair in May, but the way Theo was smiling said he was thinking about something else entirely. The glint in his eyes sent me blushing all over again.

Oh. Well. That!

So that I wouldn't die of embarrassment, I channeled my thoughts to practicalities we had to consider. "Where will we live?"

"I will find a suitable apartment. We'll decorate it with Vincent's paintings. And when we are settled in, we will invite him."

This was how I knew Theo was a man capable of great love. I could see the ocean of brotherly love in his heart. I could trust my own feelings to a man like that. He was never withdrawn, never cold, never dismissive, never too embarrassed to show his feelings. His passion burned bright, whether for me, or his work, or his family.

He cradled my face in his hand. "My dearest, dearest Jo. How lucky I am."

I thought he might kiss me again, right in front of the others—Annie and Dries had just come back—but a knock on the front door interrupted.

Dries talked briefly with a man on the steps, then returned with a telegram. He handed it to Theo. "Your lodger sent it on."

Theo read the contents at once, lines forming on

his forehead, an invisible plow digging furrows into his skin. "Vincent is grievously ill with a nervous breakdown." The words escaped him in a desperate rush. He reached for me. "Gauguin advises me to travel to Arles immediately."

I embraced him, my heart pounding against his, sharing the same rhythm.

Neither Dries nor Annie said anything about propriety.

"I shall write as soon as I arrive to Arles." Theo pulled away, grabbed his coat and hat, then launched through the door. One last glance—a look of pain—and he was gone.

"And while I wait, I shall pray for Vincent!" I rushed out into the cold, into the night, calling after him.

I clutched my hands and watched my beloved until the darkness swallowed his dear silhouette, then I stood there disoriented. I felt as if that same darkness had swallowed my heart. How could our moment of happiness end this fast?

A breath ago, we'd been admiring a painting. Then I was engaged. Then tragedy struck and Theo was gone, before we could even properly celebrate. Shivering in the cold, I looked around for proof that the proposal had happened and hadn't been one of my girlish daydreams.

Dries drew me back inside. "Vincent will recover. He has these spells from time to time."

Annie clicked her tongue. "Let us hope it's not a bad omen." She faced the mirror and patted down a few stray strands of hair. "I am glad to see no snow tonight. A dry winter is the best, don't you think?"

Oh, who wants to chat about the weather!

I wanted to burst through the door and run after Theo. *I'm going with you!* But I couldn't because we weren't married. Because I was a woman. I could have howled with frustration.

Even when, half an hour later, Dries, Annie, and I were sitting in church, I could scarcely focus on the miraculous birth of our Christ. My mind clung to Theo riding the train through the cold and the dark, alone and worried.

I could think of little else the following day, and the next. I couldn't draw an easy breath until a letter arrived from him at last.

"What does he write?" Dries was at my elbow as soon as I closed the door behind the mailman.

We had spent the morning together, just the two of us. Annie was at her seamstress.

My eyes ate up the maddeningly short page. "Theo found Vincent in the hospital with high fever. The doctors say it's from madness and are unsure whether he will remain insane. He…" I had to reread the sentence. "Cut his ear off with a razor? Theo says he will know more in a few days. Right now, Vincent is still too agitated."

"His ear?" My brother touched his own lobe, his tone bewildered. "Why?"

"Theo doesn't say. Only that I must not delay my plans to return to Amsterdam. I should not wait for him to come back to Paris." I reread the brief missive again, but I couldn't puzzle out more than on my first turn. "I don't understand."

And then *nothing* from Theo for another two days, while I fretted, and then, *finally*, a new letter, this time with a newspaper cutout from the local weekly, *Le Forum Républicain*.

"Dimanche dernier, à 11 heures ½ du soir, le nommé Vincent Vangogh peintre, originaire de Hollande, s'est présenté à la maison de tolérance no 1…"

I handed it to Dries. I only had a modicum of French.

"'Last Sunday, at half past eleven in the evening,'" he read, "'one Vincent van Gogh, a painter and native of Holland, presented himself at brothel no 1, asked for one Rachel, and handed her his ear, telling her: *Keep this object carefully*. Then he disappeared. Informed of this act, which could only be that of a poor lunatic, the police went the following day to the home of this individual, whom they found lying in his bed, by then showing hardly any sign of life. The unfortunate was admitted to the hospital as a matter of urgency.'"

I collapsed into the nearest chair, knocked down by the words, which were wholly incomprehensible. "Poor Vincent! And, oh, my poor, poor Theo."

I looked to my brother for consolation, but I found his gaze assessing. He looked exactly like Papa just then. Papa when he was ready to lay down the law.

"There can be no engagement party, Jo. You must

see that. This gives you time to think the proposal over."

The injustice of his suggestion pushed me to my feet. Battle drums beat in my brain. "I pledged my life to Theo mere days ago. I care for him too much to desert him at the first sign of hardship. You yourself said that Vincent is known for his dark moods. He always recovers."

"If drinking and brooding was all, but this kind of madness? It's in the blood—"

"Theo is *nothing* like him! He is gentle. And he is patient. He is loving…"

Dries's chin dipped and his chest expanded. Stubbornness hardened his eyes. "You have not seen Theo this past year, living to excess."

Nothing he hadn't already told me in his letters. "You are too conservative."

"You are too naive!"

"How will I learn and grow if I stay at home with Mama and Papa forever?" I shot back, then regretted that I'd raised my voice at my dear brother, so I begged. "Please, Dries. I have only just found happiness. If Theo and I are to gain Papa and Mama's blessing, we need your support. Please."

"It's an unacceptable mésalliance. I will not allow my sister to marry into the family of a madman." And then, without giving me a chance to respond, he strode away.

"Dries!" If my brother was against us, my parents would never consent to the marriage. I had to convince him and fast, before he fully set his heart on stopping the engagement. Changing his mind then would be more difficult still. *"Heaven help a woman once a man made up his mind,"* Mama always said, although dear Papa was most reasonable. Most of the time.

I ran after my brother. "Dries!"

CHAPTER NINE

Emsley

Friday began with a scare.

I climbed the stairs to Violet's fourth-floor studio, in the jeans and sweater I had fallen asleep in on the top of the covers after reading another entry from Jo's story. The true accounting of how Vincent, possibly my great-great-etc.-grandfather, had lost his ear, and given it to Rachel, possibly my great-great-etc.-grandmother.

After waking, a few seconds had passed until I remembered where I was, and remembered that Violet was gone. And then I'd cried. But I couldn't cry all day. Bram Dekker, Violet's attorney was coming over. I wanted to finish inspecting the house before he arrived. Which meant I had to face Violet's studio.

I'd always loved the large open space, the clean

lines and white walls. While the third floor was a dramatic theatrical performance, the fourth was pure peace, the kind of space where a person could reinvent herself, where one could create just about anything, including a new life.

I paused on the landing to brace myself.

Faint strains of a dramatic classical melody filtered through the studio door in front of me. *Oh.*

The hairs on my arms stood up. The music took the whole *Phantom of the Opera* theme too far.

Get a grip. The Realtor must have tuned a radio to the classical station when she'd shown the house, and then she'd forgotten to turn it off. Had she played opera on the third floor? Pretty smart if she had. No wonder the house had sold so fast.

Violins soared. I pushed the door open, half expecting a strange man in a half mask. But what I found was worse. I froze as I stared at the tableau before me. Then I screamed.

So did some of the people inside.

Instead of canvases, cameras filled the space—a small forest of tripods with a clearing in the middle. Where several women were being tortured by a serial killer.

I ran. Down the stairs. Into Violet's bedroom. Grabbed the door. *Slam!*

"Who are you?" the torturer shouted outside. "How did you get in?"

She'd followed me. A female serial killer. They exist. My mother watched documentary after documentary about them.

"How did *you* get in?" The gall of her. "This is my grandmother's house. I belong here."

"Emsley?" She sounded surprised. "Did I scare you? It's performance art. Before you call the police, look up Suugarworks. Two U's, one word."

I typed Suugarworks into my phone with shaking fingers.

Wikipedia showed up as the top search result. First was her picture—with a different hairstyle—next to the words *notable contemporary artist*. Then her name, Strena. No surname.

Bam, bam, bam. My heart couldn't slow down. A broken heart shouldn't have to beat that fast.

According to the next paragraph, Strena's work explored body art and the exploitation of women in a consumer society, women's bodies as consumer products. I scrolled to the bottom—catching my breath at last—to the long list of reference links about her.

"Are you looking me up?

I opened the door to two inches, keeping my foot planted solidly behind it. "It's not blood?"

"Melted sugar with food coloring. I use Violet's studio sometimes. We have an ongoing agreement." She no longer held what had earlier looked like a thin dagger in her hand.

She was all unquestioning self-confidence, very New York City, in her forties. *Fifties?* Her long black braids—tipped with gold highlights, swung to her waist.

Now that I wasn't running, I could see that she

had that same celebrity quality my grandmother had had, the aura that would draw strangers to her in a room, because even from a glance they would know she was *somebody*.

"I didn't realize Violet had a tenant."

"I like to keep where I work a secret. Otherwise, some photographer inevitably shows up to scoop my new show. I'm only here for another week or so."

I opened the door.

She looked me over. "You don't look like Violet."

"Nobody looks like Violet." She'd been a once-in-a-millennia compilation of genes.

"Are you all right?" Strena checked out my swollen eyes.

She didn't know.

Of course, she doesn't know.

And I desperately didn't want to be the one to tell her, but I had to, even if I hated every miserable word. "Violet passed away yesterday."

Each damn syllable was a nail driven into my chest, punching through to my lungs, stealing my air.

Strena's shoulders collapsed, as if experiencing the same effect. Silent tears flooded her face. And then she hugged me, a real hug that lasted. "I'm so sorry." She wiped her eyes. Sniffed. Backed toward the stairs. "I have to go." She climbed the steps sideways, dazed. And just before she disappeared into the studio, she said, "My sugarworks are stiffening."

I had no idea what that meant, but didn't go after her to ask. I had my own work. I would leave her to hers.

Violet's living quarters waited behind me, but I wasn't emotionally ready to tackle them, so I headed down. I'd already been scared in the attic—which the studio had been at one point. I might as well brave the basement.

My grandmother's Realtor, Beatriz Amoso, called as I plodded down the stairs.

"I just saw your text. I'm so sorry. I loved Violet." She also sounded as if she'd been crying. "May I ask if you are Violet's heir? I need to know what to do with the listing. Violet has accepted an offer, but the signing of the contract of sale was supposed to happen at the closing next week. If we're not sure who'll be inheriting the house, it'd be best to take it off the market, or the heirs might contest the sale. If they don't, then they can relist and the buyer can put in a new offer."

"I'm the sole beneficiary of my grandmother's will."

I opened the basement door and flipped on the light—not much of an improvement. The lightbulb couldn't have been more than forty watts and covered in cobwebs. *Foreboding.* If the third floor was the Phantom's den, the basement was a vampire's lair.

The building had been built in 1915. *Over a hundred years old.* The exact thought I should not have been thinking when descending into a spooky dungeon.

"Will you be contesting the contract of sale?" Beatriz asked.

"No." The farther down I went, the mustier the air. The stairs creaked, a horror movie soundtrack. I stopped at the bottom until my eyes adapted to the low light. *Definitely dungeonesque.* "I'd like everything to go ahead the way Violet wished."

The basement wall next to me was stone, the floor under my sneakers plain dirt.

The better to dig graves in.

Don't think that!

Too late.

I turned my head, and my soul left my body.

A six-foot-tall taxidermized black bear loomed on his hind legs not three steps away, paws reaching toward me. I jumped back, a delayed reaction. A real bear would have had my head by then.

"Thank you, Violet, for scaring five years off my life. If you were afraid to go alone, you could have told me you were aiming for a double funeral."

"What's that?" Beatriz asked.

I raised the phone back to my mouth. "A heart attack in the middle of a nervous breakdown, possibly with the beginnings of an ulcer."

"I'm sorry. I'm sure business talk is the last thing you want. All I need for now is a copy of the paperwork that certifies that you're now in charge of the property."

"I'll have Violet's estate attorney send over the will. I'm meeting him today." I peered farther into the dim basement.

Behind the bear, about a hundred cardboard boxes stood stacked to the ceiling along one wall, followed by about three dozen folding metal chairs that Violet used at show openings. Even farther in, an ancient wardrobe promised an alternate universe through its back panel. But the pièce de résistance waited past the wardrobe.

As Beatriz went on about rules and regulations, I only half listened, because… A carousel occupied the rest of the basement. A bona fide flat-top merry-go-round, a smaller version of the one in Central Park, but with carved horses and chariots and all.

Oh, Violet.

How had she moved an entire carousel down the stairs? Why? And most importantly, how was I going to have it transported upstairs?

Had I ever been down in the basement before? Not that I could remember. I *would* have remembered a giant carousel.

Had Mom known about this? I would have liked to think she would have warned me. *Do take a chainsaw, darling. It's only sensible.*

A hopeful thought fluttered to life in my brain. "Did the buyer also purchase the contents of the basement, by any chance?"

"No. Everything must go. The house must be empty by closing day." Beatriz's nervous laugh gurgled through the phone. "It's wild down there, isn't it? Any idea what you'll do with all those curiosities?"

"Craigslist?" With *buyer responsible for removal* tacked to the end of the ad. In bold letters.

After our call ended, I snapped a few pictures

with my phone, but the light was too weak, even with the flash. I added a stronger lightbulb to my mental shopping list.

On my way over to the stack of boxes, I skirted the bear. "I swear I'm not here to eat your porridge."

I opened the first box and pulled out a handful of flyers that advertised shows at The Gallery Velar. The graphic design carried my grandmother's style: bold lines, brave colors.

I carried the box upstairs. I couldn't do much else in the house until the packing boxes I had ordered online that morning were delivered.

My stomach growled.

"On the other hand, if you do have some porridge…" I told the bear on my way back for the second load. I loathed the thought of going to the grocery store, having to face people.

I carried up another box, then another and another.

People who said physical labor was meditative were big fat liars.

By the time I was on the fifth trip, my back was killing me. By the tenth, my hair hung into my face. By the fifteenth, my black sweater—which I'd sweated through—stuck to me like snakeskin. Dust covered me all over.

I was gasping for air at the top of the stairs when the doorbell rang.

Maybe they'd go away.

Hopeful seconds rolled by.

Then the doorbell rang again.

Bram!

I had forgotten about Violet's attorney—all the blood was flowing to my muscles instead of my brain.

I dropped the box and ran, made the mistake of glancing at the gilded mirror in the foyer as I passed it. I looked like a child's stuffed toy that had been sucked into a vacuum cleaner then rescued by a horrified parent: covered in dust, hair sticking out every which way, clothes askew. Obviously not right in so many ways.

I patted down my hair and tugged my sweater back into place. Zero improvement. Any self-respecting mother would toss that toy, order a new one online, and pretend that nothing had happened.

The bell rang for the third time.

"Coming!"

I forced a smile on my face. He *was* here to help me. Then I put the smile away. Teeth were not the way to go. Aw, damn.

Rabid honey badger. In a windstorm. Blown clear through a hedge.

No help for it now. I'd missed my chance to shower and change. My only hope was that at his age, Bram Dekker's eyes weren't what they used to be. Maybe he wouldn't notice my disheveled appearance.

"Oh." I froze in the open door, disoriented, a honey badger that touched its nose to an electric fence.

The man on the top step wasn't seventy, not even

half of that. He was *pristine*: impeccable black leather shoes, fancy New York City suit, fresh-cut dark hair.

He was far from California easy—no surfer dude, nothing like Trey—no sunshine about him. He was New York crisp. He had *gravitas*. That was the word. Steady as those giant concrete columns that held up highways. Like you could build on him.

"Sorry I'm early. I'm Bram."

He was definitely not Bram.

He smiled, a plain friendly smile, no come-on in it, and not the smile of someone who was about to sell you something either. A straightforward, under-stated, professional New York smile. "You expected my grandfather. He's retiring. I've taken over his clients. He still worked on Violet's affairs, but I've been doing most of it already."

I accepted that as a reasonable explanation. "Emsley." A platinum band glinted on his ring finger. Married. Good. I stomped out a few sparks of nascent attraction I didn't want anyway and relaxed. "Please, come in."

"I'm sorry for your loss. I've met Violet a handful of times. She was special among legends."

Someday, tears would no longer flood my eyes at the mention of her name, but that day was not today. Deep breath.

Bram glanced around. "Are you cleaning the place out yourself? I can recommend some people."

And then my mother would kill me. "I can handle it."

I led him into the gallery space, then remembered

that the only chairs were in the tiny kitchenette in the back, way too close quarters. I halted awkwardly, midstep.

While I tried to decide whether to show him back there or conclude our business standing—signing papers on his back?—he set his leather shoulder bag next to the staircase, shrugged out of his silk-lined suit jacket, and hung it on the banister. Necktie over that. Next, he unbuttoned his shirtsleeves and rolled them up to midforearm.

The unexpected shedding of clothes caught me off guard.

He gestured at the pile of boxes and the open basement door. "You're in the middle of bringing stuff up. I'll help."

I wanted to say I didn't need help with that either, but my heart leapt at the thought of not having to be alone with the bear.

"Thank you. If you're sure."

He went down the stairs in front of me and when he reached the bottom, he high-fived a black paw. "What are you going to do with Tiny Tim?"

The beast? "Try not to dream of him."

"And the rest?"

"Maybe I could sell the wardrobe to a travel agency. What do trips to Narnia run these days?"

He grinned at me. "Any plans for the carousel?"

"I think a better question is, why did Violet *have* a carousel?"

"Bought it in pieces a couple of years ago to have

it restored. I think she meant to auction it off for charity. It was her last project before…"

I nodded.

He walked to the remaining boxes. His easy manner, his very presence, made the basement more bearable. No pun intended.

"I have a cousin who owns an antique shop in the Hamptons," he told me. "I'll give you his number. He knows some eccentric collectors. He'll be able to help with the wardrobe too. Unless you're set on the travel agency plan?"

"The phone number would be great." He'd solved some of my most pressing problems in five seconds flat. The man was impressive.

And he was moving right along. He grabbed the first dusty box and didn't grunt with effort like I had.

I grabbed my own box and hurried after him, not wanting to be the slacker on the team. "I really appreciate this."

Then we did it again and again. Rinse and repeat.

After a while, he switched to two boxes per trip, stacking them on top of each other. And he did not get dirty. He didn't have to hug the boxes against his body like I did. He was strong enough to hold them out in front of him.

We fell into a rhythm, a comfortable silence. He only broke it on the last trip, setting down the last boxes and brushing off his hands. "My grandfather is heartbroken over Violet's death. He'd love to stop by and meet you. I promised I'd ask."

I tried to hide how pitifully hard I was breathing.

"He's welcome anytime. I'll be here for at least a week. And thank you again for the help. This would have taken me the rest of the day without you. Glass of water?"

"Thank you. I think I swallowed enough dust for a medium-size desert."

I led the way to the kitchenette where two barstools framed a napkin-size bistro table, three glass-door cabinets served for storage, a tiny sliver of a window above them blessed the small space with natural light.

"Tap water. Sorry. Nothing but the basics."

"Tap water is fine."

We washed our hands. When I strained to reach the glasses in the middle cabinet above the sink, Bram reached above my head, taking one glass down, and then another. He smelled like office supplies, which was pretty much my favorite smell. Under different circumstances, I might have been tempted to sink back against all that printer-paper-and-new-eraser-smelling warmth and hard chest.

Trey and I had broken up a month before, but we hadn't been *together* together a lot longer than that. I didn't miss the sex, but I missed touching, human connection, warm skin. Anyway, I didn't sway against Bram, because...*platinum wedding band*.

"How is business?" he asked as we sat. "Violet told me about Ludington's."

I wished she'd told me about him. He wouldn't have taken me by surprise. "It's great."

I needed to hang on to *some* shred of my dignity. I

looked my worst—the ghost of chimney sweeps past. I wasn't going to tell him that my boyfriend had left me for my best friend, and that I was desperate for money. I didn't want those gray eyes to turn soft with pity. "Business is business. I know I don't sound overly enthusiastic, but it's just…"

"You miss Violet."

"Yes."

"The pain gets better."

Does it? "I thought we had decades left. I had postrecovery plans."

"You feel like you've been on a train, going steadily forward on a track, and then the track disappeared."

The truth in his words hit me in the middle of my chest, the shock of the punch reverberating through my bones. He'd nailed exactly what I felt.

Then again, he was an estate attorney. Of course he knew about grief. He'd lived through it with countless clients.

"What do I do?"

"You build new tracks."

"I don't want new tracks. I want the old tracks back."

His eyes held profound understanding, and instead of the usual weak "everything happens for a reason" platitude, all he said was a heartfelt "Yeah."

And somehow, that one-word acknowledgment was all I needed.

The silence that stretched between us grew from grief laden to comfortable. Before it could have stretched all the way to awkward, Strena popped in. Her eyes were swollen, as if she'd been crying upstairs.

"Hey. Oh, hey, Bram." Then to me, "The models are gone. I have to run and take care of something. I won't be able to talk today. I'll catch you tomorrow?"

"Sure."

As Strena left, Bram checked his watch. "Can I help you with anything else today?"

I slid off my barstool. "I think I can take it from here."

I followed him out through the gallery, to his shoulder bag by the stairs. He opened it and handed me a large UPS envelope. "Read. Sign. Call if you have any questions."

"Is there something in here that proves I'm the sole beneficiary? Violet's Realtor needs confirmation, so the sale of the house can go through."

"Beatriz? I know her. Why don't I take care of that?"

"Thank you. And thank you again for all the help."

He walked to the foyer. "I enjoyed meeting you, Emsley."

I locked the door behind him, then turned over the envelope in my hand. Postage paid, ready to be dropped off at the nearest UPS box, no further personal interaction necessary.

I doubted I would see Bram Dekker again.

CHAPTER TEN

Johanna
1889, Paris

Theo and I were married on the 17th of April, in Amsterdam.

The wedding was small, just my family, my friend Anna and her new husband, Jan Veth, and some of the neighbors. Theo couldn't stop smiling. I thought he might take flight and circle around the ceiling like a bird. I was so nervous, my mother had to remind me to unclench my fingers.

"It'll be over fast," she whispered, guessing the cause of my anxiety. "It's nothing to fuss over, dear."

I held on to that and managed to live through the solemn service. All I wanted was to get through the rest and have the most embarrassing part behind me.

The reception at my parents' house was short: food, drink, congratulations. Immediately after, Theo and I left for Paris, stopping in Brussels for a honeymoon of a single day.

"I'm sorry I have to return to work so soon," Theo said as we settled into our hotel. "I dared not request more than a fortnight. I have been away from the gallery too much already this year on account of Vincent's troubles."

To schedule the wedding at the end of his break, rather than at the beginning, had been my choice. I'd hoped it would make us less of a stranger to each other on our wedding night. Yet now as I faced the large bed, I realized twice the time would not have been long enough.

"Shall we go out for a stroll?" The train ride hadn't been overly long, but our compartment had been cramped.

Theo offered his arm, and a minute later, we were walking outside.

"At least the day gifted us with sunshine," I prattled. "A good omen for our beginnings."

"Should we visit St. Catherine Cathedral?"

"As you wish." Though I feared I wouldn't be able to fully appreciate it. I would have liked to enjoy the city, truly, but I was too jittery to notice anything beyond my husband of a few hours next to me.

All my life, I'd been solitary, despite the size of my family. My brothers were never home. My sisters and I pursued different interests. Of all my siblings, I was closest to Dries, but since he'd moved to Paris, I rarely saw him anymore. Now, suddenly, I was part of a pair. Part of a tiny new family, one that would live far from my old large one, in a foreign country where I barely spoke the language. A household that would be all mine to run. And a husband to please, which would start *tonight*.

That last thought turned my face hotter than the sun.

Just as well that we stepped inside the cool of St. Catherine Cathedral.

I did my best to think pious thoughts. There was no mass, but a few of the faithful knelt in the pews, the altar magnificent. We stood in the back and remained silent, holding on to each other and breathing in that unique scent of ancient wood and books that old churches had. I enjoyed the respite very much, but we couldn't stay there forever.

Back outside, we browsed the colorful little shops that sold food and souvenirs. Then we strolled over to the Grote Markt, the Grand Palace, that contained the Baroque guildhalls, the Town Hall, and the Maison du Roi.

Theo turned slowly around in the middle. "Hard to believe that two hundred years ago, the French burned it to the ground."

I turned with him. "It must have taken an eternity to rebuild."

"The guilds had it done in four years. Only to have the Brabant Revolutionaries sack it a hundred years later."

Theo went on to educate me on the finer points of Belgian history, but it all passed in a blur.

When he noticed my inattention, he smiled at me.

"Shall we return to the hotel for dinner, my little wife?"

So soon? "Yes, dearest."

He hurried, and I kept up. Then, seated in the dining room, I couldn't eat more than a few bites.

Theo finished all his plate and half of mine. "Ready to go up to our room?"

Already? Heavens. Maybe I *could* eat a few more spoonfuls. But Theo was on his feet already. *Here we go, then.*

We walked upstairs hand in hand, and all I could think, again, was that I was not ready. Such a child I was. I was *not* going to write this silly panic in my diary.

Moonlight lit the room like in a romantic novel. The sweet scent of the red roses Theo had gifted me for our wedding perfumed the air. I had only one last brief delay left, the bathroom down the hall we shared with other guests.

I went first. Afterwards, while Theo took his turn, I changed into my nightclothes and hid myself under the covers. *Nothing for it but to suffer through it, then.*

In the room on our left, a baby cried, and a mother soothed the child. In the room on our right, a couple argued loudly over wine.

Theo knocked.

It gets easier, my friend Anna who had married last August, told me when I'd asked. The words implied that at first it was difficult. Yet I could not put *it* off forever. *Oh, why didn't I ask for greater detail?*

Theo knocked again.

"Ready!" And then, after he entered and slipped into bed next to me, I couldn't say another word.

Suddenly, he seemed very much like a stranger again. Certainly, we didn't know each other enough for *this*. Had I made the right decision? I still barely knew him. We'd spent but two weeks together in Paris before Christmas. Then two weeks around our engagement, and another two weeks before our wedding. Our joint lives stretched before us. Would I find the nights burdensome? Would I be adequate?

He ran his warm hand over my arm. "Are you cold, dearest?"

"Nervous. And embarrassed." I pressed my face into my pillow. "I don't know what to expect," I mumbled into the duck down. "I can hear everything people on either side of us are saying." I was mortified that strangers might overhear *us*.

Theo smiled in the moonlight. "My Jo, I'm inexpressibly happy that you are my wife at last. I can wait."

He brushed his thumb over my cheek, then his lips across mine. Degree by degree, I warmed to his touch. And those kisses were all he took that night.

I would love him forever for that.

I relaxed into his patience and slept.

The next morning, we rode the train to Paris. Then an open fiacre to the cité Pigalle where we were to live.

"This way, you can see your new neighborhood." Theo pointed out all the shops I might visit. He thought of everything.

He couldn't stop talking as he led me up to our fourth-floor apartment on our short, dead-end street. "I do hope you'll like your new home. I inspected a great many. How I wished you were here. This one truly seemed the best. And it's close enough to Goupil's so I can come home for lunch every day, dearest. It will be our quiet nest in the city."

"All the tiny gardens with their lilac trees are lovely. We shall be spoiled with blooms in May. Was that an artist's studio across the street?"

"Just so. I'll introduce you to the neighbors tomorrow." He unlocked the door. "Ladies first."

I moved tentatively into my new life.

Standing in our home made our marriage seem more real somehow. More irrevocable. My prewedding worries came rushing back.

"I know little of keeping a house of my own." I whirled back to him. "And I have so little French. How shall I manage the market? And I'm not as sweet natured as you might think. I had disagreements with my sisters all the time. What if I don't make a good wife?"

"Our home will be full of happiness. We will make it so, Jo. Surely, it is up to us?"

His self-assured manner settled my nerves once again. He was right. Of course, he was right. We would be happy here.

Brilliant sunshine filled the living area to the left and the kitchen to the right. This high up, the building across the street didn't throw its shade on our windows.

"You can change anything you wish." Theo tossed his hat onto the sofa, next to a pile of books and blankets. "And buy anything you think we might still need. Just before I left for Amsterdam, I received three hundred francs from an English friend, repayment for a favor in the past."

"How good of him." But where would we put anything else? The apartment was already crowded.

A multitude of paintings hung on the walls, a riot of sky blue and petal pink, flowering plum trees and peaches. Here and there, gold glinted among them, vases upon vases of yellow-petaled blossoms.

"Why does Vincent paint so many sunflowers?"

"He painted more than this. He gave the first few to Gauguin." Theo came up behind me and put a hand on my shoulder. "Vincent meant to start an artist colony in Arles with some of his Paris friends. Gauguin is the only one who's moved down so far." Theo pointed at a painting of a house, then another one that showed the interior. "The yellow house at 2 place Lamartine. My brother's yellow chair and yellow bed. Yellow flowers. In Arles, Vincent found the light."

I put my hand over his. "Then may he return to that light."

In February, two months after the ear incident, Vincent had been confined to the hospital in Arles on the order of the police. His neighbors had petitioned, saying they feared his mental state. It'd broken his heart, according to Theo, that they should be scared of him. He had nothing toward anyone but goodwill.

"He's to be discharged soon," Theo said. "But he's so wretchedly worried about going back to his old neighborhood, he's thinking about committing himself to the asylum at Saint-Rémy-de-Provence."

"I hope he—"

Footsteps in the hallway had us turning at the same time.

The fiacre driver who'd brought us from the train station dropped our luggage. "Monsieur."

Theo thanked him and paid him.

Then we were alone.

"Gratitude." Theo came back to me, putting his arm around my waist this time. "Sunflowers mean *gratitude* to Vincent. He never loses faith."

I leaned against my husband and imagined an entire vast field of vibrant golden petals. Thousands of these flowers, unworried about the world, unafraid of the storms, turned as one in gratitude toward the light, toward the sun.

The idea had me smiling.

"What do you think of my other treasures?" Theo gestured at the multitude of curiosities that made the place into a messy bachelor apartment.

He stepped to the nearest shelf and picked up a little vase. "Vincent bought this." Then a pottery bowl. "Vincent thought it was interesting."

For a moment, I felt overwhelmed, by the apartment, by the avalanche of strange and unfamiliar things around me, by the noise of the city outside—I could hear the bell of the omnibus from Rue Jean-Baptiste and the clopping of horseshoes on the cobblestones from a hundred carts and carriages, the shouts of a collier, the local coal peddler.

Then Theo was in front of me. "What a dream come true to have you here at last."

The warm light in his blue eyes settled my nerves.

"How did you manage the fresh daffodils?" A prettily tied bouquet sat in a glass on the sideboard.

"They are a mystery." But then he spied a note on the table next to us and picked it up. "Ah. Aunt Cornelie. Uncle Cent's widow. She says she also put fresh linens on the bed, and she will be gifting you her piano as a wedding present. The landlord must have let her in."

The woman's kind and generous gesture burrowed into my heart, a warm ember. "I must write her a thank-you note."

Theo took my hand. "Tomorrow will be time enough, dearest." He drew me farther into the apartment. "Let me show you the rest."

We had two bedrooms. And everything was connected to everything.

"Goodness. We have no fewer than ten doors."

"We can play hide-and-seek." Theo grinned and pulled me into the larger bedroom where the bed waited covered in fresh linens indeed. More yellow-white daffodils greeted us from their cobalt-blue vase sitting on the bedside table. The pink walls showed off yet another half dozen vibrant paintings that celebrated life in all its colors.

"Dearest?" Theo reached for the buttons of my dress.

I trembled. "And if I disappoint?"

"I love you, Jo. I am going to love you forever." He kissed me. "I know you'll miss your family, but I promise you shall not be lonely. My friends will be your friends. Pissarro and his son are coming over to meet you tomorrow. And then Isaacson and the young Nibrig. Your brother and his wife are not far. Your friends can come to the World Fair and stay with us. And you'll have me. I shall do my best to make you happy."

In that light-filled room, surrounded by cherry blossoms, I let him pull me onto the covers.

Nothing was awkward. Or difficult. It was as if we'd always been together.

Happiness.

The following morning, I was truly a married woman. Even if I couldn't, for the life of me, project a matronly air. No matter how many times I corrected the baker that I was a madame, the dratted man insisted on calling me mademoiselle.

Theo laughed when I complained. "May that remain your greatest problem, dearest."

Fate did not grant his wish.

Difficulties came for us, lined up like joined train cars, one following the other. And fast.

CHAPTER ELEVEN

Emsley

My ringing phone startled me awake. I groaned and picked up the call blind.

"I have a few minutes before work," a man I thought should be auctioned off to a roomful of PTA cougars for a school fundraiser told me. "Just checking if you've signed the papers yet. I could pick them up."

I blinked my eyes open. It was Saturday morning. *Stage-set bedroom. Car horns, police sirens, garbage trucks. New York.*

Bram Dekker.

A groggy *no* was working its way up my throat.

"I'm outside. I brought you coffee and a bagel."

"Okay." I stumbled from the bed. The cougars would have to find other prey.

I'd slept in yoga pants and a T-shirt. Technically, I was dressed. I shuffled to the bathroom for some quick maintenance, which made little difference. I'd gone to bed with my hair wet, then slept the wrong way. I looked lopsided, and consoled myself with the fact that I still looked better than the day before, sweat covered in the basement.

Anyway, Bram might not recognize me if I didn't look like a mountain troll who'd wandered into civilization and stuck her finger in a light socket.

"Hang on. I'm coming."

I hurried barefoot down three flights of stairs, vague memories of a late-night internet search floating back. Bram had won all the top lawyer awards—none of which I could recall by name, but they sounded important. He and his grandfather did a massive amount of pro bono work. Their firm had given enough money to a local hospital, I couldn't remember which one, so that they had something called the Dekker Pavilion, specializing in...*blood clots?*

Oh, and he'd been on the swim team in college. I might have spent more time than advisable on a picture of him, wide-shouldered, in a Speedo, holding up a gold medal that explained his impressive upper-body strength. No wonder carrying boxes up from the basement hadn't winded him.

I yanked the door open. "Hi."

To which I hallucinated him responding with "Bob's the man." He extended a steaming cup of coffee and a parchment paper sleeve that hugged a whole-wheat bagel. "Your shirt."

Had one of us had a stroke overnight? Going strictly by genetics and appearance, it had to be me. He was as solid and crisply put together as ever, in another stellar charcoal-gray suit that whispered high-end.

I drew a breath of coffee-scented heaven, let him in, and caught my reflection in the hall mirror. *Right.* My SpongeBob SquarePants shirt. So not the worst of my problems.

Bra anyone?

Coffee and bagel notwithstanding, I crossed my arms in front of my chest.

Bram was watching my sleep-wrinkled face. "Rough night?"

"Ever try to sleep with the ghost of Raoul?"

Humor glinted in his eyes. "I can honestly say I've never slept with anyone named Raoul." He didn't catch the *Phantom of the Opera* reference. "Departed or otherwise."

"Have you ever been inside my grandmother's bedroom?"

"I haven't slept with Violet either." He held up a hand. "I swear. She was a hot ticket, but way out of my league."

On another day, that would have made me smile. "Follow me."

My feet were cold on the marble of the entryway. I had to find my slippers under Violet's bed, and Bram's paperwork was up there too.

I discreetly scarfed my bagel on the way. By the time we reached the third floor, I had a hand free to throw the bedroom door open. *Take a load of this.*

"Wow." Bram tapped the side of his index finger against his temple. "Raoul. The Vicomte de Chagny?"

My first impulse was to like him because he knew Raoul's full name, but I resisted and didn't. I wasn't in New York to like a man, especially not one who was married.

My slippers teased me coyly from half under the bed where I'd kicked them. I curled my toes on the bare floor instead of bending until my butt wiggled in the air. Bram had seen too much of me already. Yet, I could not bring myself to say, *Pardon me while I put on a bra* either. Maybe he hadn't noticed anything.

"Let's talk next door." I ushered him into Violet's study, which had the same parquet floors as all the upper levels in the house, and the same velvet curtains. A dozen vibrant paintings, gifts from former students, balanced out the dark mahogany furniture. A proper English gentleman's lair.

I sat in the massive leather armchair behind Violet's desk that I'd covered with the yellowed letters from the mystery box. I couldn't read them, but I'd sorted them into chronological order. The little green book was by the bed in the bedroom, on the nightstand. The robin's-egg-blue, paint-splattered box, holding nothing but the strange painting of the ugly baby, rested on the floor by my bare feet.

Bram nodded toward the painting. "Where did you find that? Doesn't look like one of Violet's."

"She gave it to me before she died, along with an antique diary and these letters. I don't suppose you speak Dutch?"

"Sorry, no." He picked up a letter and scanned it. "It's a shame you can't read them."

"I can read the diary." I was back to thinking that it might be a diary after all. "It's by a Dutch woman, Johanna Bonger, who married Vincent van Gogh's brother. I'm at the part where Vincent cut his ear off and then decided to go into an asylum."

I couldn't wait to find out what happened next.

I could have googled that too, but I didn't want to. I didn't want a dry, academic summary. I wanted Jo to tell me her story in her own vivid words. She made me feel like I was there with her. Having her diary made me feel special, as if we had a connection. I doubted that, other than Violet and me, many people had read the account of Jo's life.

Bram lay the piece of paper down with the others. "You could have these translated."

"I will. When I have a minute."

My expression must have betrayed my conflicting emotions, because he asked, "Not what you expected to inherit?"

"I didn't expect anything. I can't figure out why Violet thought I should have any of this. I wish she gave me…"

"A letter she wrote you?"

Yes, exactly that. "Detailed advice on how to be a force of nature. Or her own diary, with enough juice for blackmail."

"Are you in need of money?"

"I could use a million." I chugged more caffeine to wake up my brain. Bram Dekker didn't need to know about my business failures.

"Were you hoping for a large inheritance?"

"It wasn't Violet's way. And that's not a complaint. I think she lived the way life should be lived."

"She thought the world of you. You must have been close. Did you spend a lot of time together?"

I drank the coffee, but grief filled my throat instead and threatened to drown me. "I grew up in Connecticut. My parents didn't get along with Violet. They rarely let me stay with her as a kid." I pulled up my feet and tucked them under me. "At first, I didn't want to come anyway. I thought Greenwich Village was *Green Witch* Village."

"Wicked Witch in *The Wizard of Oz*?"

"I used to have nightmares about the flying monkeys."

"We all had nightmares about the flying monkeys." Bram's laughter filled the room and cleared out the last of its abandoned vibes. "Did you spend more time with her later?"

"Once I was in high school, I fought to take the train a few times a year. But at Stanford, I was always taking extra classes, and in the summers, I did internships. It was better when I was working in New York, but Violet always had people around her. She belonged to everyone." And once Diya, Trey, and I had jumped into our startup, none of us had a minute for anything else. Maybe we wouldn't have ended up in a love triangle if we had time to date other people.

"What was the source of the conflict between your parents and your grandmother?"

"Diametrically opposing world views. And Mom felt abandoned by Violet, both in her childhood and later."

"Difficult to picture. The Violet I knew was always there for people."

Bram was right, of course. I didn't want to put either my mother or my grandmother in a bad light, so I felt the need to explain.

"You were Violet's lawyer. You must know she was financially successful. And that she donated most of what she made each year to her causes."

"She didn't believe in the accumulation of wealth."

I tapped my cup to the table, wishing I'd avoided the topic. But I'd gone into it, and now Bram was waiting for more. He might know the story anyway. His grandfather almost certainly did. Bram Dekker Sr. was a close friend to Violet.

"When I was in middle school, my father got hit with a huge malpractice judgment. A patient responded badly to a sedative during a dental procedure, a one-in-a-million reaction. My mother asked Violet for help. Violet said she'd already pledged the entire profit from her last show."

"I'm your daughter!" had been my mother's argument. Violet had responded with *"Are you saying you need that money more than people with AIDS who are homeless?"*

"Anyway, my father appealed the verdict and won, but Mom never forgave Violet. I'm sure she would have bailed us out if the situation had become a true emergency."

"Were you angry with her at the time?"

"I idolized her. I daydreamed about my parents having to downsize to a one-bedroom apartment so they'd be forced to send me to live with her. I built this elaborate fantasy life in New York. *Eloise at the Plaza* all the way. I had a schedule worked up of all the celebrities I wanted to meet. I had questions prepared."

"You wanted to be an interviewer?"

"I wanted to be a star, like Violet."

"Ambitious. My fantasy at that age was owning all the *Star Wars* action figures." Bram checked his watch. "I have a meeting across town. I should probably be going. Do you have the signed papers?"

Time to confess.

"I opened the door under false pretenses. I was desperate for the coffee and the bagel." I dug the UPS envelope out from under my pile of old letters. "I'll sign right now."

"Have you read it?"

"Sorry. Yesterday was a long day. I fell asleep."

He gave an easy smile as he stood. "I'll stop by again tomorrow."

I walked him downstairs.

He left with a smile and a wave.

I was about to close the door when a delivery truck pulled over. The driver dropped off a pile of flattened moving boxes without saying as much as a *Hey*. I dragged them inside and locked the door behind me.

Boxes—check.

Caffeine—check.

No reason not to dive into packing.

My phone rang upstairs, and I raced up three flights.

Morning exercise—check.

"I have some news," Beatriz the Realtor told me. "I'm not sure if it's good or bad. I had a call from the buyer a few minutes ago. He saw Violet's obituary in the *Times*. He wants to move settlement forward to the end of May."

"Why?"

"He always wanted a fast settlement. Violet requested the ninety days. I thought maybe she wasn't ready to let go. Or maybe because your mom broke her hip, and Violet knew how busy you were. Maybe she wanted to give you as much time as she could for packing up the place. Can I say yes to the buyer?"

"Tentatively, yes. I think I can do that."

After the call, I lunged into work as if I were competing for the million-dollar grand prize in a reality show called *House Packers*. But every time I laid something on the "give away" pile, my heart hurt. I wanted to keep everything simply because it'd been Violet's. Sadly, I had room for nothing.

Pare down. Can you live without it? Is it absolutely necessary?

I only stopped to dash over to the grocery store, and then for an actual break when Strena showed up with three models and invited me upstairs.

I was too curious to say no. Also, my back, unused to heavy lifting, needed time to recover.

While the models—wearing only tiny bikinis—waited patiently in the middle of the fourth-floor studio, Strena heated sugar in a copper pot on an electric plate on a cart in the corner, stirring with what she called her "wand," the pointy tool I'd mistaken for a dagger the day before.

"You can help with the video cameras. Just click the red button."

I did.

She pushed her cart over to one of the models. "Ready, Monique?"

She stirred the melted substance, then lifted her wand, pulling a fine rope of sugar into the air, swirled it, broke it off, and placed it on the model's shoulder.

"Doesn't that burn?"

Monique kept motionless. "Cools enough by the time it touches the skin."

"Why sugar?"

Strena was creating more ornamentation. Once again, the model responded. "The sugarworks represent the sticky ties of the past that can be a trap like a spiderweb. Or we can turn it into armor. Or wings."

Strena looked up, but only for a second. "Being a strong, independent woman who speaks the truth is a revolutionary act in this world. And then there are echoes to the sugar trade that started large-scale slavery."

Strena built a golden structure around Monique that was at the same time armor and a cage. Breathtaking. Then she worked on the others. One moment, they were the three goddesses, then the three graces, then three harpies from Greek myth, depending on how she lit them and from what angle I observed.

She lost herself in her work. I thought she forgot I was even there, until she turned to me. "This is practice for a show I'll be doing soon. Want to feel what it's like?"

"Sure?"

"Give me your arm."

I rolled my shirt above my elbow.

"Oh." The first touch made me jump. The sugar was uncomfortably hot, but then quickly cooled.

"I won't burn you. I use special additives." Strena drew patterns reminiscent of henna art, and then small, standing loops that solidified, turning her creation three-dimensional. "How is that?"

"Stunning. Why doesn't it fall off?"

"Secret recipe." She went back to her models.

"Is it edible?"

She laughed. "Go ahead."

Tasted like caramel.

She had to rewarm the sugar over and over. After she finished with Monique, Vivian, and Noemi, Strena stood back and had me turn off the video. She grabbed an old-fashioned camera and snapped a few stills. "What do you think?"

"You made the models look dejected and triumphant at the same time. Downtrodden and victorious. Oppressed and the rulers of all they survey. I don't know how you did that."

"I'm exploring the dualities of the human experience. Life isn't a romantic comedy."

"Truth. If it was, I would have inherited this house instead of being tasked with cleaning it. The brilliant artist I found in the attic would have been a handsome guy. Of course, Bram would also fall madly in love with me. Obviously, he'd be single."

Strena flashed me a curious look, then she lifted her camera and snapped a last shot. "Thank you, ladies. You can go ahead and clean up."

The three models padded off to the bathroom in the back, and I went for the door. "Thank you for allowing me to experience this." I stopped on the threshold when I remembered that I'd actually meant to talk to Strena about something. "The buyer for the house wants to bring up the settlement to the end of the month. You said you were almost done?"

"End of the month is fine with me." She pushed her cart back into the corner and wiped her hands on a rag. "Hold on."

She opened one of the storage cabinets that stood against the wall, and she extricated an old-fashioned brown-striped hatbox from under an avalanche of art supplies.

"I asked Violet if I could have this, and she said yes." Strena brought the box over. "But you can go through it and make copies for yourself if you'd like."

I lifted the lid. A trove of faded photographs and newspaper cutouts filled the box to the brim.

"Those are all about her. I want to put together a tribute to Violet's life." Strena returned to cleaning her tools. "Once I'm done with my sugarworks series. I'm thinking about something three-dimensional. A theme on how one person can touch many lives. Maybe hang pictures of Violet and articles about her in a certain formation from the gallery ceiling, then hang art from her students on the walls, connecting each piece to her with various colors of thread. And then adding in art created by her students' students."

I kept hugging the box, choked up at the sudden gift, at Strena's words. "A rainbow labyrinth?"

"A network. Like the veins in the human body delivering lifeblood from the heart. Or sap going up from the roots of a tree to a thousand individual leaves. Anyway," she said, probably uncomfortable with me tearing up. "It'll be a while before I can start. I'll let you know when I need the material back."

"Thank you." I scanned the articles on top, reading out the titles. *"Warhol's New Side Piece an Artist Herself. Greenwich Socialite, Daughter of Victor Velar, Dabbles in Art. De Kooning's New Muse Can Also*

Paint. Sounds like these are from her early career. I wonder if being defined by the men in her life ever made her want to shove her paintbrushes up people's...noses."

Strena snorted. "Knowing Violet, she found her revenge in more subtle ways."

I riffled through dozens of photos, Violet at splendid parties with all the famous people of the sixties and the seventies and later, gallery openings and award ceremonies. Each image filled a hole in my soul. They made me whole by filling out the past. I teared up all over again. "This is unexpected, and it means a lot. Thank you. Again."

The doorbell rang downstairs.

"I'd better see who is here." I grabbed the hatbox and ran.

Downstairs, the mailman handed me an envelope from the stroke care center—the final bill. The number required more coffee. Thank God, the buyer was moving up the closing. The weird coincidence was, the money Violet was receiving for the house almost exactly matched the amount of her unpaid bills and her new NYU scholarship. The math worked, as if she had managed to predict her life expectancy to the day and her medical expenses to the penny. She left neither debt nor wealth behind. She died as she'd lived: on her own terms.

I carried the hatbox, the bill stuck on top, to the kitchenette. And while I caffeinated, I picked through the contents once again. I especially scrutinized the men, willing the photos to show me my mystery grandfather.

The Tiffany's box Violet had given me had brought me nothing but questions. But the hatbox, the hatbox promised answers.

CHAPTER TWELVE

Johanna
    1890, May 17, Paris, France

"I must not stare at his ear." I poured water over the rice on the stove, jittery with nervous expectation, but talking quietly.

The baby was sleeping in our bedroom. I had set up his little room for Vincent.

I glanced at Theo over my shoulder. "I can't believe we've been married for over a year and I am just now meeting your brother. Should we have gone to visit him before this?"

"You were expecting, dearest." Theo's smile was warm with love. He bent over and tied his shoes. "Vincent would have come sooner if his meddling neighbors didn't interfere in his life. If he didn't feel the need to stay at that damned asylum."

"Poor man." I wiped my hands on the dishcloth,

then folded it, maybe too precisely, but I so badly wanted to make a good impression. "Are you certain he's ready to leave there just a few weeks after…"

He'd eaten his paints to kill himself.

"He's dragged himself up from that dark bottom since," Theo promised.

I stepped into the hall to listen for the baby, wishing desperately that I could lie down on the bed and rest. "And his recent attack of the nerves?"

Theo straightened. "They've done what they could for him." Sadness weighed down his voice. "I don't believe he will improve further at the asylum. You've read his last letter. *I no longer see any courage or hope—*"

A cough raked Theo's chest and cut off the rest of his words.

That dratted cold. I quickly handed him another cup of hot tea. "This should help."

"Thank you. Auvers-sur-Oise will be a better place for Vincent. He will be only an hour from us by train. We will have regular visits. And Dr. Gachet there is an artist himself. Cézanne and Pissarro recommended him most heartily." Theo drained the cup. "I want to be at the station when the train pulls in." He drew me into an embrace and brushed his lips over mine. "I love you, my little wife."

I rested against him for a moment. "I love you too, dearest."

We were natural with each other from the first, comfortable, as if we had always lived together. And over the past year, our love only deepened. The thought of spending every day of my life with Theo lit me up with unbridled joy. I wanted nothing more than to grow old with him. How lucky, how incredibly lucky, to have all my dreams fulfilled, to be so blessed.

Yet I couldn't stop fretting. "And if I ruin lunch?"

"He will be too hungry to notice. Don't worry, they don't hand you over to Madame Guillotine for a burned sausage, not even in France."

He walked down the stairs, coughing some more. The four long flights of steps were a trial, more so on the way up, for me too when I had the baby and the carriage. A larger, ground-floor apartment *was* available, but we couldn't afford it along with Vincent's added expenses.

I closed the door and moved to the window, pressing a hand against the stubborn pains in my abdomen. *Soon, this too shall pass.*

Then Theo stepped out into the May sunshine and looked up with a smile and a wave, and I forgot about the pain.

I waved too. "Hurry back, dearest."

He cut a solitary figure as he strode confidently down the street, to Rue Jean-Baptiste to hail a carriage to Gare de Lyon. He was always so sure of himself, while I was raked with a multitude of worries and fears.

Oh, why did Vincent have to insist on making the journey to Paris alone? What if he had another mental breakdown on the train, among strangers? And what if he arrived safely, but took a dislike to me?

My son cried out in his cradle, saving me from my worst imaginings. "I'm coming, darling."

His smart little eyes, the same sky-blue as his father's, fastened onto my face. His sweet little lips stopped their trembling. He was a small child, but perfect, from his pink ears to his even pinker toes, pure heavenly joy wrapped up in a bundle.

I fetched my tiny treasure into my arms, but by the time I reached the window to show him his papa, Theo had already disappeared around the corner. "He will be back soon, my love." I rocked him on our way back to the kitchen. "We miss Victorine, don't we?"

The running of even a small household such as ours was a challenge. The girl who helped several times a week had to go home to care for her mother. I had wished for little as fervently in my life as I wished her back.

"We shall manage lunch, regardless," I promised Wil. "What will your uncle be like, do you think? He's a great artist. Your papa named you after him." I salted the meat, praying out loud. "Dear Heavenly Father, please end Vincent's troubles."

My little son uttered a serious "Ah" as if trying to say *amen*. He was so sweet, I kissed his rosy cheeks until he squirmed. "You are the most darling boy. And I am the happiest of mothers."

I was not the greatest cook, however.

"Let us hope I shall not burn the rice today." I stirred the pot again. "If lunch turns into a disaster, I might not have enough energy to attempt a replacement." I had spent what strength I had on shopping at the market.

I hovered at the stove with the baby, who tangled his quick fingers in my hair, doing his best to make me look disreputable. "What do you think? Will your mama ever be more competent?"

I set the table for three, then stirred the pot again, then took a turn around the kitchen with Wil. He liked it best when we were moving. As soon as I dipped into a chair, he fussed.

"Shhh." I rubbed his back. "Your uncle Vincent will be here soon."

I hummed him an old church hymn. My eyes drifted closed. I caught myself.

"I won't drop you. I wouldn't." I carried him back to his cradle, handing him his tin rattle. "You play with this. I must finish in the kitchen."

As I straightened, blood gushed between my legs. I would have to change my pad before the men came, and burn the soiled one in the stove. I had been bleeding on and off in the past three and a half months since Wil's birth, sometimes more, sometimes less. The doctor told me the affliction should have stopped by now, but it had not. Yet.

"If only your grandmother lived closer." As I had wished for my mother's encouragement during my labor, now I wished for her advice. My problem was not the kind one could bring up in a letter that the whole family would read after dinner.

I focused on my tasks, then soon lunch was ready, darling Wil taking another nap, and nothing for me to do but wait. I didn't dare sit down for fear that I would fall asleep. I stood at the window, examining the occupants of every carriage.

I said many prayers until, finally, an open fiacre turned down the street with two men inside, both waving as soon as they saw me in the window. I waved back, buoyed by relief. "Thank God."

I ran to check myself in the mirror and patted down my hair. I had a minute or two while the men climbed the stairs. I even had a chance to straighten the kitchen chairs. Then the front door opened, and I rushed to greet our treasured visitor, who had the same blue eyes and copper hair as my Theo, and the same mustache. Yet he was a harder man, at a glance, with heavy-ridged brows and prominent cheekbones, reminding me of men of the fields who'd seen hunger and earned their living with physical labor.

"Welcome in our home."

"And this must be Jo?" The brothers even sounded alike.

I embraced Vincent awkwardly. He could not embrace me back. Both he and Theo were laden with bags, canvases, and Vincent's portable easel, which all poured into our small apartment.

I drew back into the kitchen, out of their way, and stood there nervously while Theo began to look through the pile, even before taking off his hat. He made approving sounds, but all he said was "Where are the rest of your paintings? You've written about more in your letters."

"I gave most of them away before I left." Vincent

sank into the nearest kitchen chair. "Too cumbersome to carry on the train."

I quickly set a bottle of wine on the table. "How was your trip? Was the train car hot?"

"And crowded." He reached for the bottle, but Theo dragged him to the bedroom, beaming with fatherly pride. "Meet my son. Vincent Willem van Gogh."

I paused my work to stand behind the men. My sweet son truly was a precious child. Even strangers on the street stopped me to admire him.

"Ah, the little one." Vincent offered a quick smile, then returned to the kitchen. "You mustn't spoil him."

Of course, small babies were not exciting to anyone but their mothers. Especially when asleep. Vincent spent most of his life surrounded by artists and visionaries, used to more intellectually stimulating company than little Wil and me.

He sat at the table and poured himself wine, turning his attention to his paintings on the walls. Then he launched into a discussion with Theo in French.

I caught only a word here and there. He might have said he regretted that he couldn't show Theo the portrait of Dr. Rey, but he'd gifted it to the man as payment for services rendered in Arles. He didn't mention his ear, and I did *not* look at the stump, but I knew Dr. Rey had been the one to treat him after the *accident*.

I thought he also said he was unhappy with how

we stored his paintings, but I couldn't make out what exactly his complaints were.

"Lunch shall be warmed up in a moment," I spoke up, not wanting to stand there mute, lest Vincent might find me unwelcoming. "I apologize for my lack of French."

I had spent a year in Paris, but much of it heavy with child. I had not gone out as much as I could have. Then, of course, my confinement and the birth, then these past months with the baby kept me at home as well.

Vincent gave me a quick nod, then picked up his discussion with Theo again.

"I hope I managed all right with the lamb." I felt the need to add at least that much, so Vincent wouldn't think I was a terrible hostess.

The men didn't hear me, their voices passionate and loud enough to set little Wil crying. I rushed to pick him up so he wouldn't bother the brothers who had waited for so long to see each other.

"Here you go, my darling." I rocked Wil from crying to hiccups, then kissed and soothed him until even the hiccups disappeared. I watched the men from the doorway. Their easy companionship made me miss my own siblings, most especially Dries.

"What I want to do first," Vincent switched to Dutch, "is paint that bookstore I wrote you about, in the yellow light of the city's new gas lamps."

I crossed to the stove and flipped the meat. The pan wobbled, for I still held the child so I could not steady it with my other hand. To think I could have upended it all onto the floor.

Don't be a nervous ninny!

I wanted to show Vincent that Theo had not married badly. Vincent was necessary for Theo's happiness. I had to find a way to make him like me, to make us one family.

Wil began making happy baby noises, but I didn't put him down. He would just cry again. Instead, I served dinner one-handed. Then, everything on the table, I collapsed into my chair, grateful for the moment of rest.

Vincent grabbed the rice spoon. "I invited some friends to call on me here tomorrow. Your brother," he told me, "Toulouse-Lautrec, and a few others. I hope that is acceptable."

"We want nothing more than for you to feel at home here." I tallied how much I had left in the household account. If I rose an hour early in the morning, I could visit the market again before the baby woke. He often fell into a deeper sleep toward dawn, after being up most of the night.

Theo brought a bottle of champagne to the table. "To celebrate Vincent's first sale at the seventh annual exhibition of Les XX, in Brussels."

He popped the cork with great ceremony, but without making much noise, so he didn't startle the baby, thank heavens.

"The very reason why I invited Toulouse-Lautrec." Vincent drained his wine to make room—

we had not purchased champagne glasses yet. "He defended my honor at the exhibition."

"Who would insult you?" Theo's voice snapped with instant indignation.

"Henry de Groux, that ox, disparaged my talent." Vincent jumped to his feet. "He *refused* to have his paintings hung next to mine. Toulouse-Lautrec challenged him to a duel, on the spot," he added with hearty satisfaction. He seemed to be energized by the naked admiration in Theo's eyes. He grabbed my rolling pin from the sideboard, thrusting it forward like a rapier. "And Signac warned the idiot that should Toulouse-Lautrec be killed, Signac would pick up the sword and finish the duel himself."

"What happened?" I barely dared to ask. "A *duel*. My goodness. So very French."

"De Groux, the coward, withdrew," Vincent said with contempt, then he discarded the rolling pin and dropped back into his chair.

And then he switched to French again, saying something about Theo paying the bill at the asylum and how much money Vincent needed to start life over at Auvers-sur-Oise.

"I should feed the baby." I could barely follow the conversation anyway, so I excused myself.

I hid a slight stagger in the hallway by stopping to kiss the baby's head. Once in the room, I wilted into the armchair in the corner and unbuttoned my dress, frustrated by my weakness. "Here you go, my darling."

His mouth made an eager sound on my breast.

My sweet and precious child. I stroked his cheek and whispered, "What do you think of your uncle?"

I'd expected a sick person, but the ruddy-faced man in our kitchen was a sturdy man, wide shouldered, healthier than either Theo or I were.

"He seems to be in good cheer." I was glad for that. Vincent's sadness and melancholy tended to infect Theo, even through his letters.

"This visit will make your papa happy." I kissed Wil's fuzzy head. "And that shall make us happy." I was just so very, very tired.

Vincent was larger than life. I could hear him extolling his latest pieces in the kitchen, his passion a brightly burning flame. I admired his focus, but, as he went on, barely taking a breath, I also found it relentless. I could see how living life with such intensity could make a person sick from time to time. Fire like that had to be carefully fed. When I left the woodstove untended because I was distracted by the baby, the flames burned themselves out in short order.

Wil finished nursing, and I buttoned up, then laid a cloth on my shoulder and propped him against me. "I hope to know your uncle Vincent a lot better before he leaves. He is my brother now as much as Dries."

I rubbed the baby's back for several minutes, as the doctor had recommended, and waited for the air he had suckled into his little stomach to escape. Then I laid him on the bed and changed his wet diaper. I barely had to rock him after that before he fell asleep again. I settled him into his cradle then rejoined the men.

Theo was holding up a large painting in the middle of the parlor, his face lit with pride. "Look at Vincent's gift for our son."

Pink-white almond blossoms sparkled against a blue sky. The colors nearly vibrated off the canvas, as intense as the artist himself. "Extraordinary. I'm sorry I'm not smarter and can't describe it better. It's… Thank you, Vincent."

"For above the piano," he said in French.

And while I ate, awake just enough not to fall off my chair, he insisted the picture be hung right then. When Theo brought out the hammer, I could have cried. Of course, little Wil woke at the first loud *bam!* I left my plate and went to console him, but an hour passed before the child was asleep again.

While Theo and Vincent laughed at some old story, I cleaned the kitchen. Afterwards, I completed my mending. The men discussed galleries and the latest artistic trends.

They didn't notice when, hours later, I rose to make dinner. After which, I fell into bed alone, setting Theo's alarm clock—a clever new invention—so I could hurry to the market at first light.

I heard them even as I was falling asleep, the conversation switching to Dutch again.

"You must tell me the truth," Vincent said. "Am I a burden?"

"Nonsense. You work harder than any man I've ever met. You will see success."

"Everything I have is yours." Vincent's voice was thick with emotion. "Every painting I brought. Everything I shall ever make."

"I am thinking about leaving Goupil," Theo told him. "I want to open my own gallery."

This was followed by a long silence, during which I fell asleep.

I managed the three days of Vincent's visit in a blur, my only relief when Dries stopped by on the second day. By silent agreement, we didn't mention Vincent's ear or the asylum at Saint-Rémy-de-Provence.

Guillaumin, Toulouse-Lautrec, and a few other of Vincent's old Paris friends also visited. Even had we room enough for me to sit with them around our small table, I couldn't have. The cooking and serving and cleaning up kept me on my feet.

Then Vincent left, and my legs might have been trembling from exhaustion, but I felt only regret that he couldn't stay with us longer. I put the apartment back to rights, then collapsed on the sofa.

Theo, returning from the train station, found me there. "Are you quite well, my dearest?" He sat with me, happiness radiating from him as if he held the sun inside his chest. "I promised Vincent we would visit him in a few weeks."

A train trip. Not long, but with all the supplies a baby required— *No, I must not always think only of difficulties and obstacles.* I laid my head on Theo's shoulder. "Then we shall. I hope Vincent's breakdowns are behind him. I hope he will paint great art in Auvers and find happiness there."

"Our time together went too fast." Theo sighed at the ceiling, then jumped up, jostling me. "The yellow bookshop in the gaslights!" He dropped back down. "We both forgot."

"He will come to Paris again. I shall improve myself and become a more proficient cook. And I will speak better French. I want to do what I can to make him like me. I want him to think of me as another sister."

Alas, it was not to be.

Two months after I had first met my husband's beloved brother, he shot himself. When the news came, I thought it would be our darkest hour. I was wrong. Beyond it waited a deeper hell.

CHAPTER THIRTEEN

Emsley

Sunday morning, Bram Dekker broke my heart.

"Good morning, Emsley." He offered a cream-cheese bagel and coffee when I opened the door. The sun hadn't yet risen over the buildings, the muted morning light shimmering around him.

He had texted the night before that he would stop by around 8:00 a.m. on his way to taking his grandfather to church.

He takes his grandfather to church. He was handsome, successful, and had a sense of humor. *And* brought me food in the morning. Did I envy his wife? Yes. But I kept that to myself.

"Thank you." I accepted the caffeine-and-carb combo, just what I needed. "Please, come in."

His grandfather walked in behind him. My hands were full so I couldn't offer to shake his. I smiled instead. "Hi. I'm Emsley. I've heard so much about you from Violet."

He was the Mr. Rogers version of his grandson: thick gray hair, charcoal gray slacks, red cashmere sweater and blue Harvard tie. Or better yet, he was Mr. Rogers's New York City attorney twin.

He put a comforting hand on my elbow. "I'm sorry for your loss, Emsley. We're all heartbroken." His soft voice cracked midsentence. "Would a grand-fatherly hug be all right?"

"I've never had a grandfatherly hug. I might embarrass myself by clinging."

"You go ahead." He embraced me, mindful of my breakfast. "You didn't know either of your grand-fathers?"

"My father's parents had him late in life and died before he married my mother. I only knew them from pictures. And Violet… She never said." To my great disappointment, the hatbox hadn't offered up any clues either.

I led the way into the first room of the gallery, which no longer stood empty. I'd wrestled down three armchairs and a few other light pieces the previous day to open up the overcrowded third floor.

"This is new," Bram remarked on the furniture.

"I'll have to have everything on the ground floor for shipping, anyway."

"Need help?"

"I won't be dragging all the furniture down myself. Whatever antique store buys the pieces will handle that. If there's anything left over, Habitat for

Humanity promised their people would do the heavy lifting." All I had to do was clear out Violet's personal effects. I put down my breakfast, then picked up the UPS envelope and handed it to Bram. "I read and signed everything."

His grandfather ambled past us. "Would you mind if I walked around? It's been a while."

"Go ahead. But there's not much to see."

"Ah." He took in the nearly empty room with hazy eyes, as if seeing not the present, but the past. "But there is much to feel."

I sat and embraced the day's first caffeine hit. "Thank you again," I told Bram. Then, "It's nice that you're close to your grandfather."

"I have the other one too. In Pittsburgh. Used to be a steelworker." He folded onto the chair next to mine. "Big football fan. Grandpa Joe used to take me to all the games. Grandpa Bram took me to the Harvard Club. That's how I grew up such a balanced person," he deadpanned.

I rolled my eyes at him and fought a grin as I reached for the bagel. Then I caught myself and dropped my hand. I'd be polite and wait.

Bram put the envelope down and pushed the food toward me. "Have you had any luck with translating those old letters?"

"No time. But I'm starting to think again that what I thought was Jo's diary is a book. I think Clara was writing about Jo. It's more than someone would jot down to later remember what happened in a given year. The author is clearly trying to tell a story.

I wonder why Clara didn't write about Vincent instead of his sister-in-law. You'd think Van Gogh would be the more marketable topic."

"Maybe she was an early feminist." Bram nudged the bagel again. "Eat."

I took what I hoped was a ladylike bite. "Could I ask you about something business related?"

"Can't promise I'll have an answer. I'm an estate attorney. But I'd be happy to listen."

I gulped some more coffee. "I signed a contract a few days ago." While I'd been sitting with Violet. "I want to buy out a partner from my startup. Trey put up the initial million-dollar starting capital. He wants it back. He also bought our third partner's shares for two hundred thousand, so I'd have to buy that too. I can scrape together two hundred grand from savings and if I sell everything I own. The rest…" I hated sounding desperate, but sugarcoating the truth helped nothing. "If I can't pay him by the end of the month, he gets the company. For peanuts."

"Why are you splitting?"

I looked at Bram Sr., who was running his fingers over a window seat. *Wonder what had happened there.* "We no longer agree on what the company should do." *Full disclosure.* "We also had personal issues. We were seeing each other for a while, and now we're not."

"How are you going to get the million?"

"I have to find an investor."

"Are you looking for wiggle room with the deadline? It might be possible, depending on how the contract is worded. Have you talked to your own corporate attorney?"

"He's one of Trey's best friends. Trey brought him onboard."

"I'll talk to an attorney friend and have her call you tomorrow. You can trust Adele."

"I don't know if I can afford a new attorney."

"You can afford a consultation at the friends-and-family rate. May I see your contract with Trey?"

I ran upstairs, grabbed it, and hurried back down. While I'd been gone, Bram put on reading glasses—dark, kind of square, all sexy librarian. He lowered the glasses and looked at me over the rim, probably wondering why I was tripping over my feet.

For a split second, I flashed over to an alternate universe where his voice dropped as he said, *These books are late. Step closer, Miss Wilson. I believe you've acquired a fine.*

I could *not* keep thinking stupid stuff like that. The corporate attorney he was recommending could be his wife. They'd probably met at law school. Or at Bram Sr.'s firm.

I handed him the contract. "I'd appreciate any advice."

Bram Sr. was rotating in a slow circle in the middle of the gallery, one arm outstretched. "You should have seen the shows Violet had here." His tone held profound admiration. "The parties. All four floors *and* the basement. At her last party, she had a *carousel* down there."

"Still there," his grandson and I said at the same time.

Bram Sr. peeked in the basement door. "I'd love to see it, but I'm afraid my knees no longer like stairs." He let his gaze roam the first floor again. "Everyone who was anyone in New York used to be here. The newspapermen would be waiting outside, shouting questions as celebrities came and went. City council-men, who were here with their mistresses, would sneak in through the back."

While his grandson read my contract, I pictured the clothes, the music, the fancy cocktails. "Wish I could have seen that."

He used his cane to point at the window at the back that opened to the miniscule courtyard of dying grass and now overflowing garbage containers. "Did you know a neighbor called the police on your grandmother for sunbathing naked out there? The young officer was hopelessly starstruck by Violet. He ruled that the courtyard was Violet's personal prop-erty, in no way public, and issued the complaining neighbor a Peeping Tom fine."

Ha! "She never told me *that*."

"Everyone was in love with her." Bram Sr.'s voice thickened with enough nostalgia to make me wonder, was *he*?

"How long were you friends?"

"Fifty-seven years."

The last bite of bagel stuck in my throat. Time stopped. *Mom is fifty-six years old.*

Bram Sr.'s hair was gray. My gaze whipped to his

grandson's. Brown, a shade close to my mother's. Wrong eye color, but both my mom and I had inherited Violet's green eyes. I zeroed in on Bram Sr.'s chin. Was that a hint of a cleft?

Would a grandfatherly hug be all right?

Did he know?

Oh-God-oh-God-oh-God. I fought the bagel down at last.

Had my grandmother told him? Or had he guessed? Was he here to tell me? Why not contact me before? Why not contact my mother? Why ignore our existence all this time? Was I Bram's *cousin*?

I gulped coffee so I wouldn't blurt those questions, gulped it too fast, and then coughing made me jerk my hand. Black liquid splashed all over the table, nearly nailing the UPS envelope next to the remains of my breakfast.

Bram snatched the envelope up and dropped it on his chair as he stood, holding my Ludington's contract safe. "I'll grab the paper towels from the kitchen." He was halfway across the room before he asked, "Mind if I use the bathroom in the back? The church bathroom is full of crucifixes. It's an uncomfortable space."

"No. Of course. Go ahead."

Bram Sr. wandered past me, toward the staircase. "Is the upstairs still the same as it used to be?"

"If by *same* you mean more drama than on Broadway." His grandson would be gone for only a few minutes. If I wanted to ask the man anything, it would have to be now. "I was—"

"You know, I think I'd like to hazard that basement after all."

I led the way, opening the door, then flicking on the light. Nervous energy pushed me forward. Impatience stopped me halfway down. This was it, the secret of secrets in my family. I had to ask. I might not have another chance.

"Were you and Violet ever more than friends? What I mean is…" I didn't want to offend him, but the question was burning through me. The clock was ticking. I wanted to have this conversation between the two of us, in private. "Are you my grandfather?"

The world stopped turning. Even the dust motes stilled in the air. My lungs froze between one breath and the next.

A moment out of time.

Then the clock of the universe restarted.

Bram Sr. grabbed the railing, as if my question were a blow and he needed support. "Oh dear." His gray eyebrows drew together in distress. "Oh, I see. I'm so sorry. I'm not your grandfather, Emsley." His voice rang with profound sadness. "But I would give everything I have to be able to say I am. Please believe me."

A dull ache spread in my chest.

He took a tentative step down, then another, visibly shaken. I went back to assist him. I shouldn't have agreed to show him down there. I shouldn't have asked stupid questions.

The corners of his mouth tilted down as if pulled by a lifetime of regrets. "I would have done anything for Violet. For us to be together like that. I was stuck in a loveless marriage for too many decades. But Violet wouldn't have had me for a husband, anyway. She never wanted to get married."

"Do you know why?"

"She didn't want to be tied to anyone. And, I think, she didn't entirely trust men. No wonder, of course, after that cursed Vanderbilt party." Bram Sr.'s eyes flashed, sharp and hard, and for a moment, he was a much younger man, one ready to charge off to battle.

"What happened at the Vanderbilt party?"

He focused on the next step and wouldn't look at me. "It's not my place to say."

"I can't ask anyone else."

We made our way to the bottom of the steps, and he turned away from me. "Well, hello, Tiny Tim. It's been a while."

The LED bulb I'd bought at the grocery store was worth the six dollars. The bear looked less intimidating, his outstretched paws threatening not so much to tear us from limb to limb, but maybe just to pat us on the head. Not that right then I cared about the bear.

"My grandmother? Please."

"She wouldn't talk to me about that night. I thought she might have told you. She loved you more than anyone."

"Told me about what?"

He weighed his words. "You understand, I was only there for the aftermath."

"Then could you just tell me the part you know?" *And fast.* His grandson would be looking for us any second. "Please."

Finally, laboriously, Bram Sr. answered. "I went to law school with one of the Vanderbilt nephews. I almost didn't go to that party. Thought it was a pity invite. I came from a modest background, you see." He leaned heavily on his cane. "Then again, who isn't modest compared to the Vanderbilts? Have you seen the building?"

"I think so." I had a vague picture of it in my head. "Seventy-third Street?"

"Seventy-second. A block from Central Park. Which always bothered the hell out of Vanderbilt. The Carnegie Mansion is not only right on the park, but it overlooks the water. Jaqueline Kennedy Onassis Reservoir. They called it the Central Park Reservoir back then."

"And the party?"

"I'd only just arrived. I was climbing the curving staircase, champagne flute in hand. I hadn't even taken the first sip." He paused as if what he was about to say hurt him, or he was worried it would hurt me. "The most beautiful woman I'd ever met flew out of the library. One moment, she was full of motion, then she stopped as if she'd lost her way, as if she didn't know where she was, which way to go next. The first and only time I saw Violet lose her wits."

"What happened?"

"I dashed up the stairs and asked if I could help.

She shied back. And every instinct I had said she was the type of woman who never shied from anything. She asked if I could get her out of there. I set my champagne glass on the floor, on the spot, and offered her my arm, asked her if she needed to gather her wrap. She cast a panicked glance at the closed library door, then fled down the stairs."

"Did she say why she was upset?"

"Just gave me her address. I escorted her home in a cab and offered to stay, but she sent me off. I went straight back to the party, burst into the library, ready to kill the man who'd hurt her."

"Why did you think she was hurt?"

"Her dress was disheveled." Bram Sr.'s voice dropped. "I thought I saw blood on the hem."

My hands curled into fists. I wanted to punch the freaking bear. "Who was in the library with her?"

"I found the room empty. Whoever was in there before, he left by the time I arrived back."

"She never told you?"

"She wouldn't even let me ask the question. We became friends. But every time I thought to ask, she knew, and the look on her face rendered me silent."

"Thank you for being a good friend to Violet."

"An honor." He couldn't say more, because his grandson was drumming down the stairs.

"You'll be late for church." The younger Bram held out a hand to his grandfather. "Let me help you up the steps."

I followed them, raw emotions screaming in my head like banshees from an Ancient Greek myth. I wanted to scream with them. *In a minute.* When I was alone.

As we passed my new seating arrangement, I absently noted that the spilled coffee had been all mopped up. Bram had cleaned my mess.

He picked his envelope up from the chair. "I'll take care of this." He scanned my face. "Talk of the past upset you. I'm sorry."

"I just miss my grandmother."

He nodded and handed me Trey's contract. "This looks pretty tight, but run it by Adele too. She's the expert."

"Thank you for all your help."

I walked them to the door. Bram Sr. gave me another warm hug. The younger Bram simply said goodbye, but he had questions in his eyes.

I dropped my gaze. By sheer chance, it landed on his left hand. *No platinum wedding band.*

"Mind if I call you later?" he asked.

Oh hell no.

If I'd ever felt a modicum of attraction toward him, it was instantly dead. Dropped from the sky like a shot pigeon. Splat on the steps. I seriously couldn't stand guys like that.

Bram had been nice and polite and funny, helpful, and I had thought he loved his wife. I liked the man I thought he was. I liked the idea that somewhere out there, a woman had a husband like him, a win for the sisterhood. And if she could have all that, maybe someday—when I was out of my current mess—so could I.

Except that now there Bram stood, ring probably in his pocket, asking if he could call me later.

"I'll be busy packing all day." Our business was concluded. "Goodbye."

I closed the door. The world was shit and everyone in it.

I'd thought I'd been so good about not sending mixed signals, not flirting in any, even harmless, way. I'd thought we'd been on the same wavelength. I'd thought Bram was a friend, at a time when I needed a friend.

I'd been delusional. We barely knew each other. He owed me nothing. And my disappointment in him was less than nothing. Not when compared to the startling news I'd just uncovered in the basement.

"Oh, Violet."

I spun on my heel in a rush of anger. I didn't know much, but I knew this: I was going to turn the house upside down for every note, every letter, every last scrap of paper. Whoever had been in that library with Violet, I was going to find the bastard.

CHAPTER FOURTEEN

Johanna

1890, July 25, Amsterdam, Netherlands

"I want you and our little son to recover." Theo embraced me with tenderness on the platform next to his train. The cool of Amsterdam misted over us. The slower rhythm of the city felt comforting, like an all-healing balm.

I loved Paris's sunshine, even if it blinded me when the light reflected off the white palaces of the Champs-Élysées. I loved swimming in the colorful currents of the greatest city in the world, where, if you listened carefully at night, you could hear life's heartbeat. But after a year, as a young mother, I was happy to be home. After running the household and taking care of Wil alone, I craved the helping hands of my mother and my sisters.

Theo had come with me for a summer holiday

with the baby, but after four short days, he had to return to Paris for work. He had a buyer for the Diaz, and we needed the commission from the sale.

Theo kissed my cheek and then Wil's head. "I love you both. Every day shall be misery without you. I promise to hurry back."

"Please do. I want us to have the grand vacation we all need."

I clung to him, my heart filled with more love than I had ever been able to imagine as a silly girl. We had not spent a day apart since we had married. I didn't want him to leave. I had found my happiness at last, that flawless state of joy I had daydreamed about as a young girl. I was certain that our luck was turning at last.

"By the time you see us again, I promise we'll be the pictures of well-being. Wil's infection is clearing up. Did you see how heartily he ate his lunch?" And my own health was improving too. Each day we had been back in the Netherlands, Wil and I had grown stronger.

Theo hung on, as reluctant to leave as I was to release him. "I will be back before you have a chance to miss me, dearest. Do rest while I am gone."

"I shall plan the rest of our vacation. Long boat rides and lovely walks along the canals, The Rijksmuseum, The Hague."

He took my hand as if he wasn't able to help himself. "And what shall I bring you for a gift?"

"I wish for nothing but for the Diaz to sell quickly

and that you hurry back." I rose to the tips of my toes for another quick kiss.

"The commission couldn't come at a better time." Theo's smile was filled with hidden meaning.

Hope should be a patient thing. Mine wasn't. It made me demand, "We are moving?"

The tips of Theo's mustache wiggled higher. "I promise, dearest. And this is only the beginning. All our dreams will be coming true and soon."

I sprang back into his arms. "Life will be so much easier in the ground-floor apartment. Oh, do write Vincent in Auvers to tell him. In a larger apartment, we will be able to store his paintings exactly as he wishes. That should make him happy."

"You read his last letter. He is happy already. He is painting every day. He found a good friend in Dr. Gachet. I am certain his new works will sell."

"I'm just glad he's optimistic about his prospects again." Vincent's happiness was necessary for Theo's happiness.

At the last warning whistle, my husband hopped onto the train. I held back tears as the steam-spewing black beast carried my love away.

On the way back to my parents' house, I held my son tighter. I worked on gaining control of my emotions, yet some stubborn tears still clung to my eyelashes as I walked inside at last. But then there, in the parlor, the happiest of surprises awaited.

My best friend, Anna, jumped to her feet and ran to me. "Jo! And Wil! How precious he is. And here is my Saskia." She reached back for her own daughter, who was sitting on the carpet. She was only a few months younger than my son.

The three carefree days that followed were full of laughter. The two babies loved playing together. My family doted on us. Theo wrote that he would be returning shortly.

"My life is a dream, the perfect idyll," I told Anna Tuesday morning, handing Wil back his wooden ball, which had rolled under my seat. "And yours too. How lucky we are."

She straightened Saskia's pretty yellow dress. "Of course, the trouble with the story of Paradise is that it always ends with being cast from Paradise."

I opened my mouth to ask if she and Jan were having troubles, but the doorbell rang.

I hurried to answer and accepted a letter from the mailman.

"From Theo. He's probably writing to tell me which train he'll be on in the morning." My gaze snagged on the return address.

Anna noticed. "What is it?"

"He writes from Auvers-sur-Oise instead of Paris."

My mother sailed into the living room from the kitchen. "Why is he there? Must he constantly travel? Your father wouldn't have dreamed of deserting me and our children."

"Theo has hardly deserted us, Mama." I opened

the letter and scanned the hastily scribbled lines. "Vincent is unwell again."

"In what way?" My sister Mien came in behind my mother.

"Theo doesn't say." I hurried to my father's desk in the corner and wrote back immediately. "I'm sending my wishes and prayers for recovery."

Mama nudged my shoulder. "And ask for details."

I did. And then two endless days, my heart alternating between the lightest hope and the darkest worry, before Theo's response arrived.

Anna and I were home alone, my father at work, my mother and older sisters out for a walk with the children. It was Anna's last day with us, so she was packing. I was in her room to help.

We were planning our next meeting, in Paris, when the maid came upstairs and handed me Theo's letter.

My eyes flew over the words.

Anna closed her suitcase. "Good news?"

"The news could not be worse." I staggered to the armchair in the corner and collapsed. I could barely see my friend through my tears. "Vincent is dead." *Breathe.* "He shot himself."

Anna's legs folded too. The bed caught her. "A tortured soul. But, oh, Jo." She sprang up and hurried over, put her arms around me. "I am so sorry. Why? Does Theo say what happened?"

I rubbed the tears from my eyes with my wrist to read the newspaper cutout that had come with the letter, from the *L'Écho Pontoisien*, but new tears replaced the old faster than I could erase them.

Anna took the piece of paper from me and translated as she read. *"Sunday, July 27, a certain Van Gogh, aged 37, Dutch national, artist, has shot himself with a revolver in the fields and, only wounded, returned to his room, where he died the day after the next day."*

The article fluttered from her hand, landing on the hem of my skirt.

I couldn't bear touching it. Not even with every instinct screaming to shake it off, as all women were trained to instantly defend against anything that touched our garments lest it be a stray spark. We no longer wore the crinoline dresses of my mother's youth that caused thousands of deaths each year, but plenty of women died still from their dresses catching on fire. All I could do was stare at the tightly printed words and shudder with the premonition that they were no less dangerous than live embers, having the power to burn down my whole life.

"But Vincent was so well when we visited him in Auvers in June." How he'd loved little Wil, had proudly shown his nephew around the animal yard. He even gifted Wil with a bird nest he found. "Theo must be broken." I struggled to breathe past the pain that hardened my lungs into stone. "I have to write Theo."

"You stay here." Anna snapped up the newspaper cutout. "I'll bring pen and paper."

I could barely see the white sheet she slid in front

of me a few seconds later. *When shall I come?* I wrote, in terrible script, with trembling hands.

Two agonizing days crawled by before a response arrived. Anna and her sweet daughter had returned home by then. My family surrounded me with love, but nothing could budge the dark burden of grief from my chest.

"Theo wishes for me to remain in Amsterdam." I was sitting at the kitchen table with my mother and sisters, numb, unable to comprehend the words on the paper. "He says to stay where I am."

Yet to be separated from him at a time like this was unimaginable. I ached to be with him, ached for the comfort of his embrace. Our broken hearts belonged together.

I barely had the strength to push my chair back, but I managed. "I am going upstairs to pack. When the maid returns from the market, please send her up to help."

The next morning, my little son and I took the first train to Paris, since Theo's last letter had been posted from there. I'd sent a telegram, so my dearest husband was waiting for us at the station.

"Oh, my love." How his clothes hung on him!

He had been growing stronger before this tragedy, and I had trusted that our holiday in Amsterdam would heal him completely. But instead of resting and recovering together, we had been apart, and Theo appeared more haggard than ever.

He looked at me helplessly, like a child. I could not lean on him, nor could I huddle against his chest.

The sight of Theo with his strength drained away broke my heart. When I'd married him, I'd been transferred from my father's care into his. He'd protected me. Two weeks ago, he'd escorted me to Amsterdam. But I came back on my own, and I could see that something had shattered inside him while we'd been apart. I would have to take up the weight he could no longer carry. I would have to step into the lead.

I had been a married woman for over a year. I had a child. But I finally grew up on that platform, in that single moment. I felt fate carve lines around my eyes with a merciless hand. I doubted the baker would ever make the mistake of calling me "mademoiselle" again.

I took Theo's hand. "Is there a fiacre waiting?"

"At the entrance."

I slipped a coin to the porter and asked him to follow us with our valises and bundles. Then, once we were settled in our hired carriage, our belongings loaded in the back, I claimed Theo's hand again.

"As soon as I lay our son in his cradle, I will run out to the market. I will cook a hearty meal. We are here now, dearest. Our family is together. You will feel better."

He held my hand and nodded without conviction, sitting collapsed next to me, his eyes glinting with tears. He twisted away so I wouldn't see them.

The fiacre rolled forward under an ominous, blackening sky.

"How did it happen?"

"On Monday, Dr. Gachet wrote to ask me to visit." Theo buried his face into my neck and his tears fell on my skin. "He said Vincent had wounded himself. He didn't die from the shot at once. He was still talking when I arrived. I expected him to recover."

I held our little son on my lap with one arm while holding on to Theo with the other.

"He died Tuesday." Theo's voice was a broken whisper. "Not long after midnight. He told me *I wanted it to end like this.*"

I swallowed a sob. "He wanted you by his side at the end. And you were there. The two of you together, always." But oh, how I wished Vincent would have spared Theo all this suffering.

"Our mother is devastated." Theo straightened and wiped his eyes. "We buried him in a sunny spot amid the fields at Auvers."

"He is at rest at last." I kissed my husband's temple. "You were without me at your brother's funeral, but you will not be alone in the rest of your grief."

We slogged through August in a haze and suffered the city's merciless heat, our plans for a holiday in the cool of Amsterdam forgotten. How strange it was for the postman not to come nearly daily with

Vincent's letters. I would see his uniformed, bulky form from the window and think *I wonder what news from Auvers.* And then I would remember.

We lived in sorrow, but at least our precious boy was well. My bleeding stopped. Theo's melancholy lifted, and his cough that had worsened after Vincent's death was easing again.

In the middle of September, we moved down-stairs to the larger apartment. Since Theo was no longer supporting Vincent, we could afford the higher rent. We lost the light of the upper floor, and everything was still a mess and would remain so until we found the right spot for each piece of furni-ture, but at least fewer stairs meant an easier daily life. And we could properly store Vincent's paintings, an important consideration, since more were on their way from Auvers.

We were discussing that, late at night in bed, when Theo had an idea that at long last brought him a small measure of happiness.

"I am going to hold a retrospective for Vincent in our old apartment while it stands empty, before it's rented out again." For the first time since the tragedy, his eyes glinted with excitement instead of being lost in the shadows of sadness. "I am going to ask Émile Bernard to help. He is writing a biography of Vincent and means to include some of their letters to each other. People are suddenly talking about Vincent's great talent."

"I hope he sees it all from heaven."

Theo kissed the tip of my nose. "I will make him

famous yet." And just like that, my husband was back to being a dreamer. He cradled my face in the palms of his hands and kissed my lips next. "Will you help me, my dearest?"

"Always, my love." My heart filled with the kind of iridescent light that Vincent painted so well. Hope unfurled its whisper-soft petals. "Together, you and I will triumph. We will leave all darkness behind. Now that we have more space…" I whispered between kisses.

"Our Wil should have a brother or sister to play with?" Theo smiled his first smile since Vincent's death. "Yes." He pulled me closer. "My darling, yes."

Later, I fell asleep looking at one of the paintings on the wall, dark skies over a wheat field. In my dream, I walked into that field, and as I strolled forward, the storm clouds cleared. Flowers opened their petals. The birds sang.

I woke abruptly to a sharp pain in my shoulder. Theo was thrashing in his sleep and had struck me. He gnashed his teeth, emitting an eerie sound of anguish that raised the fine hairs on my arms.

I shook him. "Wake up, my love. You are having a nightmare."

Instead of opening his eyes, he howled, a mournful wail that filled our home and my head, a haunting sound I shall never forget—like ghosts calling from the distance.

Gently, I brushed the hair from his brow, and I felt the heat of fever.

No, no, no. Not now.

I jumped out of bed. "I must fetch help."

Then the window caught my eye. I looked out into the darkest night. I couldn't run for the doctor until first light.

I shook Theo's shoulder. "Wake up, dearest!"

CHAPTER FIFTEEN

Emsley

How many years of life does the average person waste being an idiot?

How many hours had I wasted in middle school —spending entire evenings gazing at Timothy Dalton on the internet?

My grandmother hadn't kept my grandfather's identity a secret to spare his reputation because he'd been a married man, a famous man. She'd never spoken about him because she'd wanted to forget him. She'd never told my mother because she'd wanted to protect my mother from the terrible truth. But then, of course, the silence had hurt my mother anyway.

I was heartsick for both of them. And I was mad.

After Bram and his grandfather had left Sunday morning, I read another chapter from the little green book to settle my mind. Instead, I cried like a child over Vincent's death. His death and Violet's melded together in my mind, and I grieved all over again, as if their passing had only just happened.

Then there was Bram Sr.'s revelation, a tornado itself, swirling through my hurricane of emotions. I spent the rest of the day anger cleaning, with small breaks to answer Diya's pre-auction questions. I left the business to her and ripped the house apart. But I found no hint of the identity of the man who'd hurt Violet in the library.

I had plenty of fury left over for Monday. I stripped off the old curtains and bagged them for the garbage.

Bram Sr.'s words played over and over in my head. I wasn't surprised that Violet never reported the assault. In 1965, she'd been at the beginning of her career. If she'd made an accusation, she would have been disbelieved, blamed. Those had been the times.

Hell, those were the times still.

I ripped the last set of velvet bedroom curtains off their rod and sent them to the floor with a satisfying thud. "There."

I climbed down. The Phantom's lair no longer looked like the Phantom's lair. Without their heavy cover, the two south-facing windows bathed the room in light, the space almost as bright as the studio on the top floor.

I dragged the heavy curtains to the top of the stairs and tossed them to the landing below, burning off my frustration with hard work. Classical music filtered through the studio door above. Strena had models up there again. I left them to their practice and stomped back to the bedroom to see what needed to be tackled next.

Newspaper cutouts and pictures covered the floor. "Aw, dammit."

I must have knocked over the hatbox with the stupid curtains.

I opened the window to let out the dust that danced around me in the air, then I carefully sat in the middle of the mess and picked up the closest photo, Violet's old cherry-red Mustang convertible.

A pigeon landed on the windowsill.

"I don't have a crumb of food in here. Shoo."

He stayed where he was and stared at me.

I went back to the photos while keeping an eye on him.

Violet accepting an award. Then a picture of people I didn't know. Then a picture of Violet at thirty-something, at what might have been opening night at a gallery, dancing with a dashing man. I'd put him under obsessive scrutiny the day before already, but I had no way of telling if the man was THE man.

I returned the photo to the hatbox then reached for one that had been flipped over, and I realized it was marked on the back with names and dates. And so were many of the others.

I went through everything again.

"The award ceremony was at the MoMA in 1979,"

I told the pigeon, who watched with interest. The handsome man dancing with my grandmother was the Dutch ambassador, at a party at the embassy, not at a gallery. The strangers smiling into the camera were from Violet's Van Gogh class.

"Wonder if she ever showed the little green book to her students."

I picked up another photo of Violet, in Yves Saint Laurent's famous Mondrian shift dress. *A gift from the designer*, the note said on the back. My mother had mentioned that dress a few times. *Violet wore it to my graduation! Can you imagine? All your friends are there, and your mother shows up in a minidress and go-go boots?*

Since I'd dragged the coffee table and bedroom chairs downstairs, I had floor space in the bedroom to spread out my treasure.

"I'm going to put these in chronological order." Then looking through them would be like watching a movie about Violet's life.

The earliest image was from 1965, Violet at eighteen, breathtakingly beautiful, a smart-alecky grin on her face. She'd already been accepted to NYU.

No other photos from 1965, only an article about Violet's first show. Then nothing until 1966, the year my mother was born. Nothing in between. Nothing from the cursed Vanderbilt party.

I lay back and stared at the ceiling, frustrated. I banged my head on the floor, which earned immediate regret and a concerned *coo* from the pigeon.

Wait.

"Just because Violet didn't have photos of the

party, it doesn't mean nobody else had them either." And where did all photos end up? *The internet.*

I speed crawled to my laptop on the nightstand and made Google my best friend.

The opulent scenes my image search located could have been out of a movie made by Old Hollywood, one of those elaborate productions with Zsa Zsa or Marilyn: flowing dresses, feather boas, the occasional tiara. Too bad the photos were black-and-white, so I couldn't tell the colors.

I magnified the screen and combed through the images one by one.

"There she is!"

Violet wore an empire-waist dress, at the same time sophisticated and innocent. An embroidered silk wrap covered her shoulders, her hair pinned up in a soft twist, her eyes filled with merriment.

Once I knew what dress and hairstyle to look for, finding her again was easier.

Invariably, she was surrounded by men. My heart pounded as I scrutinized each. They all wore tuxedos. "Half look like Daddy Warbucks, the other half like Fred Astaire."

I caught no threatening vibes. I found no pictures of Violet disheveled.

I scrolled through the images over and over, determined to spot the conscienceless bastard who hid among the lambs.

And then I found him, a clean-cut twenty-something with a smug smile, caught exiting a room. The door behind him stood half open, revealing book-shelves.

He wasn't the focus of the photograph. He was in the background, half hidden behind a glamorous older couple. The more I enlarged, the blurrier the picture became, but I could see a dark line on his jaw —a scratch? And something white below his waist that looked like the corner of his shirt caught in his zipper.

I clicked on the image description, desperate for a name, but only the couple was listed. "Mr. & Mrs. Wannamaker."

I combed through all the pictures again, searching for that specific smug face. I found him with a timid-looking woman, just arriving to the party. This time, he was the focus of the picture, and he was identified.

"Taylor Wertheim, the junior senator from Mass-achusetts, with his bride."

I immediately googled him.

"He is still alive."

CHAPTER SIXTEEN

Johanna
    1890, October 12, Paris, France

Never say that life could not be worse. Nor ever say that luck had turned and nothing but blue skies wait ahead. Fate will hear and laugh.

I had told my friend Anna once that I would rather have a year of intense happiness than small moments doled out over a lifetime, and I received a year, but only that. By the time October arrived, our lives were unraveling so quickly, I couldn't catch my breath.

Theo was unable to overcome his brother's death. He fell from one malady into the next, until even his mind became affected.

"You must eat, dearest," I pleaded with him through our bedroom door, wanting nothing more than to nurse him back to health. "At least come out to the kitchen."

He no longer allowed me inside. I had been sleeping in our son's room, my only interaction with Theo when he let me pass him a plate.

"Vincent deserved better!" he shouted. "If I hadn't made the decisions I made, if I could go back... What have I done? He was fully dependent on me. I knew that!"

He yelled in Dutch, and then yelled in French, and then yelled words I couldn't understand.

The doctor had been there the day before, but Theo would not let him inside the bedroom either. I'd passed his medicine in with the previous night's meal, but had no way of telling if the potion had been taken. "Vincent is at peace. You said so yourself. He is at rest."

"I failed him. And I am just like him, don't you see?"

Something crashed inside. Wil began to cry and crawled to me. I picked him up.

"Would you eat lunch with us?" I begged his father. "Or at least take a plate?"

No response, only silence.

"A glass of milk?"

"Don't you understand?" he raged at me. "I am going mad."

My heart was drowning in all the tears I held back. "You are grieving. The pain shall lessen with time. I promise, dearest."

"And if you're wrong?" Theo's voice broke. "If I do something unforgivable?"

"You will not harm yourself. You are not alone. You have me and your son. Your life is not hopeless, Theo. You are nothing like your brother."

"Same blood, same flesh." A lengthy, dark pause followed the words. "Jo, I no longer feel in control of myself."

"Try, dearest."

Another crash, closer to the door, sent me jumping back. I clutched Wil, mumbling another whispered prayer in an endless chain of whispered prayers.

When the front door behind me rattled, I jumped again, not knowing which way to run. "Who is it?"

"Dries."

I rushed to let in my brother, rounding the piano Theo's Aunt Cornelie had gifted us, which was in the way, still in the wrong spot, too close to the hearth. The sofa sat at the wrong angle. Half-unpacked boxes held our belongings. Theo had fallen ill so soon after our move, we hadn't had the chance to fully unpack in the new apartment. If our living room was a painting, it could have been titled *Life Interrupted*.

I opened the door. "Oh, thank the merciful heavens."

"Is it as bad as that?" But then Theo shattered something else and my brother could hear it for himself.

I flitted back to the bedroom. "Dries is here. Will you not come out to say hello?"

Nothing but more cursed silence. I hated those silences, their tyranny that made me wonder whether Theo might have done something to himself.

Dries came up to stand by me. "How long has he been like this?"

"Two weeks. But he's been declining even before that." First, that terrible cough that wouldn't leave him for the past two years had grown even worse. We'd lived in fear of the flu epidemic. And he'd escaped that, but then came this dark melancholy. "He resigned from the gallery."

"Has he anything else lined up?"

I blinked back tears.

"How will you live?"

"I don't know. I don't know anything. I'm so glad that you're back." My brother had been traveling in Belgium on business. I had held off telling him about Theo, but in a desperate moment the day before, I ended up sending him a telegram.

Inside the room, Theo screamed.

"Has he harmed you?"

"He wouldn't. He is merely overcome with grief that he hadn't done more for Vincent."

Dries spoke through the door. "I say this as your friend, Theo. You did more for your brother than anyone else would have. And you couldn't have saved him if you did a thousand times more. Vincent has always been broken."

No response. At least, Theo didn't break anything else.

Dries slipped off his hat. "Would you not let me

come in? We'll have a drink. Talk about old times."

Seconds ticked by, then the door opened to a gap.

I grabbed Dries's arm. "Take food. And milk."

I set Wil down and quickly handed the already prepared plate and glass to my brother, then I nudged him forward. "Go! Or the door might close again."

It did, but only when Dries was on the inside, a prayer answered.

"Papa." Wil picked his rubber ball off the floor and offered it to me, for his father.

"Your papa and your uncle are going to have a nice talk. Isn't that lovely? Why don't I cut up an apple for you, and we shall finish yesterday's cheese? And then maybe a walk outside after that?"

I didn't want my little son to worry. I didn't want him scared. "You mustn't remember your father like this." I took him to the kitchen and washed our largest apple. "We'll make new memories, good ones, when he recovers."

Theo shouted, "You understand nothing!"

Then a heavy weight crashed against the bedroom door, as if the men were fighting each other. I dropped the apple back into the bowl, grabbed up Wil, and fled.

"Your father is a good man. He is such a lovely man. And he loves us very much. He—" I choked on raw fear, shaking on the front stoop. I had grabbed neither my shawl nor my hat. Nor had Wil any shoes on his small feet against the October chill.

I held him tightly against me. "All is well, my

cherub. Papa and Dries are merely playing a game. All is well."

I waited until I caught my breath, until my heart stopped racing so hard that it hurt inside my chest. Then I eased back inside our apartment.

Theo was yelling words I never could have imagined spoken by my dearest. They made my heart bleed.

"He doesn't mean it!" I called to Dries, on the point of fleeing again, because I didn't want my son to hear his father's rant. "Could you not make him take his potion? It's in a small green bottle."

Then more tussling inside, muffled words from both Dries and Theo that I could not catch.

"Appe," Wil babbled, squirming to the floor.

"Yes, an apple. I did promise that."

I cut the fruit into quarters with unsteady hands and handed him the smallest one, the one his baby fingers could best grab.

"Cheechee!" He pointed and scrambled onto the chair all by himself.

"And cheese too." I set the plate on the table, everything inside me straining to hear what the men in the bedroom were saying to each other.

That they were talking without resorting to raising their voices gave me hope. No more fighting. Nothing crashed. Dries was a kind and patient man. He would be able to reach Theo. He would calm Theo's anguished mind with reasoned arguments.

"All is well now," I told Wil. "Your papa is coming out to us. I will draw him a bath. That will make him feel better. Or maybe we shall go for a stroll first on the street. Would you like that? He probably needs fresh air."

I hurried into Wil's room and prepared a fresh shirt, fresh pants. Luckily, I had a load out to the laundry when Theo had locked himself in, clothes that had since come back. It was the only reason I had anything to wear.

Half an hour passed in nerve-racking suspense before Dries emerged. The door slammed closed behind him. I could not catch so much as a glimpse of my dearest.

Dries looked at me with the regretful expression people wore when they had to tell someone their loved one was gone forever. "You shouldn't be alone with him."

Pain and denial screamed through me. His words were not ones I could accept. "He loves us."

"He is not in his right mind."

"He would never harm us. You know him." I begged. "*I* know him. I love him, Dries."

"He should be in an asylum." My brother softened his tone, but he didn't soften his words. "For his own safety and yours. He should be under the watchful eyes of a doctor."

"I can't have them lock him up. I can't bear the thought. They don't know what he needs. They don't know him as I do, all his moods and fears and regrets." I rounded the table, put it between us as a barricade against Dries's merciless opinion. "The asylum didn't save Vincent."

"Didn't it? When he was inside, he was safe. When he was on the outside, he cut off his ear. He shot himself." Dries, equally frustrated, shoved a chair. "When was the last time you saw Theo?"

"When I gave him his dinner last night."

"Fully seen him. Not through a gap in the door."

"Two weeks ago?"

Dries flinched. "Do you realize he voids his bowels into a bucket?"

"But I hear him use the bathroom in the night."

"Not during the day?"

I covered my face with my hands because I couldn't bear to look my brother in the eye. And I couldn't bear to think of my Theo as debased as that.

"His mind cannot fight the darkness of grief, Jo. And his body is fading as well. He needs help."

"Then help us."

"The best I can do is obtain him medical assistance. This is beyond the two of us, Jo. You must see that."

Dries waited for my response, but I couldn't form words. The best I could do was stand there in the middle of the kitchen and not collapse.

I will not cry. I will not howl. I will not rage.

I swallowed my unbearable pain in silence.

My brother grabbed his hat and strode to the front door. "I am going to find a doctor who will admit him into the hospital. The Maison Dubois."

"Don't take us from each other, Dries. You can't." I ran to him, desperate to hold him back. "Could we not just write Dr. Gachet to come? He is a friend. He treated Vincent."

"Where is Vincent now?"

The words rang in my ears like a slap.

My brother pulled away. "It's for the best. You can't save Theo on your own, Jo. Not from this."

And then the door was closing behind him.

I staggered back. I wanted to wake up from the nightmare, shake myself out of the numbness. *Don't collapse. You can't. Not yet.*

"Mama?" Wil's sweet voice woke me. He'd finished his meal.

I could not let his father be taken. Our love would heal Theo. I would not give up on him and give him over to strangers. I had a terrible premonition that if I let him go, I'd never have him back.

I grabbed up my son and was out the door with him the next breath. "We are not going to let anyone take your papa." I shouldn't have let Dries leave. *What have I done?* "We're going to catch your uncle."

I would stop my brother if I had to beg him in the street.

I ran.

CHAPTER SEVENTEEN

Emsley

"I can't tell if it's a circus or a funeral." My mother shifted on her chair, the kind of shocked horror in her voice she normally reserved for people who quit perfectly good jobs or marriages to "find themselves." Or for when one of her friends' children chose to study liberal arts. "What kind of funeral home would even allow a carnival band? An accordion player, for heaven's sake." She tugged on my father's elbow. "Philip, stop that man."

"They have bagpipes at Scottish funerals," Dad said in a philosophical tone.

Mom sat up straighter, not a small accomplishment since she'd already been stiff enough to give ramrods inspiration. She'd been holding her solemn-Nancy-Reagan expression for so long, I feared her features might freeze that way permanently. I'd mistakenly called it a discreetly-grieving-Jackie-Kennedy look when she'd arrived. She'd corrected me with *"Don't be crass, Emsley. I would never look like a Democrat."*

She wore one of her black Nordstrom suits. I wore Violet's blue-red-yellow Mondrian dress that I'd found the day before in the wardrobe in the basement, along with her white go-go boots and navy-blue pillbox hat, all in attendance. My new sunflower earrings sparkled in my ears.

"I can't believe you squeezed yourself into that old rag," Mom said.

Despite Bram's bagel deliveries, I'd lost a few pounds. I kept forgetting to eat. Also, as it turned out, cleaning counted as exercise.

The May afternoon was nice enough to have windows open in the back, and the faint notes of a different kind of music filtered in. A merry-go-round revolved endlessly in the funeral home's parking lot, similar to the one in Violet's basement.

Mom nudged Dad again. "Why can't they close the windows, at least? You should talk to someone about that."

My father simply patted her hand.

Violet had a detailed plan for her Celebration of Life service, from beer on tap to a carnival band and a fortune-teller. A hot dog cart provided food, and a cotton-candy maker offered dessert.

She'd left her old friend and attorney in charge, and Bram Dekker Sr. had followed Violet's instructions to the letter. Including a sign in the entry hall, a quote by Stan Laurel: "IF ANY OF YOU CRY AT MY FUNERAL, I'LL NEVER SPEAK TO YOU AGAIN."

Black-clad people filed by us in an endless line, then by the cherry-red-and-chrome coffin reminiscent of Violet's old Mustang. Violet looked peaceful, fabulous, and mysterious—a diva to the end.

I tried not to look at her so I wouldn't cry. She'd been clear that she wanted the day to be festive. *A joyful celebration*, her instructions specifically said.

Her funeral notice requested that people donate to her scholarship fund in lieu of flowers, so I filled the dozens of easels that surrounded her with her own paintings instead of wreaths. The paintings came from private collections, on loan for the day. The overall effect was stunning: color and light and life, movement, joy, adventure.

After reading about Vincent van Gogh's death in the little green book, I grabbed a volume of his works from Violet's bookshelf. Mixed in with the artist's spectacular creations was a short biography that mentioned his funeral. He had his art instead of flowers at his gravesite. I thought something similar would be fitting for Violet.

"Goodbye, my friend." A middle-aged woman I didn't know slipped a tube of paint into the coffin.

Another mourner told her, "We'll see each other again."

And the next: "I'll miss you, Violet."

Next to me, my mother rubbed her hip.

I'd almost told her of my suspicions about her father a dozen times. Each time, I held back. Not the right topic for a funeral, not even one like my grandmother's. And Violet had never told anyone about that night. On this day, of all days, I had to respect her wishes.

Louis from the stroke center rolled up with tears in his eyes. "She was..." he said in a soft Cuban accent. "Love at first sight."

I'd talked Mom out of suing over the hot tub incident. Violet had always made her own decisions. It would have been unfair to blame anyone else for them.

Mrs. Yang came next. "I'm so sorry, Emsley. Violet left a hole in all our hearts."

"Thank you." I peeked at her bulging pocket. "Is Lai Fa here?"

"About that..." She cast a surreptitious look around. "Do you have a purse?"

I nodded toward the messenger bag at my feet.

"The nurses are starting to suspect us." She looked around again. "The jig is up."

She bent down as if to adjust a tennis ball on the foot of her walker, and slipped the chick into my bag, moving smoothly, as if she'd practiced.

"Come by the center sometime and sneak her in for a visit," she whispered, then shuffled on before I could protest.

Nurses, orderlies, and physical therapists from the center offered their condolences. Violet had a way of making a friend of everyone she met. Even Trey and Diya flew up from LA.

"Truly sorry, Em."

They hugged me too. I let them.

They didn't come out to the cemetery with us after the service, but two hundred other people did—not to mention the carnival band. An up-and-coming rap artist rapped a prayer so sublime, you could hear angel wings flap to the rhythm.

A holy silence followed, several seconds passing before anybody moved, as if waking from a dream.

Dad offered Mom his arm. "Let me help."

He guided her to the grave, where they each threw a handful of dirt.

Then it was my turn. My determination not to break down wobbled. I felt as if I were throwing my heart into that dark hole with the crumbling soil. "You can haunt me, if you want," I whispered. "I won't be scared."

I returned to the chicken sleeping in my bag. Bram Dekker Sr. and his grandson went next. Bram Sr. said a silent prayer, then threw white rose petals, cast soft and wide like a blessing over water.

Strena threw art brushes she drew from her pocket. "The sky is your canvas, my friend. Make something magnificent."

The tall man, about Bram Sr.'s age, who stopped in front of me to step up to the grave next seemed familiar. Hair colored dark to cover the gray, a door-to-door salesman's practiced smile, paired with the expensive leather shoes and crisp suit of a stockbroker. Every nod and gesture he made looked practiced. Most of my grandmother's friends were in the arts, and a strong vein of authenticity ran through them. This guy was as fake as a politician.

Between one breath and the next, I knew where I'd seen him before: on the internet. I had googled him just the night before, in fact.

Senator Taylor Wertheim.

I froze, immobilized by his sheer audacity. *How dare he come here?*

Then hot rage filled me, and I lurched forward without a plan. At the same time, Bram Sr. swayed next to me and tumbled. He crashed to his knees before his grandson could catch him, his walking stick shooting out in front of him.

The carnival band in the back started another lively tune.

"'Beer Barrel Polka'?" Someone a few rows behind us barked a laugh.

Time stretched, a Hollywood special effect. In slow motion, right in front of me, Wertheim tripped on Bram Sr.'s walking stick and tumbled headfirst into Violet's grave.

Around us, people gasped in horror.

"Help, dammit!"

I was the closest. I crouched and offered my hand, the former senator atop the coffin no longer distinguished looking, but stunned, bruised, and disheveled. I grabbed his outreached hand, others stretching to support him from the side.

I heaved as hard as I could, looking down at his upturned face. Anger glinted in his eyes that some fool had done this to him. And then all I could see was the old photo I'd found on the internet, his self-satisfied smirk as he was leaving the library. I let my hand slip. I'd held most of his weight, so despite the others, he crashed back into the coffin.

"Don't move, Senator!"

I was pushed out of the way as more men rushed to assist.

"His nose is bleeding!"

Trouble was, no one could jump down next to him, not without stepping on the coffin lid, which nobody dared.

I covered my face with my hands, making stricken noises, and backed away, all the way to my parents.

My father muttered, "Oh, dumpling."

My mother shot me a look that said if we weren't at a funeral, she'd be shouting at me so loudly, damned souls could hear her all the way in hell.

I hung my head, the picture of contrition. "I was just trying to help. He's too heavy."

Mom scrambled forward, calling for my father to lend a hand.

Bram Sr. and I exchanged a glance, Innocents-R-Us stamped all over us.

Utter pandemonium all around.

And the band played on.

I raised my eyes to the sky and managed to feel joyful at last, fulfilling my grandmother's last wish.

Farewell, Violet. Farewell.

CHAPTER EIGHTEEN

Johanna
    1891, January, Utrecht, Netherlands

Theo was admitted to the Maison Dubois. Dries had been relentless. Then, when more help was deemed necessary, the doctors moved my love to Faubourg St. Denis. And when he didn't improve, to the clinic in Passy. And finally, so I could be closer to my family and the help they offered, my beloved husband was transported to the Willem Arntzkliniek in Utrecht in the Netherlands in November—on the night train, in a straitjacket.

Little Wil and I went with him, the three of us escorted by two attendants. Then Theo was spirited away, and we traveled on to Amsterdam. And then months of heartbreaking visits began.

I wanted to help him recover. I wanted my dearest back.

"He is improving," I told Mama as the year came to a close and a new one, which I prayed would bring us relief, began. I was packing my bag at her kitchen table, my son napping upstairs.

"You should tell Dries." She was embroidering a handkerchief for one of my sisters, blue cornflowers on white linen. "The good news would cheer him. He says you're not answering his letters."

I loved my brother with all my heart, but I wasn't sure I could ever forgive him for having my husband committed.

"I wish Theo back in my own loving care." The weekly visits to Utrecht were as unbearably bleak as they were insufficient. And I was turned away at the slightest whim of his doctor. *"The patient is not feeling well."*

"But Theo *has* improved. You said he sits calmly and listens."

"He still barely talks. I want him home. He *will* come home. Today, I shall get the doctor to commit to a discharge date."

Mama sighed and patted my hand. "And then what? How will you live? Theo has quit Goupil."

"They know he was sick already when he handed in his resignation. Once he improves, they'll take him back. I can't worry about anything right now but that he recovers."

"I'm sorry. Of course, dear."

"When Wil wakes up…"

Mama smiled. "I've raised my share of children."

I picked up my bag, and then the white chrysanthemums, the symbol of loyalty and love. They had been preserved from my mother's fall garden. "I will be back on the six o'clock train the latest."

"Are you certain you don't want one of your brothers to escort you?"

"No, Mama. I can manage." I'd become a self-sufficient woman at last.

On the train, I composed what I would say to my beloved.

You mustn't worry about us. All you have to do is regain your health. And then you will come back home, and everything will be as before. You'll see. It'll be even better.

Across the compartment, a young couple sat, smiling at each other and holding hands. They engaged in a whispered conversation, punctuated by frequent laughter.

I closed my eyes. I bitterly envied their happiness.

What I hear from Paris is all good, dearest. All the big names are talking about Vincent, more than ever. His talent is widely acknowledged. He is missed. He will not be forgotten.

I gripped my bag tightly on my lap.

Little Wil is healthy. And so am I. And soon you'll recover, and then we shall go home. Wil asks about you. He looks around. Papa?

And then I imagined what I would say to Theo's doctor, what questions I'd ask. And I imagined how the doctor would answer.

The prognosis, Mevrouw Van Gogh, is entirely favorable.

I refused to entertain anything else.

The news will be good, the news will be good, the news will be good, I repeated to myself.

I deboarded the train with that very mindset. As I hurried down the platform, protecting my fragile dried bouquet, I was filled with nothing but optimism. And I swore that after this was over, I'd never again return to Utrecht.

I resented the city's gray sky, the insidious cold winds that blew down the medieval streets and narrow canals, the dark Dom Tower that loomed over all like a menacing angel. I had disliked Utrecht when I taught English at their school for girls three years before, and now I disliked it even more for stealing my Theo.

On my way to the clinic, I practiced smiling. Theo must not see me worried. At first, I feared passersby might think I was demented, but nobody paid attention to me. I must have looked like a crone: wearing all black in mourning for Vincent, shoulders hunched, eyes red.

And then, all too soon and not soon enough, I was there.

"Meneer Van Gogh is having a difficult day," Theo's doctor told me, offering a metal chair in his spartan office. White tile covered the spotless floor, everything as clean scrubbed as if he expected to perform surgery.

His white coat covered him to the knees. No bright colors were allowed in the room, all life drained away. The sea of nothingness swallowed me whole, whitecaps of worry washing over my head. "How bad?"

"A visit would not be the wisest course of action today." The doctor watched me with beady brown eyes that rarely blinked, as if he was fixated on seeing inside me.

He couldn't mean to keep me from my husband, could he? "I haven't seen him in a week."

"Even so." The man folded his hands over his portly belly.

"But I found him improved on my last visit."

"He has suffered a setback since."

The news will be good, the news will be good, the news will be good. The mantra I had repeated endlessly to myself on the train had taken root in me. The doctor ripping my hard-won hope out by the roots brought breath-stealing pain. "What kind of setback?"

The doctor sighed. "I am afraid he is raving. He has reverted to the stage in which he arrived. He is nearly incoherent."

Shoulders back. Spine straight. I had to will my body to obey. Then my mouth. I only had enough strength for one word. "Nevertheless."

"I would not recommend it." The man spread his hands, annoyance flashing in his tone. He didn't like that I argued. "The truth is, your husband doesn't wish to see you, madam."

A merciless chill had been growing inside my chest since I'd walked through the door. At the doctor's latest pronouncement, my frozen heart cracked. Theo didn't want me to see him in his current condition, didn't want me to witness him weak, feared that I would think less of him. I wouldn't. I couldn't. *Never.*

"I must see for myself what state he is in."

"You wouldn't find it reassuring, Mevrouw Van Gogh. Rather the opposite, I fear. You should not come again." He leaned forward, trying a fatherly smile that I found the opposite of comforting. "If I see improvement, I shall send a letter."

I rose to my feet, clutching the dried flowers so hard, I was crushing the stems. I would not be brushed aside. I would not be sent away like a child. "I demand to see my husband."

The doctor stood as well. "When he was told that you would visit today, madam, he flew into a rage. He destroyed his room. We had to remove him. For his own safety, you understand."

My throat burned, and when it contracted, it hurt, as if I'd swallowed thistles. "Remove him where?"

"To a safer space." The doctor's tone dipped into patronizing. "Where he can find nothing with which to harm himself."

"I shall not leave without seeing him." They couldn't make me, could they? "I insist."

He snapped his teeth together. "As you wish."

He shoved his office door open, and I hurried to keep up with him down the sterile white hallway. When we reached a pair of locked double doors, he yanked a key ring from his pocket. "These sights are not meant for ladies such as yourself."

I clutched my bag in one hand and my flowers in the other. "I am determined."

He opened the door, and we walked into hell.

The smell hit me first, as if something foul and rotten had been thrown into my face. I caught my breath, too late. I gagged.

The doctor strode forward. "I recommend you hold your handkerchief to your nose, madam."

I followed him past a row of cells...no, worse, *cages*. More than half of them had men in them. Some of the patients rushed to hide in corners, others pressed their faces to the bars and stared. Most remained silent, but a few moaned and shouted for help.

A single word echoed through my head: *purgatory*. If it existed, it was this, and I was there. And so was my beloved.

I found Theo at the very end.

His cell held a stained mattress on the cement floor and a night pan tipped over next to the back wall, the totality of comforts he'd been afforded. A torn nightshirt hung off his bony shoulders. He stared into nothing—a wraith, a ghost of himself.

"Theo!"

I hadn't meant to disturb him, only peek at him to ensure he wasn't mistreated, but I could not help myself. The flowers fell from my hands, broken dry petals scattering like blossoms thrown onto a grave.

My dearest slowly turned his head.

An animal cry issued from his mouth, a howl of fury and despair, a sound of agonizing pain that entered my body and shredded its way through my chest.

"Theo…"

He picked up the night pan and hurled it at the bars with a soul-shattering clatter. I could find no love in his eyes, nor care, nor fondness. The mindless rage inside him was directed at me.

Why?

Was he mad at me?

I couldn't fathom it. I loved him with all my heart. Yet what burned in his eyes was perilously close to hate.

The beginning of his mental anguish had been blaming himself for Vincent's death. Did he now blame me?

Was I to blame?

Vincent had had Theo's full support, full attention. Then I'd come along. And then little Wil. And I had asked for that larger apartment, to make living with a child easier.

The night of Vincent's first visit with us, as I had lain in bed, I'd overheard the brothers in the kitchen.

"Tell me the truth. Am I a burden?" Vincent had asked.

My knees buckled.

The doctor kicked through the bars, rolling the night pan back.

"Lucky it was empty." His tone held a strange satisfaction. *I told you so.*

I struggled for breath.

Theo shouted words that had no meaning, no

beginning, no end. His raving upset the other men. They began to shake their bars and yell at us as well.

"Enough." The doctor grabbed me by the elbow and dragged me stumbling out of there.

I couldn't fight him. I had no strength left.

I must not lose hope.

My dearest will come back to me. He will come back to his wife and his son. We will move back home, to Paris, together. This darkness too shall pass.

I had to keep faith, both for myself and little Wil.

This could not be the end. We had lost Vincent. We could not lose Theo. God would not be so cruel. I willed myself to believe in deliverance.

The doctor and I were far down the hallway by the time I gathered myself enough to ask, "When will he recover?"

My soul trembled as I waited for the answer.

CHAPTER NINETEEN

Emsley

Bram Dekker, the younger, called me the day after Violet's funeral. "Care to tell me why you and my grandfather assaulted Senator Wertheim at the cemetery?"

I'd only picked up the phone because I thought he might be calling about a legal matter. And because I'd been crying over Violet and needed to stop, needed to be distracted from the hollow cave of pain in my chest. I was alone in the house. My parents had gone home to Hartford. I'd suggested that they stay for a few days, but Mom couldn't deal with the stairs and definitely couldn't handle staying in a house with a chicken.

"A terrible accident," I told Bram, petting Lai Fa on my lap. We were working in Violet's study. "I never have time for the gym anymore. I have no arm muscles. Is your grandfather all right?"

The way Bram Sr. had dropped, he could have broken a knee.

"He's fine. He claims he felt faint."

"Low blood pressure."

"Was it? I'm thinking coordinated attack."

"When would we have coordinated?"

"Good question."

"Do you know how the senator is?"

"You haven't seen the papers?"

I opened a new window on my laptop and googled the *Times*.

My grandmother's funeral hadn't made the cover, but it made the society pages. With a picture. "Taylor Wertheim, former senator, rescued from Violet Velar's grave. 'Intoxicated,' says anonymous source." I cleared my throat. "Who would call the paper with an allegation like that? People are mean."

Exasperated silence on Bram's end. Then, after several seconds, he asked, "Did the band play the theme song to *The Benny Hill Show*?"

"'Beer Barrel Polka.'"

"I would ask how you even know 'Beer Barrel Polka,' but I have a dozen more important questions."

I liked talking to him, and I shouldn't have. I refused to miss our nascent friendship. He wasn't the man I'd thought he was. There was nothing there.

"I'd love to take you out for coffee," he said.

"Thank you, but I'm drowning in work."

"All right." He didn't push, which I appreciated. "Let me know if you end up needing a criminal lawyer."

I only smiled because he couldn't see me. "I haven't done anything."

"You might want to look up assault and battery, or even attempted murder."

"As I said, an unfortunate accident."

"My grandfather and you stick with that. It's probably the best strategy." Sounded like he was laughing on the other end. Then he asked, "How is the Van Gogh book?"

"It's a Jo Bonger book. Difficult to read at times. She had a rough life. I thought women in the eighteen hundreds sat at home and embroidered. And, speaking of exceptional women, thank you for Adele." The corporate attorney had called that morning. Bram had asked her to contact me. I'd googled her while we'd talked on the phone—one of the highest-rated attorneys in the city, part of a power couple. Her wife was a councilwoman. It would have been childish to refuse her just because of her connection to Bram.

"You're welcome. You're in good hands. She knows what she's doing."

"Thank you. Again. I have to go. I have a ton of work."

"Let me know if you need anything. And try to stay out of trouble."

"Expect nothing, and you won't be disappointed."

I hung up and set Lai Fa on the floor so she could stretch her legs, but she plopped down on my foot.

"I hope you're not developing abandonment issues." I petted her. "I don't want to have to ask my mother to ask her psychologist about chickens and separation anxiety."

In response, Lai Fa pecked at a loose thread in my sock.

I left her to it and worked on a list of talking points for potential investors until lunch, which I ordered from a nearby Chinese restaurant.

"Don't look at me like that," I told the chick. "It's broccoli *beef.*" I attacked the food with my chopsticks and mentally catalogued the office.

"I am going to keep the paintings from Violet's students. The furniture will have to be sold. And I'll have to go over Violet's papers to figure out what to do with them."

I ordered a shredder online—under forty dollars, overnight delivery—while I finished lunch. I was thinking about licking the sauce from the bottom of the container when Strena popped in.

Had she seen me stretching my tongue toward the empty box? I decided not to worry about it unless she brought it up. "Hi. I didn't realize you were coming over today."

"I want you to be one of my models. Hi, Lai Fa."

"To practice on?"

"Practice first, yes. But I want you to be in my next show."

"The show that's in ten days?"

"The one after that. I'm working up a new concept. I can see the entire performance in my head. I see you in the picture."

"I don't do naked in public." It was important enough to repeat. "I don't do naked in public."

"Come to the MoMA with me."

"Right now? I'm working."

"Come to the MoMA with me after work. I want to show you one of Violet's paintings."

"I've seen my grandmother's paintings." Including the ones at the MoMA. Multiple times.

"I want you to really look."

"I have."

"You didn't look hard enough."

"How do you know?"

"We're having this conversation."

"We could just look on my laptop."

"It's not the same." She flashed impatience at me, a look that said she was disappointed she had to explain.

"All right." Every minute I wasn't thinking about work, I was thinking about Violet. Her art would make me think about her life instead of her death. "But I need another hour."

"I'll meet you there."

"I'll call you when I leave."

She nodded and walked away.

"But I'm not going to be naked in public!"

I settled back into work and read through the weekly reports and schedules at Ludington's. Then I started researching potential investors.

"It's hard to find venture capital," I told Lai Fa. "Angel investors don't just put themselves out there. They don't want to be bombarded twenty-four seven by people begging for money."

It took me the full hour to scrounge up a single name. I needed a break.

I nestled Lai Fa on the folded blanket in the bathtub to keep her safe. I topped off her food and water, told her she was on her own for a while and to go wild, then texted Strena that I was on my way.

I was in the Uber when Bram called again. "I had an idea. Instead of looking for one investor to put in a million dollars into Ludington's, you could look for ten people at a hundred thousand each. Why don't you pitch to me?"

"Thank you, but no."

"Is everything all right?"

"I'm on my way somewhere."

"Did you ever call my cousin?"

I hadn't, but I should, so I did, after I hung up with Bram.

I told Sergei Prokhorov, antique shop owner, that Bram sent me, and what I had in my basement.

"When would be a good time for me to stop by for a visit?" Sergei asked. "Tomorrow morning?"

"That would be great."

"I hope I'll be able to help."

"I hope you like stuffed bears."

We ended the call on a laugh. His was amused, mine was desperate.

At the MoMA, Strena led me straight to a

painting some people nicknamed Lady Godiva because it depicted a naked woman on horseback. *Excalibur.* "What do you think?"

"Sure brushstrokes, no hesitation, no unnecessary ornamentation—an artist in her full power. Energy, movement, life." Violet's art was as different as possible from the row of still lifes by a different artist on the next wall.

I moved closer, until *Excalibur* filled my entire field of vision. Not only was the woman riding her horse into battle, but she was enjoying it, laughing into the wind. The swirls of color transmitted something that could never come through the internet, as if Violet had left a piece of her soul on the canvas.

I felt that if everybody around us would fall quiet, I could hear the painting breathe. "I've always wondered why she didn't paint in the sword. That's what Excalibur means, doesn't it? King Arthur's weapon that he drew from the rock?"

"Who do you think the woman is in the painting?" Strena watched me.

"Arthur's queen, Guinevere?"

"It's Violet. Look at her. She painted this when she was thirty, in her full power. Unlike Arthur, who pulled his weapon from the rock, Violet pulled her power from herself. She is Excalibur."

"Okay. That's deep."

I'd seen the painting before, but I'd never examined it closely. You couldn't stare at a life-size naked woman in a museum that long without people starting to think you've been looking at it *too* long.

With Strena at my side, I examined every inch. It *was* Violet. A younger Violet, with much darker and longer hair. How had I missed that?

Out of nowhere, an unreasonable jealousy burned me that Strena had insights about *my* grandmother that I didn't.

"What does *Strena* mean, anyway?" I sounded peeved, and I didn't care. "Why don't you have a last name?"

"Strena is enough. Lets me have a private life. It means *storm* in Papiamento. I was born in Aruba, during a hurricane. Any other questions?"

I was never going to be as cool as she was. I gave up. "Thank you for telling me about the painting."

I pondered it on my way home. Since the weather was warm enough, I walked.

Power from within. You are the sword.

Forget Trey taking Ludington's from me. Over the past few days, my grief over losing Violet had sapped my strength. But this auction wasn't over yet. I had to reach deeper inside me and find something more to bid.

I was the sword. I didn't want my life to be a still life. I wanted it to be one of Violet's paintings. I wanted the kind of strength and joy she had. Power from within.

When I reached the house, filled with newfound optimism and firm resolution, I found a visitor waiting.

"Hi. Beatriz Amoso. You must be Emsley." Violet's Realtor was about my age, tall and slender in a dove-gray dress and matching high-heel shoes. A magnificent heron, taking a break from gliding over a silver glen.

I tugged my shirt straight. "Hi."

"Had an open house on the next block." She flashed a sudden maniacal smile—which ruined the serene image in my head—like someone who desperately needed to sell some bad news. "I was about to call you."

I let her in. "What's wrong?"

"Nothing! A minor slowdown. Maybe even an opportunity," she twittered as we walked to the makeshift living room, but the way she collapsed into the nearest armchair belied her chirpy attitude.

"The buyer just called." She cast me a please-don't-fly-off-the handle look.

"And?" I asked as calmly as possible. Judging by her state, she must have had some difficult clients in the past.

"He's pulling out."

Hi, calm. Bye, calm. I dropped into the chair next to hers. "Can he do that? Why?"

"I think he's a speculator. I'm sorry. Talking with his agent just now gave me the impression that the buyer was going for a quick flip. He had a buyer of his own lined up, from overseas. Your buyer was going to take possession of the property, then immediately sell at a premium."

"Why?"

"There could be a number of reasons. From money laundering to the secondary buyer wanting to remain anonymous."

"And then the secondary buyer changed his mind, so my buyer pulled out too?"

"He might not have a choice. Might only have a short-term loan. A few months? Then he would have received his money and paid everything off."

"I don't know much about real estate speculation. Does this happen often?"

"Not often, but it's not unheard of either. Especially in New York."

The buyer withdrew the offer. No sale. No money.

I thought of the stack of stroke center bills on the corner of my desk upstairs and felt a sharp pain in my middle.

"We will, of course, immediately relist." Beatriz struggled to sound reassuring. "If you still wish to sell."

"I do."

She apologized again, then again and again, before she left.

I didn't want to deal with Bram, but called him anyway—all business, strictly professional. I told him about the buyer for the house stepping back. "Is there anything I need to do before I relist?"

"Violet's assets will have to go through probate. You have to officially inherit the house and have it transferred into your name. It could take a couple of months."

I dropped my head into my hand. "The stroke center already sent me the bill."

"I could negotiate on your behalf. They might agree to small monthly payments until the house sells. They had a similar arrangement with your grandmother."

"I'll do that. But thank you for the suggestion."

"You know I'd be happy to help any way I can. With this, or anything else."

He kept telling me that. But what I wanted from him was to be the man I'd thought he was. At least we could have been friends. I missed Diya and Trey.

"Thank you," I told Bram. *But no, thank you.* "I'm sorry. I have to go. I have too much work."

I brewed more coffee, retrieved Lai Fa from the bathtub, and brought her to the office with me. I settled in with my laptop and rolled up my sleeves. I had to expand my meager list of potential investors, and then I had to start making calls.

In the end, I was able to come up with six names, which I thought gave me a fair chance at success. I only needed one of them to bite.

I dialed the first one, Bill Wesner. His father invested in vineyards, the son dabbled in startups, with considerable success. He was a frequent bidder at our auctions, so he knew me.

"And you'll be the CEO?" Wesner asked.

"Yes."

Less than five percent of CEOs were women. I wasn't trying to make a statement. For now, I had no money to bring anyone else on board.

"Who else is attached to this new project so far?" Wesner meant known entities, other major investors or a serious venture capital firm.

His tone reminded me of the could-I-talk-to-the-man-of-the-house tone I'd heard all through my childhood from salesmen who'd come to our door and found themselves face-to-face with my mother.

"You're on the top of my list, so you're the first person I called."

He wasn't flattered. We went on talking for another ten minutes, but ultimately, Wesner's answer was *no*.

I moved on to the rest of my list. All five potential investors declined. I didn't book a single in-person meeting. They gave me the distinct impression that they would have preferred to talk to Trey.

I drew a line through their names, then another and another, until my pen went through the paper. Then I tossed the list into the wastebasket.

I needed a million dollars, and I only had twenty days left.

CHAPTER TWENTY

Johanna

1891, January 25, Utrecht, Netherlands

"Never, Mevrouw Van Gogh. Never," Theo's doctor had told me when I'd asked when Theo might return to his former self, when he might be discharged.

I refused to believe him. I wrote to our landlord in Paris and asked him to hold our apartment. No matter what I had to do, I would find a way to restore our family to our home.

At my parents' house, in my childhood room, when nobody could see me, I cried, but I kept returning to Utrecht, undeterred by what I might find each time.

As January drew to an end, Theo improved again, justifying my faith. I talked to him about our little son. I pledged to help protect his brother's legacy, to assist in building a name for Vincent as soon as Theo was released from his confinement. I pretended that I was one of Vincent's sunflowers, and I turned my face to the light in gratitude. I forced myself to see only hope. I skirted around all the dark corners of despair.

When I rode the train to Utrecht once again on the twenty-fifth of January, I had in my bag the photograph taken of me with our son in Paris, at the studio of photographer Raoul Saisset, on Rue Frochot. It would remind my beloved to fight harder so he could return to us sooner. If he remembered how much he loved us, maybe he would forget the accusations he'd shouted in his rants.

"This way, Mevrouw Van Gogh." The orderly led me straight to the doctor instead of my husband, which usually meant Theo was having a bad day. I remained undeterred. For any illness, it was normal for the patient to take a few bad turns before he finally recovered.

The doctor stood up at my entrance, his expression even more somber and pitying than usual.

"I regret that I have bad news for you, Mevrouw Van Gogh." He rounded his desk. "Your husband, most tragically, passed away this morning."

…passed away this morning.

Shock punched me in the chest, my lungs flooding with fire, no air left in the room as I desperately gasped. I clawed at the collar of my dress.

…passed away…

Grief squeezed me like a corset sent up from hell.

Fate had ripped from me my love. All hope died. The horizon held no faint dawn.

…passed…

The room spun around me.

Help!

"I was just writing you a letter," the man went on. "Please accept my condolences. We will, of course, assist with the transportation of the body for the funeral."

My mind struggled to accept the words that flew at me like daggers. My heart shattered into shards too small to ever be fitted back together again. How could my fervent prayers be so utterly futile?

I collapsed into a chair.

"A glass of water?" The doctor hurried to the door and shouted for assistance.

A nurse arrived, then water shortly after.

"A sedative?" The doctor offered a pill.

"I have to ride the train home." I shook my head. "I wish to see him."

"The body has already been removed to a different building."

The body. As if my husband had ceased being a person. Ceased being my Theo.

I was too broken to argue with the doctor. Or maybe too scared to open my mouth for fear that I would scream at the man.

"You've had a shock, madam. You must stay until you recover," he said, less of a suggestion and more of an order.

I handed him back the glass of water and pushed

to my feet. If they wouldn't let me see Theo, there was nothing left for me there. "Thank you. I shall manage."

Yet I couldn't, in the end. My eyes blurred, I lost my way on those narrow medieval streets, and instead of the train station, I ended up at the foot of the looming Dom Tower. A menacing dark angel indeed.

Tears raced down my face. How was I going to find my way through life when I couldn't even find my way to my train?

I was a widow at twenty-eight, without funds. My little son had no father. What would become of us?

Thinking hurt. Breathing hurt. Standing hurt.

Every heartbeat was a punch of pain.

CHAPTER TWENTY-ONE

Emsley

Sergei Prokhorov stopped by Thursday morning to look over the contents of the house. My age, reddish-blond hair, angular features. He took one look at me and asked, "Have you been crying?"

"Theo van Gogh died. And so soon after Vincent."

"The Library of Alexandria burned. That's what gets me going."

He was so serious, somehow I ended up laughing.

He laughed with me. "Bram told me a lot of nice things about you."

I refused any pleased flutters. Bram could be impressed with me all he wanted. I was *not* impressed with him.

Lai Fa was pecking at my heel, so I picked her up.

"This is Lai Fa. Come in, please. Bram said you were cousins. You don't look alike."

"I was adopted from Russia. With love. Hello, Lai Fa. Aren't you sweet?" Sergei petted her fuzzy head, then looked around with awe. "Violet Velar's own diva den. I've been anticipating this since Bram told me he gave you my number. He said the goodies were downstairs?"

Lai Fa squirmed, and I let her go to hunt for stray ants, whose existence by the back door she'd only just discovered earlier.

"This way." I directed Sergei to the basement door.

When we reached the bottom of the stairs, he stopped in his tracks. "You weren't kidding about the stuffed bear. You know, it has potential. There are a couple of interior designers I know who specialize in trust-fund-baby bachelor pads."

I thought of the ultramodern penthouse condo Trey's older brother had bought as an investment in San Diego the year before, the giant stuffed moose head over the modern marble fireplace "for contrast." Sergei was right. I could see the bear in that glass-and-steel foyer.

"How are you going to take it upstairs?" I didn't want him to think, even for a second, that I'd be doing that.

"I have a crew." Sergei walked to the wardrobe and ran a finger over the wood. "The walnut inlay is exquisite. Charles the Tenth."

I could have pretended that I knew all about

Charles the Tenth. *Oh, that guy?* But Sergei was so instantly disarming, I didn't think he'd judge me for my ignorance. "How old?"

"From around eighteen thirty." He opened the doors and panned the cavernous inside with his cell phone light. "Was there anything inside?"

"Vintage fashion. All mine."

"I will work through the pain. Because I am a professional." He tilted his head as if calculating. "The wardrobe alone is worth anywhere between ten and fifteen thousand dollars, if I can find the right buyer. Would that be acceptable?"

For a single piece of furniture? I let go of the tension I'd been holding in my shoulders all morning. "That would be great."

"Ah." He was moving on already, heading for the carousel. "You have a beauty here. An Allan Herschell." His nostrils trembled like a hound on the scent. "See the horses? Nobody carved like Daniel Muller." He snapped pictures. "Thirty feet in diameter. Twenty-two individual horses, two chariots. From the early nineteen twenties."

"Is that good?"

"Excellent."

"Where do you think it came from?"

"I'll have to research that. Maybe Coney Island?" Sergei looked into my eyes as intently as if he wanted to hypnotize me. "The question is, are you going to let me have this beauty?"

"That's the idea."

"I love you. I mean it," he said the words with sincere passion. "This is the best day of my life."

He was utterly without artifice or affectation. He was funny. And he was going to help me empty out the house. "I like you too."

"Life is so unfair." His lips twisted. "Bram made me swear I wouldn't hit on you. Would you marry me, skipping the preliminary steps?" He pressed a hand to his heart. "I do have my Aiden. But he'll love you too. He won't be able to help himself. We'll move to Utah. I'll marry you both. You'll be sister wives."

"I don't think that's how it works."

"Polyamory. Google it."

Violet would have loved him.

He swiveled back to the carved horses. "All I'm saying is, think about it." He carefully tested the boards, then stepped up. "Condition is excellent. Obviously restored, but that won't affect the price. Touch-ups are expected for a piece that's a century old."

He aimed his phone light at the nooks and crannies. "Come here."

I climbed the carousel and followed his awed gaze. The light illuminated a date. "Nineteen eighteen?"

"This," he said with reverence, "is what we call a jackpot in the business."

"I can't take the suspense. Just tell me."

"Mid six figures. I'm going to call a few serious collectors to see if I can encourage some healthy bidding."

I sucked in a loud breath that sounded like a sob. "I wonder why she didn't sell it. She sold the house to pay her bills."

"She might not have realized it was a Herschell. Or that the paintwork is by Daniel Muller. I doubt she was aware of the true value."

"Are you sure about that value?"

He scoffed. "What am I, an amateur?"

"You're an angel. You might have just saved my life. I don't suppose you speak Dutch?" At that moment, nothing seemed impossible.

"Would it make a difference as far as our marriage prospects go? I could learn. Not too late to toss Bram aside and run away with me. Just kick him to the curb. *Bam!*"

"It's not like that between me and Bram. I wouldn't." I hopped off the carousel. "He's married."

I hated the obvious disappointment in my voice that gave me completely away. I hated feeling pitiful, being attracted to a man who was unavailable. But what I hated the most was that I kept thinking about him, even knowing he wasn't the man I thought he was. I had daydreams about us in an alternate universe.

Sergei followed me. "Why is it a problem that he was married?"

I stopped. "Was?"

"His wife died two years ago. He didn't tell you?"

"He wore a wedding ring. I thought…"

Sergei watched me with as much interest as if I had a second carousel hidden behind my back. "A number of people who love him, including myself, have been trying to convince him to take the ring off ever since the first-year anniversary. We've been worried that he isn't moving on. He told us where to put our unsolicited opinions. Hint, it's a place where neither sun nor moon nor stars shine. Then Bram met you, and the ring disappeared." He paused for emphasis. "Everyone who thinks that's significant, raise their hand."

Both of his arms shot into the air.

Later, I could not recall what we talked about after his revelation. All I could remember was that Sergei had an appointment, so he eventually left.

While I had to go back to work and *not* think about Bram.

CHAPTER TWENTY-TWO

Johanna

  February 1891, Paris, France

"You don't want to leave Paris because your memories of Theo are here?" Dries's tone betrayed his impatience. We were walking close enough to each other so our shoulders brushed as we hurried down Rue Jean-Baptiste Pigalle.

"His *dreams* are here. I have to see those dreams come true. I have to make sure."

Theo's dreams for Vincent's legacy had become mine, living stubbornly in my half-dead heart. My dreams were part of Paris, as the city's cobblestones were part of the streets. My hopes were carriages racing down the Avenue des Champs-Élysées. I had found my life's purpose at last.

In my grief, I had forgiven my brother. If any of my siblings had ever understood me, it had always been Dries. His presence made even the bitter cold more bearable. Everything was going to be all right with him by my side. He was going to help me sort out my dire circumstances.

"What should I do?" I would follow his advice. I had to do only that, to stumble forward and follow the lamp he would lift to light my path through the darkness of grief. "How should I manage all those paintings? All of Vincent's art?"

My toes were going numb, tingling as we parted to let a bundled-up washerwoman pass between us, carrying her overloaded basket and singing. Then she, and the sweet scent of absinthe on her breath, passed, and I could hear only the snow crunching under our boots and the wind whistling over the rooftops.

"Dries?"

He was watching the woman's muddy footprints in the snow instead of looking at me. "Burn them."

A squall hit us, coming around the corner, where we turned. We had but walked to the nearest market, a couple of blocks away. Wil had upended my last bottle of milk that morning, startled by Dries's booming voice upon arrival.

I tucked my wool shawl closer around my sleeping son in my arms. Dries tugged up his collar, unaware that he was breaking my heart.

"*Et tu, Brute?*" I said the words in quiet shock, but the squall died, and he heard me.

His face was red from the cold. He swung up an equally red hand in frustration. "I am hardly stabbing you in the back, Jo. I am giving you advice, per your request."

"But you were a friend to Theo and Vincent."

"We cannot turn back time. We cannot go back. The machine that can fly into the past exists only in fiction."

"Anacronópete." I remembered the name from Enrique Gaspar's book. "If only we had that."

The frigid wind flung snow at us again and brought tears to my eyes. I walked faster.

"We should have waited for the omnibus or taken a carriage." Dries kept up. "You must learn to accept the present. Do be reasonable." He shifted to block some of the wind that had changed direction. "You have to rid yourself of some of your clutter. Your room at home will not be able to hold all you have."

"*I* do not fit in my old room."

I could not return to my old life, for the simple reason that one could not return to the past. I couldn't go back to playing duets on the piano with my younger sisters and become one of them again. They didn't yet suspect the true harshness of life, how it could strip off your very skin. I wished not to ruin their blissful blindness.

I was *not* the same as I had been. I had known the love of a good man and the startling brilliance of another, the feel of my very own babe in my arms. *Never* would I return to the time before. Eyes once opened would not be forced closed again.

"I want to accomplish the task Theo set me. Vincent's work needs another agent, and my best chance for finding one is here. Did you think I've come back to Paris to pack? I'm sorry for the misunderstanding. I don't need you to decide my life for me." We reached the house, and I fumbled for my key with frozen fingers. "I need you to help me work out how to best preserve Vincent's legacy."

Dries threw up his hands. "I would understand your attachment if the paintings were Theo's own."

"They might not have come from his brush, but he carried them in his heart."

"They have little value. Nobody wants them." The gentle light in Dries's eyes begged me to see reason. "You have to let them go, Jo."

I wanted to argue, but every art dealer I had talked to agreed with my brother's pronouncement. They had all offered the same advice, in fact. I refused to believe those people. I chose to believe my husband. "Vincent was on the brink of being discovered before he died. He had his first solo show last month."

"At your own apartment."

"Anna Boch bought *The Red Vineyard* for four hundred francs. She knows great art when she sees it. She's an artist herself."

"She's an heiress to the Villeroy & Boch ceramics empire. She can afford to indulge friends."

I finally unlocked the door. "Word is going to spread. I will not toss aside a single painting."

"You have a mountain of canvases, Jo. Do be reasonable."

A bitter laugh escaped me. Life had stolen the

man I held most dear, and in the most cruel way. I was supposed to be reasonable?

A bent-back crone passed us and cut me a sharp look. I was wearing widow's black, laughing with a handsome young man on the front stoop of a rented apartment. I turned my back to her and went inside, stepping out of the wind at last.

"Theo was an art dealer." Dries tapped the snow off his boots on the mat before crossing the small foyer. "With a whole roster of collectors. And with all that, remind me how many of Vincent's paintings he sold altogether?"

"Theo ran out of time. I can find Vincent another agent."

"I will not be here to help. I tendered my resignation, Jo. Annie and I are returning to Amsterdam."

The news knocked me off balance. "Why?"

"Father arranged an opportunity for me in insurance there. I start in Amsterdam at the beginning of next month." He removed his hat and brushed the snow off the top, better on the black-and-white tile than inside the apartment. "Don't look at me like that. Wanting her children around her doesn't make our mother a monster. I don't want to leave you in Paris alone."

"I'm perfectly capable."

"I worry about the anarchists." He brushed off his shoulders next.

When the front door opened behind us, Dries removed his hat again. "Madame Biset."

"Monsieur Bonger," the landlord's wife returned

his greeting, focusing on me next. "Madame van Gogh."

Don't say it, please. Not now. Not in front of Dries.

Of course, she did. "*Le loyer*?" The rent.

"*Bien entendu.*" Certainly. I gathered my excuses, nearly expiring from embarrassment that my brother would witness such a moment, that he might tell our parents.

"Allow me, madam." Dries handed Madame Biset a handful of bills from his pocket with a flourish, as if he had the money in there precisely in the hope of running into her.

"Merci beaucoup, monsieur." She shot me an unimpressed look that spelled *about time*, counted the money, then bustled into her own apartment.

Dries's pleasant expression disappeared. "Theo shouldn't have left you without sufficient funds."

"Thank you for that. I mean the rent. I will repay you as soon as I am able." I pressed my lips together as I unlocked the apartment door, but could not hold back the rest for more than two seconds once we were inside. "Theo was not an irresponsible man."

"He paid for Vincent's lodgings, his every meal, his medical care, the paints, the canvases, every last pouch of pipe tobacco. Maybe if he did less for Vincent, there would be more left for you." Dries clicked his tongue. "I introduced you. I feel responsible."

His shoulders sloped, and I could nearly see the cloud of guilt that sat on them, too much guilt for the confines of the kitchen. Not enough room for it all, not with my own mountains of guilt already there, crowding the space, thinning the air.

"I should have done more," Theo had shouted when he'd raved. The words took root in my own heart. *I should have done more.* I owed it to Theo to see his life's work succeed. I had to finish his quest, to redeem myself.

The paintings on the walls reminded me daily why Theo believed in Vincent. Winter might have ruled outside, but our home was bathed in summer. The pale pink of almond blossoms were joined by the robust blue of irises, and the indomitable yellow of sunflowers. At times, I felt as if the colors were singing together and calling me to dance. I swore the miracle of Vincent's paintings would not remain forever locked away in our apartment.

"Theo was the best husband I could have dreamt of. I was made better because he was in my life. He saw me as I was and saw me for what I could become. He educated me. He opened my eyes to so much culture and art…" I placed my hand on Dries's for a moment. "Theo paid for his brother's care. As would I, should you need it and had I the means. And when he himself fell ill… The rest of our funds were spent on hospitals."

Brain infection had been the official cause of death given, instead of *gone stark raving mad*, to spare the legacy of a good man.

Wil squirmed, and I kissed his rosy cheek, then set him on the rug at my feet. I checked his hands to make sure he hadn't been too chilled, but his tiny fingers were warm. I checked his feet too, removing the second pair of socks I had put on him for our outing. Then I removed the simple white hat and coat I had knitted for him. He fussed at being tugged this way and that, but as soon as I finished, he picked up a wooden block to play with, instantly content. He was a year old. I swore to keep him healthy and happy.

"I must remain in Paris," I told my brother. "Theo's friends will help me finish his work."

"Have they been able to help so far?" A grievous sigh escaped him. "Theo's artist friends might represent the most brilliant development in art in our lifetime, but they themselves have not yet been discovered. They cannot even help themselves. They cannot help you, Jo."

"And you? Could you not lend me sufficient funds to last the year?" I shouldn't have asked. He had his own wife, his own children now. And he'd only just told me that he'd left his job in Paris and would not start the one in Amsterdam for some weeks. "I'm sorry. Please forget I said anything."

He bent down to run his fingers over Wil's silky blond hair. "I will help any way I can. But I can help you more easily in Amsterdam. Would home be so bad? You will take care of our parents as they grow old. And you might yet meet a widower who needs a mother for his children. Surely there would be some fulfillment in that? Mama says Garrit still asks about you."

Because I loved my brother, I tried to imagine the

future he painted, but everything in me protested. My mind would grow dull, every last spark inside me dying one by one. No time to read my books, no time to think and write, no time to visit a gallery or an exhibit, no time to accomplish the great task Theo had set for me, the task of a lifetime.

"I think I would go mad."

"Mama has always been content."

Frustration had me yanking my hat off with force, pulling some hair tangled in the ribbon. "I love our mother, but I don't wish to become her." I set my snow-wet hat and shawl on the chair near the warm stove. "Is there no other way?"

Dries hung his own hat and coat, then rubbed his hands together over the heat. "You are a widow with a babe, in a foreign country, without any means of supporting yourself."

"I have over a hundred paintings left to me by my husband." Most by Vincent, some by others, alas none worth much. The artists Theo had most admired were the ones the art world least recognized.

The walls were crowded with still lifes, land-scapes, and portraits, and we had more, in every cupboard, and piled under the bed. In more than one corner, they towered to the ceiling. They had become the structure of our lives, defining the edges.

"What else do you have?" Dries asked.

"Some four hundred drawings? Also from Vincent."

My brother shook his head. "Worth nothing." He

looked around. "You can't seriously wish to live in this mess."

"I will set everything up the way Theo had intended. And I can live frugally."

Dries didn't respond, but his eyes said I dreamed of the impossible.

"I will move back up to the fourth floor." I spoke as the solution occurred to me, but Dries had already turned away. Still, I could not quit. I offered my deepest, darkest pain. "I don't need the larger space without Theo. There will be no more children."

Cold spread over my chest, and I brushed at the front of my dress, thinking snow was melting into the black fabric, but there was nothing there.

I busied myself so I wouldn't scream at the unfairness of life. I poured a bit of donkey milk in a pan, then placed it on the stovetop to warm, adding a pinch of sugar. "I am still convinced that Wil's illness last summer came from contaminated cow milk." How Dries's wife, Annie, had mocked me for that opinion. "As soon as we arranged to have a woman bring her donkey to the back door every day, getting the milk fresh, he quickly recovered."

My son was the picture of health these days, but I still bought donkey milk when I could—now at the market. I stirred the frothy white liquid for a moment or two. I needed that much time before I could look at my brother again.

Dries said, "I want to take you home with me when I go at the end of the week."

Defeat robbed me of words.

Of course.

He hadn't stopped by merely to ensure I had not sunk under the turbulent waves of widowhood's despairs.

"You've known happiness," he said quietly.

I could not argue. I'd had joy in my marriage, more than most. In this apartment, and the one three floors above, I'd woken every day with the man I loved. We rose together, made eggs and tea together, laughed together. When he left for work—selling everyone's paintings but Vincent's, because despite his repeated entreaties, Goupil would not carry them—I could hardly wait to have him back for lunch.

"I have known true love. And you had none." Annie continued to make him miserable. Even having children hadn't helped.

"You could leave Vincent's legacy with one of his other siblings."

"I don't think Cor is coming back from South Africa anytime soon." Cor was the third Van Gogh brother.

"Wilhelmina, then. She was Vincent's favorite sister."

"She works as a nurse and can barely support herself. She has no connections to the arts, nor the time or funds to take on such a quest."

I waited for my brother to finally acknowledge that my way was the right way, the only way, but instead, his mind always on practical matters, he said, "We could strip the canvases. The thin wood used for stretching, I can easily break over my knee and reduce to kindling. You could gift it to your neighbors. The folded canvases can be fed into your stove one by one. They'll provide you with a night of warmth. The very act might set you free from the past. Consider it a way of saying good-bye."

For some reason, my numb mind could only think that since Vincent preferred painting outside, on his easel, at least his canvases were of a reasonable size. "Imagine trying to burn one of Claude Monet's giant pieces."

"Oh, many people do imagine," Dries said with thick irony. "He is still criticized for the unfinished quality of his work, for not making his lines more precise." He waved the idea of Monet away. "If only he didn't buy that house and lock himself away in Giverny. Now he wastes half his time gardening. Do you know he's having ponds dug and plans to paint waterlilies? It will be the end of him in the profession."

"How sad." Monet was the most successful of the group of Parisian artists who'd broken with academy tradition. He had tasted poverty and even bankruptcy, but he was beginning to sell. His house was far from Paris, in the country, but still, unheard of riches compared to Vincent's earnings that never paid a single month of rent. "I'm happy for Monet's success."

I hoped it wouldn't be as temporary as my brother predicted.

Wil grabbed my ankle. "Milly."

"Yes, darling. More milk."

He didn't speak clear words yet, but soon. Those words, however—if Dries had his way—would be spoken somewhere else.

The room spun, the walls closing in. I looked out the window, needing to see the familiar redbrick houses of cité Pigalle, to assure myself I was still in Paris. But a merciless dusk was falling outside, covering the city and my dreams, stealing them away from me already.

Wil smacked his lips together, and I smiled at him through a sheen of tears. "Are you blowing kisses for your mama?"

I picked him up, all softness and warmth, the living half of my heart. As we stood in the middle of the kitchen, I saw the happy home the apartment could have been, the home Theo and I had built from hopes and dreams. Except, those hopes and dreams were beginning to blink out one by one, like Paris's gaslights in the morning.

No. I refused to let them.

When the lights went out on the streets, the sun came up.

I looked from one sunflower painting to the other on the wall. I would not sink roots into worry and fear. I would turn to the light with gratitude.

I had my son, I had my health, and I had Vincent's art.

"Thank you for your concern and advice," I told Dries, holding Wil close. "Nevertheless, I cannot move back with Mama and Papa. And I am not going anywhere without the paintings."

"Don't be a fool, Jo." Exasperation drew tight lines around my brother's eyes.

I did not wish to fight with him, so I held my peace.

He sighed. "What do you propose to do?"

CHAPTER TWENTY-THREE

Emsley

I called Bram.

After Sergei had left, I'd gone back up to the office to work, *determined* not to think about his cousin. But then I decided I was allowed to think about Bram in a professional capacity. And I reconsidered his suggestion of small investors.

Startups tended to avoid them.

Anyone who put in money wanted a vote in everything and needed to be pleased. TAFB. Time Away From Business. One guy putting up a million dollars was easier to manage than ten guys putting in a hundred thousand each.

However, startup beggars could not be venture capital choosers. Johanna had found her life's purpose, and so had I. She'd fought her battles, and I would fight mine.

Bram answered on the first ring. "Emsley. Everything all right?"

"Sergei was just here. Thank you for giving me his number." I petted Lai Fa at my feet, half hoping she'd talk me out of what I was about to say next. She gave me an expression closer to a smug smile than I'd expected from a chicken. Fine. "Would you still be interested in hearing a pitch?"

"Absolutely."

"I don't have a formal presentation prepared yet."

"I don't need anything formal. May I bring my grandfather? He'll probably be interested too."

"Yes, please."

I'd been trying to figure out how I could engineer another meeting with him. I wanted to ask about his "accidental" tripping of the senator. I suspected Bram Sr. knew more about the incident in the library than he had admitted.

"Is seven o'clock too late?" Bram asked. "I have an end-of-the-day meeting I expect will run long."

"Seven is perfect."

He didn't respond for a few seconds, then, "Sorry. I'm at court again. We're going in."

"No, I'm sorry I'm bothering you at work."

"You can call anytime. You're never a bother. See you tonight."

We ended the call, and I picked up Lai Fa and kissed her head. "This is happening."

I was going to give a presentation. Trey usually did that—tall and confident and *next Bezos* written all over him. My job was to run the auctions and, if necessary, coddle our clients. I was so not a saleswoman.

For the phone pitches I'd done from New York so far, I just used handwritten notes. I had no slides. No charts drawn up. No projector.

I set Lai Fa on the floor. "Hold on to your fuzzy feathers. We're about to have a busy afternoon."

I switched on Violet's ancient printer in the corner, and it came alive with a whirr. Lai Fa peeped at it, curiously. She hadn't been startled, showed no fear. And if she could be brave, so could I.

"I can't be more chicken than a literal chicken. Right?"

While Lai Fa settled down on my feet for a nap, I ran through Ludington's numbers for the past year. Then I worked up a new, aggressive marketing plan.

Strena popped her head in the door, with two of her models, Monique and Vivian, smiling from behind her.

Lai Fa ran over, and they went to their knees, making a gratifying amount of fuss about her. I felt like a proud parent.

"We're going to work a couple of hours." Strena straightened. "Have you thought about the show?"

"Thought about it, yes. Made a decision, no."

She didn't push me. She took her models upstairs.

I needed a break, so I packed up Violet's bathroom—antique perfume bottles, candlesticks, ceramic statues of Greek goddesses—for Goodwill. Lai Fa stalked a small spider under the tub. When she finally snatched it, she let out a triumphant chirp.

"And this is why we're an unstoppable team."

The hour we spent cleaning cleared my brain. I reassessed my presentation with fresh eyes. This time, Lai Fa seemed interested, tilting her head. Maybe she'd gained enough self-confidence from the spider hunt to tackle entrepreneurship next.

I simplified my spreadsheets into a handful of easily understandable charts. "Visuals are always appreciated."

At six, I set up downstairs, quickly showered, then dressed in a pair of Audrey Hepburn-style black slacks and tailored white shirt—both saved from the antique wardrobe in the basement.

The woman in the mirror could be a CEO. She could be anything she wanted.

"Strength from within," I told Lai Fa. "The power comes from me."

I grabbed my printouts from the office, then the doorbell rang, and I hurried to let in my potential investors. I'd been carrying Lai Fa up and down the stairs, but this time, before I could pick her up, she went for it, flapping her wings. "Hey, your feathers are growing!"

We opened the door together. Bram, his grandfather, and his cousin filed in.

"Thank you for coming."

"Hope you don't mind that I tagged along." Sergei flashed that charming smile of his that made it impossible to mind anything he did. "The antique trade can be fickle. One year, antiques are trendy, the next, all the designers want handmade, fair-trade folk-art pieces from overseas. I try to invest a little away from my own business when I can."

Bram picked up Lai Fa and settled her into the crook of his arm. "Sergei told us you got a chicken. My aunt in Jersey keeps half a dozen for eggs."

"Her name is Lai Fa." Because he was a lawyer holding my chicken, the legalities of poultry in the city occurred to me for the first time. "Does New York have livestock restrictions?"

"Chickens are legal in all the districts, as long as they are hens. No roosters."

"Blatant discrimination," said Sergei.

Bram patted Lai Fa's fuzzy head. "Strena here? I saw her van up front."

"Upstairs."

Then I thought *Why didn't I invite her?*

"Take a seat," I told my potential investors. "I'll be right back."

I invited Strena *and* the models. The models declined. Strena said, "I'll be down in a few minutes. We're in the cleanup stage."

I hurried back downstairs and distributed the handouts, then I served coffee with my impulse-purchase chocolate chip cookies I still had from my first grocery trip. Better someone else ate them. I wanted to wear the Mondrian dress at least one more time before I inevitably gained my lost pounds back.

Sergei was telling Bram Sr. about Daniel Muller, the artist who'd carved the horses for the carousel. Bram was giving Lai Fa a drink in a water bottle cap.

I was glad and grateful for every single person in the room, but my gaze kept returning to Bram.

There were details about him that I had not allowed myself to notice before. Like that he had sensual hands, square-trimmed nails, no hairy fingers —strong hands, with veins and tendons standing out when he flexed his muscles. I'd never been attracted to a man's hands before. Thank God, Strena glided down the stairs with her models before anyone could notice my freakish obsession moment.

Vivian waved goodbye, then left.

Monique offered a shy smile. "Could I change my mind and stay? I've been thinking about starting a modeling agency for plus-size models and models of color. If I do it, I'm going to have to pitch, but I don't know how. I want to see how you do it. Would you mind?"

"The more, the merrier. Just remember I've never done this before either."

Bram Sr. and Sergei immediately stood to offer the ladies their armchairs.

Bram put Lai Fa down, then he got up too. "I'll grab the barstools from the kitchen."

I made the introductions. Everyone picked up their handouts, while Lai Fa pecked around on the floor for crumbs of bagels past.

When Bram returned with the barstools, he asked, "How is Jo Bonger?"

"Down but not out. She had grit."

"Any luck finding a Dutch translator?"

Strena answered. "I speak Dutch." At my

surprised look, she rolled her eyes. "Born and raised in Aruba. Aruba is part of the Kingdom of the Netherlands?"

"The Dutch have a king?"

"Willem-Alexander. *Christ. Americans.*"

"Since I can't possibly get any more embarrassed now, I'm going to just plunge into my business presentation." I fixed a bright smile onto my face. "Thank you for coming."

Then I told my audience about how Ludington's had begun. How we targeted a niche market. How we built our current client list. I asked them to open their handouts and refer to the appropriate pages.

I finished with "Any questions?"

Bram Sr. went first. "Is the business named after Sybil Ludington?"

"Yes. Her story is a patriotic story, which appeals to our politician clients. Also, she symbolizes that you don't have to be big and important to do good work. Sybil was sixteen at the time of Paul Revere's ride. Paul Revere rode twelve miles. Sybil rode forty, through dark, hostile woods, fought off a highwayman, and alerted troops that the British were coming."

Violet had told me about her. I'd written a paper on Sybil in middle school, with all my youthful outrage that Revere was still celebrated while she'd been forgotten. I used to daydream about being Sybil, riding through the night like a Valkyrie.

Bram Sr. had another question. I answered that too. And then I answered another.

"I think we'll be here for a while." Sergei pulled out his cell phone. "How about dinner? A friend of mine has a Russian restaurant a few blocks over."

Until he mentioned food, I hadn't realized that I'd forgotten lunch. "What's good Russian food?"

"What isn't?"

Strena, her nose in the handouts, said, "I vote yes."

When, twenty minutes later, the doorbell rang, I thought it was food delivery. Sergei dashed to answer and called back from the open door. "Someone's here to see you, Emsley."

And then Trey loped in, one hand in his pocket.

"Are you having a party?" He stopped on the threshold of the gallery, in his usual casual wear: five-hundred-dollar sneakers, jeans, the latest hip brand hoodie.

I used to like his style. I used to think he had style. But for a man of thirty who was a CEO, he was trying too hard for the I'm-just-one-of-the-bros vibe.

Bram, only a couple of years older, acted infinitely more mature. Bram was an adult. Trey was adulting.

"Why are you still in New York?" I joined Trey in the foyer, while Sergei returned to the coffee table where my potential investors engaged in conversation to give us privacy. "I thought you and Diya were going back to LA after Violet's funeral."

"We decided to stay for the rest of the week at my father's condo. Diya wants to do some shopping."

Sounded like Diya had already landed a new job, one with a sign-on bonus. How long had she been looking? I didn't ask. I didn't want to sound snarky and juvenile. I was channeling more of a *mature businesswoman, CEO* vibe for the evening.

Then I caught, belatedly, the weird dip in Trey's tone when he'd said *shopping*. *Oh*. "As in shopping for a ring?"

He bent his head, doing his weird looming. "Are you going to pretend that you regret the end of our relationship?"

"What do I have to regret? I didn't cheat," I said between my teeth.

"Fine. If you can't give me a break, at least give Diya one. She still wants to be your friend. Can't you just let the past go?" He shook his head as if I disappointed him. "Anyway, it's not why I'm here." He scanned the room behind me and did a double take. "Why is there a chicken roosting on the balustrade?"

"She just learned to fly today. Trey, meet Lai Fa. Lai Fa, meet Trey," I introduced them because I knew being introduced to a chicken would irk him.

His gaze slid past Lai Fa. "Who are these people?"

"An impromptu investors' meeting. Would you like to come in?"

"Could we talk in private?"

Before I could respond, Bram spoke up, "I'm her attorney."

"Business partner," Bram Sr. put in.

"Ditto," Sergei added.

"Me too." Strena also decided to have my back. She probably read the tension in my shoulders.

Monique caught the undercurrents too. Her eyes

telegraphed, *Could I please stay and watch this train wreck?*

I wasn't about to send anyone off, despite Trey's tightening expression that betrayed how much the audience annoyed him. Or perhaps *because* I knew the audience annoyed him.

He stepped closer to me. "I heard you've been calling around to investors, without any success."

"LA didn't work out. But New York seems interested."

"I had the agreement drawn up for an early handover. We both know you won't be able to raise the money. Let's cut to the chase and take some stress off your shoulders. You must be crazy busy here with the house."

"Handover?"

"You can't buy me out, so I'm buying you out. The company itself has value beyond the auction business. It's a brand associated with politics. I can raise enough money from my family to retool it into a polling agency." He drew a folder from his bag. "This is the contract."

"We can look at the papers, but there won't be a handover."

Trey's confident smile never wavered. "You really want to stay in the auction business and run the company alone? Chance having a massive failure attached to your name?"

"Yes."

"Come on, Emsley. Be sensible."

He sounded like my mother, and it was the exact worst moment to sound like her.

My mood snapped from irked to angry. "Why do you care?"

"I hate seeing you make a bad business decision."

"But it's a good decision to keep Ludington's for yourself?"

"I have enough sense to take it into a profitable direction."

"Ludington's was my idea. I'm not giving it up."

He glanced at Bram, then Bram Sr., then at Sergei. "Which one of you is going to put up the money to buy me out?" He ignored Strena and Monique.

For a terrible moment, the question hung in the air like the blade of a guillotine after the catch had been released, the weight of the metal just waiting for gravity to bring it down on the victim's neck.

Then Bram leaned forward in his seat. "I'll put up a hundred thousand."

"Same here." From Bram Sr.

"Me too." Strena's cold smile said she didn't appreciate being discounted.

"I'll put in two." Sergei spoke up. "Two hundred thousand."

"And I can scrape together roughly that much too," I said.

Trey waited another second, but Monique remained silent. "That's it?" He laughed at me. "You have half?"

An idea sparked in my brain. I'd been in paring-down mode for the past few days, going through

Violet's belongings, watching everything through the lens of *What's the minimum I absolutely have to keep?*

I needed to apply that lens to Ludington's. I silently ran through a few scenarios in my head, then asked, "How about half?"

"Half is not enough. I want the whole million point two, as specified in our contract. Otherwise, you forfeit."

"I have until the end of May. I raised half in a day. I'll set up another presentation, and I'll have the rest. Then all of Ludington's is mine." I bluffed my heart out. "But what I'm offering right here, right now, is half the company and six hundred thousand dollars. You'll own the LA operation. I start a New York office."

He laughed. "You think you can compete with the big houses?"

"They do everything. Their names aren't synonymous with political fundraiser auctions. Ludington's will be. I'll undercut them on commission. They take fifteen to twenty percent, I'll take ten."

"You couldn't hack it in New York four years ago."

"As a newbie. Now I have an auction house that's a known name in its niche."

"Obviously, I'll have to discuss this with my attorney. It's not the deal I had in mind when I came here." The look in his eyes said he thought I was a fool. "Would you walk me out, Emsley?"

I stepped out onto the front stoop with him and wrapped my arms around myself. A cold mist was drizzling from the night sky. The air had a wet-dog tang, the smell of city streets in the rain.

Trey didn't seem to feel the chill. His cheeks were flushed with heat. "You're never going to make money here with the kind of competition you'll have in New York. And I thought you were smarter than to trust strangers. I have no idea who these people are or why they talked you into this. They're exploiting you."

"For what? My vast fortunes?"

"Your ideas."

"You're the one walking away with half my company."

"It's all you ever cared about, isn't it? The company. I was just a convenience. I was there, in the house, and you didn't have to go far, waste time on actual dating. Minimal TAFB, Time Away From Business. I was just an easy solution to a problem."

"You weren't." I shook off his words. I wasn't going to go down that rabbit hole while standing on the front stoop in a drizzle. "Does it matter, at this stage?"

He drew back. "You're right. It used to matter to me, but it doesn't anymore. Diya sees me in a way you never have."

"I'm happy for you both." My response came out snarky, so I tried again. "I mean it."

Trey glared at the half-open door behind me. "Are they really going to cough up all that money, or was that just bluff and bravado back there? Sign the contract, Emsley. Then you're out, like Diya, free and clear. As long as you're bent on staying in New York, why not start over completely? Go into something less competitive."

"Or why don't I just volunteer? Why don't women stay far away from arenas of power, like politics? I know my own mind. Stop pressuring me."

"Stop taking on more than you can handle. Stop following bullshit advice from five-minute acquaintances." He grabbed my shoulders. "We've been friends for a long time. I want what's best for you."

"Please don't tell me what's best for me."

"And do take your hands off her," Bram said behind me, his voice Pittsburgh steel.

"I wouldn't mess with her," Strena added. "She's already put a senator into the grave this week."

Trey dropped his hands. "What is she talking about?"

I didn't explain. "You'll have the LA side of the business and six hundred thousand dollars," I reiterated. "Or pocket a million point two and Ludington's is all mine."

An eternity passed before he nodded. Of course, he couldn't leave it there. "You're going to fail in New York. You're going to regret this."

"My business. Mine to regret."

The rain picked up. Trey ran down the steps, casting a *you're crazy* look over his shoulder.

Behind me, Sergei said, "Bam! Spanked and running away red assed."

I backed into the foyer and closed the door so Trey wouldn't hear me laugh.

Bram and his grandfather, Sergei, Strena, and Monique stood around me. Bram had Lai Fa back in the crook of his arm. He set her down, shrugged off his jacket, and put it around my shoulders, then picked up the chicken again. And Lai Fa went along, as if they were a circus act.

My shirt clung damp and cold, but the jacket transferred Bram's warmth to me. The fabric carried the scent of fresh-shaved pencils and new notebooks, as if, at work, he kept his jacket in the supply closet.

Monique made a shooing gesture toward the door. "Boy fluttered away like a pesky fly."

"Minced like a constipated beaver," Strena corrected.

The last time I'd laughed that hard had been over a dirty joke Violet had told me. I hadn't expected to laugh like that again for a long time. If I hadn't already liked Strena, I would have liked her for just that sentence.

"Thank you. Thank you all. I appreciate the backup. And the investment. I hope you meant that."

"Meant every word," Bram said.

His grandfather nodded.

Strena squinted at me. "What? You don't think I have that kind of money?"

"I have no idea how much money anybody has. I'm just grateful to you all. And relieved."

I had about half a second to luxuriate in that relief before Sergei cleared his throat. "I only have half of what I promised. But I have an idea for raising the other half."

Strena bumped his shoulder. "Feel free to elaborate before she hyperventilates."

She wasn't exaggerating. Between one breath and the next, I was halfway to a panic attack.

Sergei pointed behind him at the stack of boxes Bram had helped me drag up from the basement. "What are you doing with those flyers?"

"I was thinking about using them as wallpaper when I find an apartment."

"How about selling them?"

"Who would buy them?"

"Who wouldn't? They're good quality prints by Violet Velar. They have all her hallmarks, the color, the movement, the boldness. And..." He cleared his throat again, his expression turning apologetic. "Violet is gone. Sorry. It's deplorably insensitive to say, but she won't make any more art. Everything she created in the past is already in museums or private collections. The flyers could be a way for new collectors to have a piece of her legacy. People would eat up a sale authorized by the family, with letters of authenticity. She was the quintessential New York City artist."

Strena walked over to the boxes and examined a handful of flyers. "He's right. And if he can't move all of it, I have friends who can. The museum shop at the MoMA, for one, would probably stock them. How many different designs are there?"

"A couple of dozen? But all the boxes aren't in good shape. The ones that were on the bottom have some water damage."

"Even better." Sergei's eyes glinted. "The fewer copies of each design, the more they're worth. I—"

The doorbell cut him off.

All I could think was *It'd better not be Trey coming back.* I didn't have it in me to go another round with him. I would rather have spent the night in the basement with the bear.

CHAPTER TWENTY-FOUR

Johanna
     August 1891, Bussum, Netherlands

In the end, I did leave Paris. I wanted to see Vincent's talent recognized and celebrated, but I also wanted to raise my son in happiness and health. With a child in tow and with my imperfect French, I could not find respectable work in France. I returned to the Netherlands, but not to my parents' home. I embarked on my own venture. I faced the future with a straight back, ready to be tested.

"I saw Janus at the baker's this morning," my friend Anna told me with a meaningful look as she walked through my kitchen door, holding a crock under one arm and carrying her daughter, Saskia, in the other. "He said to tell you that he would be by to see you today."

Anna and her husband, Jan Veth, had settled in the village of Bussum and tempted me there.

She set her daughter down, then held out the crock for me with a smile. "The sauerkraut, as requested."

I slid my treasure box farther from Wil, who was spooning turnip mash into his mouth at the kitchen table, then hurried to accept the crock. One of Anna's neighbors sold sauerkraut at the weekend market.

"Thank you. I'm making *zuuerkoolstamppot* for dinner."

"You could do worse than Janus. He likes you, and you need a husband."

"It's only been seven months. I don't need a husband. Have you seen the postman?"

Saskia tottered forward. "We-we!"

"The postman is married to some old English hag. Honestly—" Anna caught herself. "Oh. Are you waiting for something in the mail?"

"I sent a letter to Goupil in Paris last week. Theo had worked for them so hard, for so many years. I hope they can finally see Vincent's worth and champion his work. His art needs a gallery."

"Mm." Anna shrugged off her silk shawl and hung it on the peg by the door, then tilted her head toward the stairs. "It's quiet here today."

"Everyone is out."

My boardinghouse in Bussum, the Villa Helma, had few boarders so far: the Kerkhovens, who were already renting in the other wing when I'd arrived in May, and a widow.

"You need to find some nice bachelors for the empty rooms." Anna lifted her daughter onto a chair so the children could share the turnip mash, and then she kissed Wil on the top of his head.

Her cobalt-blue dress, a contrast to my widow's black, swished around her ankles. The spring breeze had teased a few tendrils of chestnut hair free around her perfectly oval face. She was beautiful even swollen with her next child, or maybe even more beautiful because of that radiance some expectant mothers were lucky to possess. Vincent would have wanted to paint her. He would have liked the cobalt of her dress, how it complemented the peach of her skin.

The children began babbling at each other in baby talk.

"Sasa no!" Wil pulled his bowl away, then immediately changed his mind. "Sasa here."

Anna and I smiled at each other.

I pulled out a chair for her. "Come sit."

"My back hurts less when I am up and walking." Her gaze ran over the sizable box on the table, her lively dark eyes glinting. "And what is this? Love letters?"

"Vincent's letters to Theo. Theo saved them all."

"Where are Theo's letters to Vincent?"

My heart had been hurting nonstop this past year since Vincent's death, then Theo's so shortly after, but now it managed to bleed some fresh blood yet. I ran my fingers over the box's edge. "Vincent tended to be

273

messy and disorganized at his best. He had his mind on greater dreams."

We both fell silent for a moment.

I picked up the folded letter at the top of the pile. "He was not a bad man. If only people knew him..." I sounded pitiful, begging Anna to understand. I let the letter fall from my fingers. "A few weeks ago, on the first anniversary of his death, I could find no rest after I went to bed." I'd fallen into a nocturnal gloom. The air had held a mournful restlessness that chased the sleep from my eyes and chased me from my room. "While Wil was asleep, I went for a walk in the drizzle."

"You could have caught a cold."

"Vincent walked a lot, did I tell you? An unhealthy amount, Theo sometimes said. He would walk for days, to towns where he wanted to see a friend, through storms or freezing cold, eating only a slice of bread here and there, spending his nights out in the open."

"He was healthier in the body than he was in the mind."

Anna might have been right about that. "As I ambled through the evening by myself, I noticed the lit windows around me. I could see the happy families inside. I understood at last how lonely Vincent must have felt. Theo knew, of course. But until then, I didn't."

"Oh, Jo. You couldn't have."

"It broke my heart. Vincent had always stood on the outside, lost to all. I don't want him to remain lost. If people could read his letters, they would love him as much as Theo and I did. Even strangers would be able to comprehend the thoughts and emotions that went into his works. How his sunflowers are gratitude and his wheat fields are loneliness. If only I were clever enough to explain."

"You're the cleverest woman I know. Clever enough to know that it does no good to keep living in old memories."

"But his words are so full of tenderness and brilliance and rage and despair. And, Anna, so much *faith*." I slipped my treasure box on top of the cupboard where it obscured the bottom of Vincent's *The Harbor* hanging on the wall, but was at least safe from sticky little hands. "Vincent reminisced a lot in his letters about the times he and Theo spent together."

Anna was taking a turn around the kitchen, a hand at her lower back, but she stopped to cast me a curious glance.

My fingers moved in a helpless flutter. "I don't know how to explain."

"Vincent's letters make you feel as if Theo is still with you." Her voice softened.

"Yes."

"I know you hated to leave Paris, but maybe it's good that you did. Everything there would have kept reminding you of him."

"I *want* everything to remind me of him." And everything did, even here.

When I left our Paris apartment, I lost Theo's

presence that had lingered around me there. But I found Theo again the day our furniture finally arrived from France. Our bed could not be assembled right away because the screws had been mislaid. I spent the first night in the boardinghouse sleeping on the floor, inside the bedframe, under Theo's blanket. And he was with me again. His presence was so strong, it was as if he were lying next to me.

I placed our furniture exactly as it had been in Paris. And I hung all the pictures the same, which took me the whole spring. All that time, I imagined Theo with me.

I did not tell Anna that sometimes I pretended that my husband was still alive, at work, and he would walk through the door on his lunch break.

All life is a dream.

"Of course, you miss your Theo." Anna started walking again. "He was a loving husband."

"He did not die as peacefully as I led everyone to believe." My voice dropped to a whisper.

"What do you mean?"

I said nothing.

"Jo?"

"I don't believe Vincent committed suicide because he suddenly lost hope for his work." The words rushed from me then. "Yes, for most of his life, he lived with such dark torments. And he had been in and out of various institutes. But his life was turning for the better. Monet himself spoke highly of him and praised his work. Vincent was on the brink of success."

"Why would he kill himself?"

"After Theo married me, after we had the baby…" My voice broke.

"Vincent must have loved Wil."

"Of course, he did. But you know Wil was named after him. Vincent Willem van Gogh."

"To honor him. The sentiment must have brought him happiness."

"I'm not certain." I pressed my lips together. I cursed myself for ever broaching the subject.

Anna watched me with endless patience.

"Vincent had an older brother who was still-born. Vincent was named after him, as if he was nothing but a replacement. And he knew it. His mother took him to his brother's grave often enough. What must it have felt like for a child to look at his own name on a gravestone?" I shud-dered. "When our son was born, Theo wanted the same name. Were we trying to replace Vincent? Of course not. We didn't mean it like that. But was it how Vincent took our well-meant gesture? He'd been sick. He'd been in the hospital for so long. And here came a newer, better, healthier version, ready to take over. Did Vincent see that as a signal that it was time for him to go?"

"Did he say anything?"

"No. But the more I read his letters…" I clasped my hands on my lap. "I used to just read the parts where he reminisced about Theo in the past. But this week, I read them in full. And I can *feel* his anguish."

"He had to have known how much you cared

about him. I know it well from how much you care about him still."

"All I ever wanted was to be a new sister to him. But did he understand that? He felt too keenly the weight of having to be supported by Theo. Did he worry that it was too much? That with Theo having a wife and child, he was a burden? Did he kill himself to free us?" I voiced the question that had kept me up the past two nights.

"Oh, Jo."

"Theo talked about wanting to quit Goupil to open his own gallery. We saw it as a chance to earn more. But Vincent saw it as exchanging a certain income for an uncertain one. He felt his existence threatened. He says as much in one of his letters." Was it all my fault? "Theo was willing to take a risk for higher earnings so we could better afford the larger apartment. Which *I* wanted. Had I not married Theo, Vincent might not have taken his own life. And had Vincent not died, Theo would not have been so despondent that he succumbed to his illness. They would be both alive and happy without me."

"Don't think like that, Jo. Guilt is a slow poison."

I could not let go of the guilt, but I set it aside and whispered my darkest fear yet. "What if Wil inherited Vincent's and Theo's illness of the mind?"

"He did not," Anna said in the firmest tone possible. "He is a kind child, sweet and smart. And he has the most exceptional woman for his mother in all the Netherlands."

"I miss Theo." I sniffed.

"Visiting his grave didn't help? It helps when I visit my sister."

Wil and I had taken the train to Utrecht and laid red roses on his father's grave. Theo had given me red roses on our wedding day. Grief lay thick as fog all around us, exhaustion heavy on my shoulders. I'd been tired of the big house in Bussum and the work, and the loneliness of the years yet to come. I'd wanted to lie down on the cold dirt. I'd wanted to lie down and stay.

In the end, my little son had led me away.

Anna placed a gentle hand on my arm. "Don't escape too long into those letters, Jo. You wouldn't want to lose yourself completely in the past."

"Wouldn't I?" *Despite the end?*

"The future has so much to offer."

Easy for her to say, her husband still alive, the two of them awaiting the birth of another child.

I was happy for her, I truly was, but I still grieved all I had lost. She was right, however. I could not remain mired in that pain. I kept reminding myself of the sunflowers. *Fear no storms, turn in gratitude toward the light.*

I wiped my eyes and set the cast iron pan on the stove, having learned that keeping busy was the best medicine. "Émile Bernard wrote a biography of Vincent after his death. He even published some of the letters they exchanged. I wrote him to thank him one more time." I nodded toward the shelf by the kitchen door where my letter waited for the postman. "When they were published, Émile's words generated interest in Vincent's art for a while. He might be willing to help again. All I want is to accomplish the task Theo left me."

"I would think it must be easier to popularize a living artist." Anna was walking again. "They can talk to people and convey their passion for their art. They can appear at events and make declarations that might appear in the papers. They can endear themselves to collectors by paying personal attention to them."

"Probably not Vincent. He had a difficult personality." I could admit that. "At times, even Theo despaired. He didn't think I knew, but he had to *pay* Gauguin to live with Vincent in Arles so Vincent would not be so alone."

"The brothers must have had a deep and abiding love between them."

"Truly. In their letters—" I'd been reaching for the wooden spoon, but I spun and faced Anna. "Their letters!" I retrieved the box. Where I'd seen well-read pages before, now I saw gold treasure. The dark clouds of grief and guilt parted. "This is the answer. Émile's publication of Vincent's biography and a handful of their letters made a difference. People talked about Vincent's art. I can revive that talk. I will publish letters too. I have a lot more of them than Émile does."

Anna eyed the pile. "You might—"

"I will start by editing, organizing, and publishing what I have here." A sudden confidence filled me, lent me support like whalebones to a corset. "And then I will write a new biography of Vincent. I will present him the way I knew him."

"Writing a book is not like writing a diary. How many letters are there?"

"Seven hundred."

She stared at me in shock, but she didn't tell me the task was impossible. Of course, she didn't know the worst about the letters.

"It's unfortunate," I told her, "that Vincent rarely bothered to date them."

"How will you put them in order?"

"I shall have to guess by the events described in each."

Anna rubbed her back. "You have a boarding-house to run and a child to care for. Nobody would blame you if you gave up. If there is no hope…"

"I believe with everything I am that Theo was right about Vincent," I rushed to say. I did not want the words *no hope* to hang in the air.

"Mammmmaaa!"

I grabbed the dishcloth and wiped the turnip mash from Wil's eyes. "There you go, my sweet."

Saskia laughed. She was the cleanest child I'd ever seen. She had been dipping her finger into the food, but not a speck landed on her face or her dress.

I kissed her rosy cheek, then snagged the wooden spoon off its peg on the wall at last and ducked into the pantry for a spoonful of lard.

The lard in the pan, I fetched a bowl of potatoes. I had delayed peeling them for the *zuurkoolstamppot*, in case Anna was unable to bring the sauerkraut.

Although, I had no idea what I would have made instead.

She strolled to the back door and looked out at the garden, then glanced at the basket of wet clothes I'd forgotten about when she'd come in. "Aren't you going to hang the laundry?"

"I'll put on the food first."

"Every time I see you, you are juggling at least two tasks, if not three."

"I am still learning how to run a boardinghouse. Maybe it will be easier with practice," I told her, then, "No, Wil," to my son, who was trying to shove the small spoon up his nose. Then back to Anna, "Did Janus tell you *when* he was coming?"

I needed to run out for fabric to make a couple of summer shirts for Wil, who was growing fast, but I wanted to be home when Janus arrived, in case he had any questions about the work I had set out for him.

"No. Nor did he tell me why he was coming." Anna peeked into the sitting room, where Theo's sofa held pride of place, covered in an oriental carpet as was the latest fashion. In the evenings, if my heart could bear it, I sat there.

Behind the sofa hung a Gauguin—in the bright colors of Martinique—but Anna had only a cursory glance to spare. She strode to the mantelpiece and paused in front of Vincent's *The Potato Eaters*, *Vase with Flowers* next to it, then she moved on to the *Boulevard de Clichy* over the door, before returning to the four Monticellos that hung over Theo's aunt's piano.

Except for the Gauguin and the Monticellos, Guillaumin's and Bernard's self-portraits next to the cupboard were my last remaining art from Theo's friends. I had to sell the rest to rent the Villa Helma and give us a chance at a self-sufficient life.

"I am glad you took a chance on the boardinghouse." Anna read my thoughts. "I love having you here."

I filled my large pot with water. "I had the idea from Theo. He took in a lodger after Vincent moved from their shared Paris flat to Arles. But I am starting to learn that managing an entire boardinghouse is quite a bit different from managing an apartment. The villa comes with a list of never-ending problems."

Wil began feeding Saskia with the spoon—better than he had fed himself, since he could see her mouth, but he could not see his own.

"Say thank you, Saskia," Anna patted her daughter's little head before addressing me again. "What has gone wrong now that requires Janus's assistance? The Widow Ballot complaining about her drafty windows again?"

I left the water on the stove to boil, then settled down next to the potatoes at the table. "All repaired. Now she complains of mice."

Anna snagged my spare apron from the peg by the stove, slipped it on, then took the chair across the table and held her hand out. "She has six cats."

I handed her a paring knife from the drawer. "She wants a seventh."

"And you will allow her?"

"She pays the rent. The room is hers. I cannot very well refuse. The vagaries of running a boarding-house, I'm afraid."

"But you don't regret moving here?"

"There's violence in Paris." Dries had been right. Mere days before I moved to Bussum, troops had shot at the May Day crowd demonstrating for an eight-hour workday. The bullets killed nine people and wounded thirty. "The papers predict more trouble on the way. And here, I'm closer to my family." Only twenty-five kilometers from Amsterdam.

"Even your parents can't complain."

"Mama does, as if I moved to Saint Petersburg."

Anna laughed. "Well, I am glad that you came."

"I'm glad too. Thank you for bringing me out of my melancholy."

She stopped by often with Saskia. And I was invited to her home, always filled with visiting artists and poets. It had healed my heart some to be included in their lively gatherings. Unlike in Paris, everyone spoke Dutch, so I could understand everything.

I was bettering myself, learning.

"Did I tell you my book starvation has been solved? Martha and Frederik van Eeden offered me unlimited use of their library."

Martha was a writer and translator, while Frederik was the top editor at the *New Guide*, the publication with which most of the members of our group of intellectuals were, in one way or the other, associated.

"Aren't they a lovely couple?" Anna pushed the curled potato peels back from the edge of the table so they wouldn't fall on her lap, and in the process squinted toward the darkest corner of the kitchen. "Do you really have mice?"

"Who knows? I might."

She watched me with suspicion as she peeled her next potato. "And you called the village carpenter to catch them?" She was teasing again. "Janus would do anything for you. I dare say he will catch those mice barehanded for a smile. I might stay just to watch."

I shook my head at her and set a worm-eaten potato next to the peels I'd saved for the neighbor's pig. "I hired him to frame more paintings."

My words did nothing to put Anna, an incurable romantic, off the scent. "Just how many paintings do you need to have framed?"

"All of them. Galleries won't take an unframed canvas." I was having the work done in stages. The rent from my borders covered repairs to the old house and provided a small income to take care of myself and Wil, but the money hardly stretched to the kind of frames Vincent's paintings deserved, and I refused to give them worse.

"Will Janus be here all afternoon?" Anna's tone was suspiciously innocent.

"It's not as you think."

"He is not taken with you?" she asked just as a

knock sounded on the door, Janus's distinct, masculine rap.

My friend jumped up with a muffled squeal to answer, pausing only to wipe her hands and whip off her apron.

"Anna!"

She put her finger over her lips, a silent promise that she wouldn't drop hints and embarrass me. Then she flew to let the carpenter in with a speed that belied her condition, as if torturing me energized her.

"Good afternoon, Janus."

"Ladies. G...good afternoon."

Anna pressed a hand to her heart. "My goodness. I must rush. I just remembered. I left the ham in the oven."

She hurried back for Saskia, then grabbed her shawl and swept out of the room with the flair of a trained actress.

Janus closed the door behind her, hat in hand, his shirtsleeves rolled to his elbows. He carried his materials, the lumber strapped to his shoulders, his box of tools under one arm. He had carpenter arms, muscles built for swinging the hammer. I was used to softer, more civilized sort of men.

Janus's formidable figure was only saved from being intimidating by his light hair that stuck up like a child's in the back. I had to turn for a moment to hide my smile as he strode inside.

"Front gate was s...starting to stick again. Fixed it on my way in." He stopped by the table, pulling a pumpernickel roll wrapped in wax paper from his pocket, and setting it next to me. "For the little one." Then he walked on. "I'll b...be in the back."

"Thank you."

He had kind eyes and callused hands, the kind of straightforward man country boys grew into. I didn't think he'd ever been farther from his hometown than Amsterdam. He had no flowery talk, no gentlemanly compliments. What few words he did say were usually about his work. He had a coarseness to him, like rough-cut wood, his planes not sanded to a smooth finish.

He paused at the door of the back room to peer inside. "Just the five? I could f...frame all you need. You can pay me later, as sales come in."

"Thank you, but five will be enough for now." I would not live on the village carpenter's charity.

I planned on sending the paintings to Goupil in Paris, if they refused the last batch I had mailed them.

"Mamaaaa!" Wil cried again, another spoonful of mash in his eyes, and up his nose too this time.

"What have you done, you silly boy?" I hefted him from the chair and over to the sink, splashing water into his face. He squirmed like an eel caught in a trap.

"Oh, you're big. All right, all finished." I plopped him back into his chair.

By the time I turned around, Janus had disappeared into the back room. Wil moved on to the pumpernickel roll with great relish. I poured milk into his bowl so he could dip the bread, which he did. He only had six teeth.

"Mama too." He held out the soggy roll.

He said that every time he had food. *Mama too.*

"Thank you, my darling, but right now, I am full."

I picked up my knife and the last potato, nearly stabbing myself when the widow Ballot burst through the door. "Would you look at these sweet babies?"

"*Two*, Mevrouw Ballot?"

She held the brown tabbies toward me, her cap askew, a lock of her gray hair trailing to her shoulder. "They are brothers. The last of the litter. I could not separate them."

Two wriggling kittens were more than Wil could bear. He dropped his half-chewed roll into his bowl and was off his chair and running forward, arms outstretched. "Mauw! Mauw!"

To the woman's credit, the sticky fingers didn't intimidate her. "Wipe your hands on my apron, Wil." She helped. "The child is welcome to totter over to see the kitties settled in. I will be happy to keep an eye on him."

"I would be grateful." I splashed the last potato into my white-blue enamel bowl.

As the widow was about to turn out, she caught sight of the envelope on the shelf by the door. Her eyes rounded, like a hen spotting a golden kernel of corn. "And who is the letter for? Who is this gentleman by the name of Émile Bernard?" She peered at me. "I see the address is Paris. An artist?"

"A friend." I washed the potatoes.

"Do you think he might help?" Like everyone else who spent even a minute in my company, she was aware of my quest. "Is he well known in France?"

"He is becoming known." I dumped the potatoes into the boiling water, careful not to splash my hands. "He exhibited at the Salon."

"Oh, he has connections. What is it that you ask of him? And is a letter not too bold? To write a man out of the blue like that with a personal request?"

"I wrote him to thank him for the kind words he said of Vincent. I asked—but only in a sentence—if he might stop by the gallery where my husband worked, to lend his support to a showing of Vincent's paintings. His recommendation might make all the difference."

"I see." She handed a begging and blubbering Wil one of the kittens before looking back at me. "Be careful of asking favors from strange men."

"Of course, Mevrouw Ballot."

I had, actually, asked George Seurat too, but then heard news of his death some weeks later. Another visionary gone. Another great to grieve.

"Oh, I nearly forgot!" The widow patted her pocket, then pulled out two envelopes. "I passed the postman at the gate. You have letters from Paris. One from some Matisse and one from a Goupil."

"Thank you." I fetched them from her and set them on a dry corner of the table, my heart running away with hope.

I was certain Goupil's letter meant they would

honor Theo's memory and help me, and even without Émile Bernard having to put in a word. I would rewrite his letter and leave out my request. My missive could be a letter of pure gratitude then.

Goupil!

Was not life just like that? The moment one nearly gave up on a pursuit, a breakthrough.

"Well?" The widow waited for an explanation for the letters, which I did not give, only wished the postman might one day learn to hand my letters straight to me instead of passing them along to my boarders.

"I shall read them later."

She didn't move from the threshold, even though Wil was scampering down the hallway with one of her kittens.

"Behave for Mevrouw Ballot, you hear me?" I called after him, but he was too excited to answer. I slipped into my outdoor shoes. "I best hang that laundry."

The widow's mouth puckered as if someone had stuffed a pickled herring between her lips. She couldn't believe I was so rude as not to invite her into my private business.

"Hmpf. I shall see you at dinner." She marched out with undisguised disappointment.

I picked up the basket of wet clothes and my bag of wooden pins.

I hung the pillowcases first, then moved on to the sheets, and was almost finished when Wil came looking for me. "Mama!"

"I am here, my darling."

He didn't like being without me for long. Did my little son remember how his father had disappeared from his life without warning? I told myself he couldn't possibly. He had been only a year old when Theo had died.

"Mauw. Mauw." Wil still held the kitten the widow had given him.

He ran around the garden with the cat, investigating every flower and ant, and I hung the rest of the wash on the line between two plum trees, working as quickly as I could manage, impatience driving me back into the kitchen, to those letters.

I carried a laughing Wil and sleepy kitten in the empty basket. "You are so heavy. You are growing too fast."

I set them down inside the door, and they stayed right there, Wil pretending to be a boat captain and the kitten his crew. I grabbed the correspondence.

Oh, I should have waited. I should have lived longer in that pocket of joyful expectation. My hopes evaporated with the first sentence.

We regretfully inform you… Goupil's letter began. And the message did not improve the further I read. I sank onto a chair.

Goupil refused to represent Vincent. And if the place where I had the most personal connection wouldn't help me, then nobody else would either, the dark voice of despair whispered.

The rough sounds of the handsaw died away in the back room, replaced by the soft blows of the rubber mallet. *Thump, thump, thump*, like a heartbeat, *thump, thump, thump.*

I wanted to cry, but I could not cry with Janus there.

And not in front of Wil either, although he was half-asleep in the basket.

I opened Matisse's letter next. I should have thrown it into the fire instead. *Tarnation and damn.*

I peeled the onions, sunk in my own misery until Anna walked through the door again.

She listened to the thumping in the back room. "He is still here." Then she said, "I saw the postman hand Mevrouw Ballot some letters while I stopped to chat with the milliner on the corner. Good news?"

"Goupil is sending back the paintings I shipped them, asking me not to send more."

"I'm so sorry, Jo. And after all Theo did for them. All those years of work and the money they earned off his back."

Her sympathetic outrage was a balm to my battered soul.

"I also had a letter from Matisse." I could barely repeat the words. "He has been traveling, retracing Vincent's steps. They had been friends in Paris. Anyway, he found one of Vincent's paintings in Arles, the portrait of Dr. Rey. Vincent painted it as payment for the doctor for treating him after his unfortunate ear incident."

"Oh?"

"Matisse bought the portrait."

"The doctor didn't like it?"

My eyelashes trembled with outrage. "Dr. Rey's mother has been using it to patch a hole in her chicken coop."

"Oh, Jo."

"I cannot give up," I said before Anna could suggest just that. "I have to keep going."

"But what else can you do? Paris is too far. How can you fight war from a distance?"

"You are right. Paris is out of my reach now. I must look closer." I sank back into my chair, and she sat next to me, our chairs turned together. An idea blossomed slowly in my mind. "Who better to appreciate Vincent's talent than the Dutch, the Netherlands, the country of his birth? I shall start over right here."

"In Bussum?" Anna drew back. "Of course, Jan makes do, but Bussum is no center of the arts. If Vincent was too advanced for Paris to appreciate him, then how will he be received here? Even Jan has some trouble, and he paints portraits, which are easier to sell. The rich tend to be in love with themselves, he says. And yet his paintings cannot pay the bills. He has to teach too, and sell his poetry when he can."

"Maybe not Bussum." Inspiration struck me. "But how about The Hague? Theo managed to include Vincent's work in exhibits in The Hague, twice. They must remember him."

Anna gave my suggestion several seconds of careful consideration. "Jan has a good friend there.

Richard Roland Holst, a commissioned artist. He painted a mural in The Hague."

My heart thrilled. "Then he has influence."

"You should write him a letter. And I shall also have Jan write a recommendation." My friend's smile was the very smile of spring. She stood, tall and confident, ready to go into battle on my behalf.

I stood with her and hugged her fiercely before I let her go.

Wil tottered over. Our voices must have woken him. He left the kitten behind in the basket this time. "Sasa?"

I looked from him to Anna. "Where is Saskia?"

I had never seen anyone turn so white, so fast. "I left her at the milliner's—"

And then she ran.

I watched her from the window, patting Wil's head. The milliner was a mother of four, her two older daughters always in attendance at the shop with her, learning the trade. I had no doubt sweet Saskia had been sufficiently fussed over and spoiled in Anna's absence.

I picked up my little son. "She will be fine. But I am glad you remembered her."

"Sasa love."

"I know, my sweet. Now, how about you finish your nap?"

He scrambled toward the kitten in the basket.

"How about you finish your nap in your own bed? You can take the kitten with you."

The smile he gifted me held more sunshine than

any artist could ever capture. Its brightness warmed my heart. However badly I stumbled with everything else, at least I was succeeding at motherhood. My son was a happy child.

I carried him up to our bedroom while he cradled the kitten. We passed by painting after painting, my conversation with Anna echoing in my mind. *The Netherlands. The Hague. Vincent, a celebrated genius in his own land.*

"This new path feels right," I told my son. "I only wish I'd thought of it sooner."

Holst had to have the right connections. He would champion Vincent. Why would he not, his own countryman?

I smiled and kissed Wil's head. "I think we might be on the brink of success."

As soon as I settled my son down, I went back downstairs and wrote Holst a heartfelt letter. I ran down the street to give it to the postman.

And then I waited for the response, holding my breath.

CHAPTER TWENTY-FIVE

Emsley

Trey hadn't come back. The second time the doorbell rang after my investor presentation, it was food delivery.

Our Russian feast included salad olivier, borscht, pelmeni (the Russian version of tortellini), blini (crepe with smoked salmon), beef stroganoff, pirogi, golubtsy (stuffed cabbage), and plov (a rice and meat dish). Sergei had been right—*spectacular*. Dear Russian food, where have you been all my life?

"When you're at the point where you need legal advice for your agency, let me know," Bram told Monique next to him. "I have a couple of friends who might be able to help." He handed over a card.

"Thanks."

Sergei looked at me across the table. "Would you and Trey own the LA and New York offices jointly?"

"No. Think of the two companies as two restaurants in the same franchise. But I'm taking the client list. And initially I might borrow some employees. I need the IT staff to set me up here. I'll negotiate that into the contract."

That brought more questions, and some excellent suggestions. I was having dinner with my new investors. Except, it felt as if I were having dinner with new friends, even if the conversation mostly revolved around business.

Monique had to leave first, had another modeling gig early in the morning. Then Strena said goodbye. And then Sergei drove Bram Sr. home because he had to pick up some antique books from Bram Sr.'s apartment.

"I'll help you clean up." Bram collected the empty containers for the garbage.

I stashed the leftovers in the fridge in the kitchenette.

Lai Fa refused cleanup duty point-blank. She supervised from her kitchen nest, an old cookie tin lined with a towel.

"How did you meet Trey?" Bram asked.

"Stanford, grad school, through his roommate, Christopher." A sun-bleached surfer dude who sat next to me in Econ Stats. "I liked Chris. But then Diya, my best friend, met him. She said it was love at first sight. A week after I introduced them, they were officially a couple. A week after that, we all went out, including Chris's roommate, Trey. Trey asked for my number. Maybe it was just convenient." I considered the possibility for the first time. "Two sets of best friends."

Peep. Lai Fa hopped out of her cookie tin, pecked at a dark spot on the tile, then hopped back in and settled down again.

Bram leaned against the counter. "Is this her coop?"

"I have nests set up for her on every floor. She's a roamer." So far, the cleanup had been minimal and well worth the company. I laid the damp dishcloth over the back of the barstool next to me. "I want to apologize to you. I was rude earlier in the week. You were trying to help me, and I kept brushing you off."

"The investment I pledged to Ludington's is not conditional on the two of us spending time together."

"I didn't think it was."

Bram watched me as closely as if he had to write a legal brief about me later. He didn't say anything. He waited until I found the right words and managed to put them in the right order.

"When I first met you, you wore a wedding ring. And then all of a sudden, you weren't wearing a wedding ring."

"You figured I was an opportunistic bastard."

"I shouldn't have jumped to conclusions."

"It's understandable. You don't know me that well." He picked up a bottle of water from the counter, then he put it back down. He rubbed a hand over his face. "My wife, Tessa, died two years ago."

"I'm sorry. Sergei told me when he was here yesterday. But just that," I hurried to add. "Nothing more. I wasn't trying to pry into your private life, I swear."

"It's not a secret." He picked up the bottle again. "She went on a girls' ski weekend to Colorado and broke her leg. A blood clot traveled into her lungs on the flight home." Bram's tone was rough, as if the words had sandpapered a layer off his vocal cords. "She was gone by the time the plane landed." He drank.

His wife's death explained why he knew so much about grief. What he'd said when Violet had died, about the train of life running out of tracks, hadn't just been a sentiment he'd heard somewhere. He understood loss on a personal level.

"I'm sorry." I didn't know what else to say.

I'd already said too much. I'd admitted that I'd been holding him off because I'd thought he was married. My attraction to him was out in the open. I'd admitted that I kept track of his marital status, that I'd asked his cousin about him. I might as well have told him I'd been nursing a secret crush on him since we'd met.

We were standing too close to each other in the small kitchenette. My heart beat too fast. I stepped back.

Bram stepped after me, refusing the distance between us. "When Trey was here, I meant what I said. Except one thing. You can't be my client. You're going to have to work with Adele. I have a nonprofessional interest in you. I don't want to be breaking any codes of ethics."

My back hit the wall. A tingling warmth spread through my body. "Adele is great."

Silence. Then more silence. I couldn't look away from him.

"I'm ready to move forward," he said seriously, with a finality, like only a lawyer could, like his words would be entered into court records. "How do you feel about going on a coffee date with me?"

Did he say date, *or did I hear what I wanted to hear?* "Sounds like it's pouring outside." Then common sense caught up with me. "You didn't mean right now."

Of course, he didn't. Way to look overeager.

"I know just the place. Unless it's too late for you for caffeine?"

"I could drink caffeine at midnight and sleep like a baby."

He popped a pod into the coffeemaker on the counter. When, in a minute, the coffee was done, he made another one—sugar, cream—he remembered what I liked. "Follow me."

Surprise, I followed him.

"The basement?" But I went after him, down the stairs.

He headed straight for the carousel. "I've been dying to check if it works."

"What if we break it?"

"At worst, we trip the circuit. I asked Sergei what would happen if someone were to turn it on, *theoretically*. He said sitting on it is fine, but nothing wild. He also said, if we damage his baby, he'll murder us in our sleep."

"That sounds like Sergei."

Bram went around to the back wall and plugged in a thick cable. "I knew I saw a 220V outlet over here the other day."

I gripped my cup, too nervous to even sip my coffee. The lights flickered on first. Wurlitzer-style music filled the basement. Then the horses lurched forward. "I can't believe it's working."

Bram looked inordinately pleased. "My grandfather told me he'd seen it down here at a party, fully functional. He remembers a billiards table and a jukebox too, among other entertainment. And a movie theater popcorn machine." He checked around. "Wonder where they went?"

"Sometimes Violet sold things to buy art supplies for her students."

Bram held out his hand. His grip was warm and gentle.

I followed him onto the slowly moving carousel. "Horse or chariot?"

"It's easier to make out in a chariot." He drew me to the nearest one and helped me in.

Then he left me. He crossed the basement to the light switch by the stairs, and a sudden darkness fell.

My heart pounded. "Don't trip on anything."

"I'm here." He hopped onto the platform behind me and took his seat. "How's this?"

"Magical."

The basement was black around us, the carousel's small color bulbs the only light.

"Like a fairy tale." I set my mug on the flat front edge of the chariot, leaning back in the seat.

He paired his cup with mine, slid closer, and put his arm around me. Our surroundings were invisible. The entire world outside the two of us disappeared. We were alone in the night. *And Bram promised to kiss me.*

"How are you coping?" he asked. "Beyond the present moment. It's been a rough week."

"I miss Violet so much. I'm heartbroken. And freaked out. Everything's happening too fast. I'm starting a new company. In New York."

"I have faith in you. If I didn't, I wouldn't have invested. You'll figure it all out."

"How do you know?"

"You figured it out the first time around, when you left New York and went to LA."

"I think you should kiss me."

The fairy lights reflected in his eyes. "Should I?"

"The suspense is killing me."

He rubbed his thumb over my shoulder. Then he leaned in.

CHAPTER TWENTY-SIX

Johanna

October 1891, The Hague, Netherlands

I refused to allow Vincent's art to be consigned to the trash heap of history. I was going boldly out into the world and fighting like the Amazons of ancient myth. Or, at least, fighting the crowd on the platform at the train station at The Hague.

"Pardon me. I must go through."

I traveled to ask Holst for his support, determined to gain it before the day was over, but as I reached the street at last, I thought again about Gauguin's unread letter in my bag.

I had written to Paul Gauguin, the artist friend with whom Vincent had shared the yellow house in Arles, for help before I'd given up on France. He had never replied, and I thought he might have sailed back to Martinique to paint its saronged women.

When we had last met, he'd talked about moving to the islands for good.

I had mostly forgotten about him until his letter arrived just as I had been rushing off to catch the train.

No matter what his response was, I feared I might not be able to manage my reaction, so I hadn't dared to read it among my fellow passengers. I didn't want to weep—either with relief or desperation—in front of strangers.

Yet, what if the response was positive? I could use it to bolster my argument with Holst.

See? Prominent French artists are arranging an exhibit and including Vincent. Surely The Hague should do the same, or risk people thinking the esteemed gate-keepers here do not know great art when they see it.

A servant pushed past me, loaded with baggage. "Out of the way!" he shouted at the half a dozen street children who were hacking wrinkled newspapers. Then to me: "Excuse me, madam."

I moved aside, shifting my heavy bag from one hand to the other. One thing was certain, I could not read the letter whilst standing on a corner, for the same reasons I could not read it on the train.

Especially, if it was another rejection. I might curse out loud. I wished I could ask Theo how he had handled being rebuffed over and over. He had managed, always, to stay strong. He had never lost his faith.

I missed him so much, my soul ached. Thinking of him brought to mind the perfect place to read the letter. I lurched into action and immediately bumped into a man who was stepping around me since I'd been standing still. "Oh, pardon me." Then I raised my gaze to his face. "Janus?" I blinked at the Bussum village carpenter. "What are you doing here?"

He snatched his hat from his head, color tinting his cheeks. "I am p...picking up tools. I snapped my b...best carving gouge last week." We took advantage of a lull in traffic and crossed the street. He had a rolled-up newspaper tucked into his pocket, and it kept catching on his sleeve, so he switched it to the other side. "Where is Wil?"

"Anna is watching him for the day."

A coach thundered past behind us. I had to duck a lady's parasol; Janus had to stop to allow a young boy and his coal cart to pass by.

"Too many p...people," Janus muttered. "You came to talk to that Holst fellow?"

I patted my carpet bag. "I brought him a couple of small paintings."

"From the ones I framed?"

Heavens, no. Frames would have made the weight unmanageable.

"The one with the sprig of almond flowers in a glass, and Gauguin's portrait." To better remind Holst that well-regarded artists in France considered Vincent their equal. Now, if I could add a favorable letter from Gauguin to that. "Theo always talked to people in person." Yet all this time, I had been sending letters and drawings and paintings in my stead. No wonder I'd received so many rejections. I was determined to change that. "He always said rapport was important."

I mentioned Theo in conversations with Janus often, to make sure he understood that my husband still lived in my heart. "Before Holst, I thought I would walk the polder along Trekweg Road, by the old canal. Do you know how I could reach it from here?"

"I can show you. After the train, I wouldn't mind some sea air." Janus held out a hand. "May I?"

I let him take my bag, and thanked him for his assistance. My wrist ached from scrubbing the floors the day before, and the heavy bag was doing the sore ligaments no favors. A family of five had moved in, a lot of work, but I was earning sufficient income at last.

Janus and I talked about the family and the work that needed to be done at the villa, until we reached the sea.

"It's nice to have sunny days like this in October." I barely needed my wool shawl. "The Americans call it Indian Summer." I'd learned that from Frederik van Eeden when I had last visited him and Martha to borrow a new batch of books from their library.

"My Catholic grandmother used to call it St. Luke's Little Summer," Janus said as we passed a couple of seagulls fighting over an empty crab shell. "Why Trekweg Road?"

"When Theo was fifteen, he came here with Vincent." I couldn't visit the polder with my beloved, but I could walk with the ghost of his memories. "After Vincent dropped out of school, their uncle helped him into a job in The Hague. Theo told me they walked here, in the rain. Somewhere here on the polder, they swore to support each other always."

Vincent had taken Theo outside the city, to this land made by human hands, reclaimed from the sea with dikes and dams and draining—a perpetual task, for the sea would always fight to claim it back. *Land in constant danger.*

"Sometimes I think Vincent was Theo's polder. Theo tried to reclaim him over and over from malaise and dissatisfaction and even madness, always hoping to restore Vincent to happiness."

Yet, at the end, Theo hadn't been able to reclaim his brother. And the bullet that killed Vincent killed Theo too. This I knew for certain.

And now here I am, fighting to reclaim both men from a world that would too easily forget them. This was my atonement.

I breathed the air Theo and Vincent had breathed. I walked the very ground. I let the mud stick to my boots, because the same mud had stuck to theirs.

Janus walked beside me, a quiet companion. He didn't seek my attention. He was content to allow me to feel what I had come here to feel.

We walked to the nearest windmill that spun tirelessly, pumping water. Vincent had reminisced to Theo about it in one of his letters.

My throat burned. "They used to sell milk and fried eels."

Now the windmill's door was locked, the faded sign hanging on its last remaining nail.

"It's difficult to run a successful business," I mused. "Even for something as basic as food, which everyone needs every day." How much more difficult, then, to sell art?

I imagined myself in the little windmill shop, selling Vincent's paintings to passersby. Except, his art wasn't like milk and eels, was it? Once the collection was gone, it could not be replenished.

My little son's heritage would be gone.

Vincent's paintings would be dispersed, one by one, into private homes. Wil might not even remember them when he grew up. We might never see any of them again. And neither would the world.

What would happen to Vincent's legacy that Theo had so wanted to preserve? How I wished he were with me, that he could explain things to me.

I headed to the bench where the brothers might have sat. "A letter arrived as I was leaving. I brought it with me. Would you mind if I read it?"

"I will walk around the m…mill. The old joint work on the sail stock looks interesting." Janus set my bag next to me, then lumbered away.

I dug out Gauguin's tardy response with a surge of optimism. He hadn't been ignoring me. He'd probably been traveling and only recently received my note. He must still think fondly of Vincent. And he would certainly feel some gratitude toward Theo. Theo had bought several of Gauguin's paintings simply to support him. Gaugin would help me.

Even if the letter contained but a few vague promises and some friendly praise of Vincent—which, surely, good manners required—it might be enough to bolster my case with Holst.

I drew my lungs full of salt air, then unfolded the paper.

Dear Madame Van Gogh,

Thank you for remembering me. Unfortunately... You know how he never took my advice... stubborn...most resistant to constructive criticism...

Anger propelled me to my feet. I ripped the letter apart and tossed it into the wind, satisfied when a downdraft slammed the pieces into the mud.

I would not admit defeat. Not on this piece of land that symbolized Dutch ingenuity and persistence. I refused to fail.

Janus rounded the windmill and saw me standing. "Ready?"

As we walked back, a gust whipped around us from the sea, nearly knocking me into him. I put more distance between us, then realized the gesture for what it was, a cowardly act. A little distance, little hints that my heart would never be free. Honest words were what the man needed. If I were to be like the Amazons, I had to have courage.

I faced him. "My wish is to dedicate my life to Vincent's legacy and my husband's memory."

He nodded, looking away.

When, minutes later, he left me in front of Holst's office, his somber gaze carried understanding, no anger or blame, only acceptance. He was a fine man. I walked inside, praying he would find a woman who could love him back.

I hefted my bag and strode straight to the secretary behind the desk, a young man who couldn't have been long out of school. "I would like to speak with Meneer Holst."

"Is he expecting you?"

"I am a friend of Jan Veth from Bussum."

The young man sauntered away, his back straight with a sense of his own importance.

I waited, willing myself into a hopeful mood. Richard Roland Holst was a respected Dutch artist. He would recognize talent when he saw it. And once Vincent's paintings had Holst's support, doors would begin to open.

As soon as I was seated in Holst's office, however, I knew the visit would not go well. He looked at me as one looks at a bug found among the bedsheets.

"Mevrouw Van Gogh. How can I help you?" he asked in a tone of *how can I rid myself of you the quickest*.

He was a handful of years younger than me, in a handsome light suit, his face made more mature by a gentleman's mustache. His mahogany desk spoke of his importance, and so did the inlaid clock on the wall behind him. He wore a gold signet ring and a ruby pin in his cravat, the trappings of success.

"Thank you for receiving me, Meneer Holst. I understand you are a busy man. I thought, instead of waiting for you to respond to my letters, it might benefit you the most if I brought you some of Vincent van Gogh's paintings myself."

I pulled my bag onto my lap and produced the paintings, laying them on the desk in front of me, side by side, as if they were brothers.

"You can see the brilliant way the artist used light on the almond blossoms and through the glass vase, how the image makes one not only see but feel. If you would kindly champion his cause as a supporter of his art, others could see and admire his work."

Holst's face remained unchanged, as if I were selling him coal for the winter and extolling the virtues of smaller clumps versus the larger.

I would not let my desperation show. "And in Gauguin's portrait..." What could I say about it? I was hardly an expert. "Vincent painted him while Gauguin was painting pumpkins. See the flash of yellow here? I met Monsieur Gauguin myself. He most respected Vincent for his talent. The impasto work..."

Holst barely cast the paintings a glance. He stayed standing through my entreaty, enjoying his position, steepling his hands in the gesture of a professor about to correct an errant student.

"Vincent exhibited in The Hague, twice, before his death," I quickly added. "As part of group shows." Shows Theo had set up with great effort.

"I seem to remember sunflowers." Holst made a dismissive gesture. "Garish. Common. Peasant material."

"All the most exciting new artists in Paris claim him as their equal."

"How many paintings did he sell there?"

"One." Well, in Belgium, and to a friend, but the important point was that Vincent *had* sold a painting, in fact.

"And at the group shows here, in The Hague?"

I remained silent.

Holst picked up his pipe and gave his full attention to tapping it, as if he couldn't bear to look at the paintings. "You will never sell them." He lit the tobacco. "If your dream is sudden riches," his scathing tone cut, "you might as well abandon it, madam."

"I do not wish to sell them." I had come to a decision just in that moment. Theo had been wrong to try to sell the paintings as the works of a new artist as bargains. Tastes must grow up to recognize Vincent's genius.

"I am confused." Holst took his first puff of tobacco. "What do you wish to do with them?"

"I'd like to ask you to help me arrange loaning the paintings to the best museums for exhibits."

"To be hung next to the works of the masters?" He laughed. "You know, I almost admire you for your audacity, madam."

I fisted my hands in the folds of my dress. "I want Vincent's works in their rightful place."

"In one of your letters," Holst sucked on his pipe, "you mentioned over a hundred works. The canvases stretched? Framed?"

"All of them stretched, and about half of them framed." At great cost.

"I could take them." His expression turned magnanimous. "For the cost of materials. I could scrape the canvases and reuse them, although, all the impasto would require considerable work."

More work than it was worth, his tone implied.

"I would like to be able to help you," he added, "but I am afraid that is the most help I can offer."

The inlaid clock on the wall ticked loudly in the pause that followed his words.

I had to break my silence, lest he thought I was considering his ridiculous and insulting suggestion.

"Thank you for the offer." I stood. "But no."

"My dear Mevrouw Van Gogh," Holst said as we faced off. "You are a charming little woman, aren't you? And such enthusiasm for the arts. Most commendable. Yet, I fear you are blinded by sentimentality. I understand your sorrow over the loss of your husband and his brother. That in your distraught feminine state of mind you misjudge the art is certainly forgivable and most understandable. But as an expert myself, you see, I cannot afford to make the same mistake—"

I barely heard the rest.

He finished, watching me with a speculative gleam in his eyes. "One hears rumors about the circumstances of Vincent's death. And his brother's as well. I have wondered…"

Was he, and as shamelessly as that, fishing for gossip?

I grabbed the paintings, wanting nothing more than to shove them into my bag as quickly as I could, but I drew a deep breath and handled them with care. I barely said farewell as I stormed out of there.

All the way that morning from Bussum to The Hague, in the crowded, smelly train car, I had been so sure Holst would help. I had envisioned returning to Bussum triumphant. I had hoped to claim Vincent's great art for the world and justify Theo's belief in his brother. But, like Gauguin, Holst refused my pleas, and not only that. He hadn't merely rejected me, he'd humiliated me and enjoyed the process.

My face burned. I stumbled across the marble foyer and out onto the street. While I had been inside, St. Luke's Little Summer had ended; the sun had disappeared. Cold wind whipped my skirt around my legs. I walked forward, carrying my bag with one hand, holding my wool shawl tightly closed with the other.

Janus found me on the train.

"How did it go with the Holst fellow?"

I simply shook my head, too dispirited for words.

He sat down across from me and pulled his rolled-up newspaper from his pocket. "Would you like to read it?"

"Thank you."

The front page featured a man's picture. *American Inventor Thomas Edison Demonstrates His Kinetoscope for the National Federation of Women.*

"What is a kinetoscope?" I asked Janus.

"An app… apparatus that produces moving pictures. A b…box if you will, with a hole. You p… press your eye to the hole and view a photograph inside, but the p…people in the photograph move."

Such a marvel, and demonstrated to a *women's club*. While in the Netherlands, I was ridiculed, on account of my gender, for daring to have an opinion.

I turned the page, but instead of the next article, all I could see were the bright paintings I so treasured, sinking into a dark sea of obscurity.

If even our own countrymen refused to recognize Vincent's genius, then I would turn elsewhere yet. I was going to… I would…

I looked Janus in the eye and announced my next grand plan. "I'm going to America."

I would not abandon Vincent.

CHAPTER TWENTY-SEVEN

Emsley

"So…" Sergei watched me over Violet's boxes of gallery flyers. He'd come over with his team first thing Friday morning. "My cousin finally found his balls and seduced you."

I sipped my coffee, then bit into my cream cheese bagel, courtesy of Bram, who sent them via Sergei. "You don't know that."

"Listen, I'm a huge fan of borscht. But I've never seen a smile that big on anyone's face the morning after beet soup."

"Maybe it was the pirogi."

"Maybe it was Bram."

Workmen pushed an industrial-size trolley with the Narnia wardrobe past us, then through the open front door. I had Lai Fa locked up in the office to make sure she didn't run out into the street.

The stuffed bear was already in the moving van. *Goodbye, Tiny Tim.* I wasn't going to miss him. I would, however, miss the carousel. I had some outstandingly good memories of a blue-and-white chariot.

Sergei picked through another box. "I might have a buyer for the Herschell."

The two restoration experts he'd brought were disassembling the ride downstairs, since it could only be brought up piecemeal. We couldn't puzzle out why Violet had it down there. It would have to remain one of her mysteries.

"What's the offer?"

"Too soon to talk money. I haven't even shown him pictures yet. I want to wait until our beauty is in a showroom, cleaned up, fully restored, under the right lights. I want love at first sight." He snapped a picture of the red-and-blue flyer in his hand. "If I sell the carousel for a good price, am I still in the running? You'll consider being my second wife?"

"Tempting, but no."

"Bram, that dirty bastard."

I laughed. "He didn't do anything dirty. I swear."

We'd kissed. All right, more than kissed. He'd had his hand under my shirt. He'd been... I didn't have the words to explain.

Diya was a great cook. She could make a gourmet meal out of anything. There could be a carrot and two potatoes in the fridge, and Diya would come up with a three-course meal. She said she'd learned the skill from her immigrant grandmother.

In the same vein, Bram could make a full orgy out of kissing and second base. My brain fogged up thinking about him.

Sergei muttered. "Doesn't even know how to properly seduce a woman."

I didn't contradict him, because my evening with Bram was private, all ours, sparkling shiny, a hot ember in my heart. "And you're an expert?"

He thought about it. "I'm better with men than with women. But I'm pretty good at both. It's like being ambidextrous."

"A born-with talent?"

"Exactly. This is why I like you. You get me."

"Friends?"

"If you must choose Bram." He heaved a dramatic sigh. "Anybody surprised, raise their hand."

Neither of us did.

He shot me a pointed look, but then he grinned. "Shouldn't you be upstairs working on building your new business?"

"I'm nervous about the carousel."

"Nothing bad is going to happen to it. Shoo." He waved me away. "For love's sake. I'm a professional."

He was. I trusted him. "If you don't mind holding down the fort here, I'd like to go for a walk."

The dangers of transporting the carousel wasn't the only thing preoccupying my mind. After I'd woken up, I ferreted out Senator Wertheim's current address. The distinguished gentleman from Mass-achusetts had chosen to live out his retirement in Manhattan.

I'd told myself I was not going to see him.

I was usually good with keeping resolutions. Unless they were *I'm not going to have that second cupcake.* Or, apparently, *I'm not going to get arrested.*

I grabbed my bag from the balustrade and left Sergei to his work. If Jo Bonger could march off and face dragons, then so could I. What I read nightly about her kept returning to me during the day. She came to America. That would explain how the little green book ended up in New York. Maybe she'd found Vincent's secret love child and brought him or her too. I was still holding on to the daydream that Vincent was my great-great-great-grandfather.

I thought a lot about Jo.

Her struggles. Violet's. Mine.

Johanna Bonger lived a hundred years before me.

And yet…

The more things changed, the more they stayed the same.

Half an hour of brisk walking carried me to the right building. Then all I had to do was get past the royal-butler-look-alike doorman, Fred, according to his name tag.

"I'm here to see Mr. Wertheim. Emsley Wilson. Violet Velar's granddaughter."

Fred's frown said he judged me for my yoga

pants, but he called up. "Mr. Wertheim would be happy to see you. Apartment thirty-six."

The elevator had enough brass to outfit a brass band and enough mirrors to make me rethink the yoga pants and agree with Fred. I tugged my sweater down before I knocked on door #36.

Shuffle, shuffle inside, then the door opened. "Miss Wilson."

"Mr. Wertheim."

He let me in, sporting a black eye and walking with a stiff gait. His apartment had that musty old-man smell.

"No need to apologize." He gestured me toward a brown leather chesterfield. "Accidents happen."

I stayed where I was. "I'm not here to apologize. I'm here to tell you that I know what you did to my grandmother."

He hesitated. "I'm not sure I follow."

"Nineteen sixty-five. New Year's Eve party at the Vanderbilt Mansion. You and Violet in the library."

A quick glint in his eyes. "What about it?"

"You should have gone to prison for that."

He inspected me with more care, measuring me up. "I assure you, the act was entirely consensual. You can spare me your MeToo nonsense. I no longer have a political career. You can't blackmail me over five minutes of fun I had five decades ago." He huffed. "I supported her. I went to several of her gallery openings."

"How much she must have loved that. Did you buy her art?"

He flattened his lips.

I wanted to punch him in the mouth. "You support an artist by buying their work."

"You want money?"

"I'm not here to blackmail you. I'm here because I didn't want you to die thinking that you got away with what you did without anyone knowing what a piece-of-shit slime you are. I know, and so do others."

He gaped, his head a hue of purple that reminded me of one of Violet's paintings.

According to his online bio, he'd never had children. I could have told him that he had a daughter, that I was his granddaughter. I didn't.

Violet had told him nothing, and I was going to respect her wishes. I left Wertheim without looking back. I was finished with him. I never wanted to think about him again.

Outside, I whispered to the cloudless sky. "I had to come. I hope you don't mind, Violet." And I walked away with a spring in my step.

Back at the house, I yelled down to the basement for Sergei. "I'm back!"

Then I sprinted upstairs. As soon as I opened the office door, Lai Fa rushed over, flapping her wings and stretching her neck.

"Miss me?"

I sat at Violet's desk and lifted her to my lap. She hopped on the table, then walked up my arm, and settled into the crook of my neck. She was a tiny fluff of love, but she made a difference. Almost as if love had no size. Like when you had a candle—no matter how small the flame, you were no longer in the dark.

"I love you too. Let's work."

Peep.

I separated my challenges into two categories: Ludington's business and problems created by the sale of the house falling through. I was good at being methodical. Bram was right. I could do this.

"Let's tackle the house first."

I opened the packet of documents I'd received from Bram the first time we'd met and paged through the papers until I found the summary of the mortgage.

Violet had inherited the house from her parents, but she mortgaged it over the years to fund various initiatives in the arts. If Violet believed in a cause, she would do everything she could to help.

The estimated value of the house—the expected sales price once it finally sold—was about the same as the mortgage plus her medical bills, with enough left over for that last-minute NYU scholarship. I emailed the dean and explained that there might be a short delay.

Next, I checked the mortgage. I had sufficient emergency funds to make payments for several months. "The house is great. Right?"

Peep.

"Exactly. Beatriz will find another buyer before we run out of money."

That eased my mind. I felt confident by the time I

dialed the accounting department at the stroke care center.

"Oh, you're Violet's granddaughter!" a woman called Maribel cooed. "I'm so sorry about your loss, honey. How can I help?"

"My grandmother had an agreement with the center. She was going to pay off her bills when her house sold."

"Yes?"

"But then payment came due immediately on her death. And the house sale fell through. I'd like to work out a payment plan."

Maribel's keyboard went clickety-click on the other end. "How much could you afford per month?"

"Five hundred dollars?" I put my hopes into Sergei's sales skills. "It would be only for a few months."

A second passed in silence, then another, and another. Was my offer too low? Did I offend her?

Then, before I could promise more than I might be able to deliver, she said, "How about four hundred? As you said, you'll find another buyer. Violet showed me pictures of that house. It's gorgeous. I wish I could afford it."

"So do I. Four hundred would be great. Thank you."

"You're welcome, Emsley. Did Violet ever tell you she helped my granddaughter get into the Tyler School of Art at Temple? She wrote my Gracie a refer- ence. Made a couple of calls, even."

As Sergei would say, *Anybody surprised, raise their hand.*

By the time I ended the call with Maribel, a huge load lifted from my shoulders. I was on a roll.

"Okay, Wonder Chicken. Ludington's is next."

I pulled up our last financial report and pored over spreadsheets and numbers. "We're not in great shape."

Lai Fa tilted her head in a way that said if she had a worm, she would give me half.

I moved on to human resources. "Seventeen employees."

I made a list of the people I needed to help me start up the New York office, then emailed Trey with what I wanted: IT support who could work for me remotely, etc. I also told him that if he went in the political polling direction, and if our auction-specific staff were willing to move, I wanted them with me.

And we'd share the client list.

I had his response in two minutes. *Deal.* He attached a draft agreement his attorney had drawn up.

I leaned back in my chair, if not exuberant, at least optimistic. I closed my eyes. "I miss you, Violet. I wish you were here to see me make it."

I wanted to go downstairs to see how Sergei was coming on with the carousel, but I had one last thing to do first.

I emailed Trey's contract to Adele. I copied Bram.

He immediately responded with, *Dinner after work?*

Me: *Who's cooking?*

Bram: *The Thai restaurant on the corner?*

Me: *Are we going out?*

Bram: *Either that or eat in bed.*

That last bit distracted me pretty much for the rest of the day. The man knew how to get into a woman's head.

CHAPTER TWENTY-EIGHT

Johanna
   November 1891, Bussum, Netherlands

If life was a rolling river, friendship was the life raft. Alone, I would have drowned, gone under. But when I'd nearly given up on my country, new friends found me. I stayed in Bussum. I saved the promise of America for when my little son was older.

There had to be more I could do where I was, something I hadn't thought of yet. And I was going to find it.

"I don't know how you manage it all, Jo," Jan Veth, Anna's husband, said. "But well done."

"Here, here." The small group of Dutch intellectuals filling my living room and the attached kitchen raised their glasses—Jan, Anna, Piet, Max, Antoon, Jozef, Frederik, and Seb.

"When I first assumed the running of Villa Helma, I feared I would become a domestic machine." I cut short a nervous laugh. "I thought I'd never have time to read or think of anything else but household matters again. I don't think I've written more than twice in my diary."

I stood and checked on the rather ambitious dinner I was preparing. I wanted my guests to like me and accept me as one of their own, despite my tenuous connection to their universe. I had no talent, nothing like they possessed. I felt an interloper in their circle. "But then I had a revelation."

Seb pulled his pipe out of his mouth. "And what was that?"

"If I am to become a machine, I would become the most efficient machine possible. Household chores are done twice as fast if I think of them as a dance. Remember the dances at school?" I asked Anna, who'd left her new baby daughter, Alida, with the neighbor for the first time, so she could come along with her husband.

"School dances?" A crash upstairs had Anna glancing at the ceiling. Saskia was up there with Wil, playing with the kittens in the hallway. "Heavens, they seem a million years ago. Have we ever been such silly chits? What I do remember is that those dances were a great deal more fun than any house-work I've ever done. I can't see how you draw a connection between the two."

I moved to demonstrate. "Stir the soup. One, two,

three steps to the dishcloth so I can take the apple cake out of the oven. Turn. One, two, three, four." Bend to take a lump of coal that had fallen from the pail and I had accidentally kicked into the middle of the kitchen. "Rinse my hands. Check on the soup. Needs salt. Back to the table. One, two, three."

In between sentences, I hummed a tune under my breath. "I learned to place everything at hand. The work that used to take me all day, now leaves me several free hours in the evening."

"Dare we hope you spend it resting?" Jan asked.

"I'll have you know that I read *Utamaro* by Edmond de Goncourt." I enjoyed the biography thoroughly. "Theo had a small collection of prints. Vincent copied them to learn different techniques."

"The greatest Japanese artist next to Hokusai," Jan conceded.

"I also read a new book by Oscar Browning, *Life of George Eliot*." Who'd actually been a woman, Mary Ann Evans. But while reading about the brilliant translator, poet, journalist, and novelist fed my soul, I had a need for intellectual work of my own.

I grabbed my treasure box from the top of the cupboard. "I'm still organizing Vincent's letters, but I've begun to translate too." I showed Jan the previous night's work. "A brand-new venture."

He scanned the first page and handed it along to Max, who was holding out his hand.

"For whom?" Max asked.

"An opportunity brought my way by one of Theo's uncles, translating short stories from the

French into Dutch. He has connections at De Kroniek.
I already mailed my first batch."

"Didn't you say you taught English at Utrecht
once? You should translate from English." Max
looked up from the page. "A friend sent me the
summer issues of *The Strand Magazine*. I am enjoying
a curious story about a fellow by the name of Sher-
lock Holmes, penned by Arthur Conan Doyle. Not a
literary masterpiece, by any standard, but amusing in
its own way."

"I shall happily translate anything De Kroniek
asks me to translate."

Max passed my translation to Antoon. "Very well
executed."

While Jozef and Frederik quietly read over
Antoon's shoulder, Piet, a struggling writer, pulled a
small book from his pocket.

"Look what I've brought back from England."
He brandished the volume with unbridled enthusiasm. "H Ford Hueffer's *The Shifting of the Fire*." And
then he lurched into such vigorous praise that his
cheeks flushed pink. And he went on about it at
length.

My eyes glazed over. "I quite enjoy the Scottish
authoress Mrs. Oliphant."

"Oh, sentimental drivel." The consensus from
the men.

"She turns out books like a butter churn." Piet
dismissed her. "How many novels has she now?
Eighty? A hundred?"

"Her husband was an artist."

At this, the artists in the room paid closer attention.

"Oliphant?" Seb squinted, trying to place the name. My translation was with him by then, and he handed the pages back with an approving nod.

"A stained-glass artist, but still," Anna put in. She had read the books first, then lent them to me. "And Mrs. Oliphant, what a woman! Bore six children and lost three early on." Tears gathered in her eyes. Her own daughter's birth had been difficult two months prior, and I knew how bone-deep her fear had been that the night would end in tragedy.

"When her husband became ill with consumption," I picked up the tale, "she moved to Italy with him for the climate. And there he died, leaving her without means to make her way back home. Yet she managed."

"She wrote so many novels in order to support her family." Anna glared at Piet. "And even now, after she's lost two more children, she keeps writing because she still supports her only remaining son, and also her ruined brother and his family. Now tell me women are the weaker sex."

The men fell silent at last.

I could barely speak past the tightness in my chest. "The thought that a mother could lose so many children is unbearable."

I wanted to run upstairs and check on Wil.

Piet stood and opened his book. "I must concede to the ladies." He nodded to Anna and me. "Your Mrs. Oliphant is a commendable woman. Yet we must consider quality of work as well, and not only quantity. If I may…" He began to read. *"Without the house the wind was blusteringly bringing down the few leaves that remained on the trees, skirting the north side of the park, and occasionally beating in a solid mass against the sides and windows of the house, or playing with undulating shrieks round the chimney-pots."*

He lowered the book with a dramatic shiver. "Can you not feel the cold?"

I exchanged a look with Anna, my mind still half on the unfortunate but eminently admirable Mrs. Oliphant.

Piet raised the tome again. *"The air was filled with a mighty rustling—"*

And, well, I did shriek then—much like the wind in the book—because someone pushed in the door, and a snow-covered creature appeared.

"Janus!" Wil barreled down the stairs and into him, hugging his leg, looking with childish adoration at the man who was a giant to him.

Janus ruffled Wil's hair, then, seeing the company, he snatched off his wet hat and gave an embarrassed greeting, adding, "I thought I would cut up that walnut tree the wind t…twisted out in the front yard yesterday."

"Thank you, Janus."

A squall blew snow in from the roof, and he stepped back out, closing the door behind him.

Wil looked at the closed front door, as forlorn as a child could be, then plodded up the stairs.

Piet read, *"Without the house the air was grey with*

twilight, and hazy yellow high up around the street lamps." He sighed. "*The air was gray with twilight.*" He carried his gaze around, daring us to contradict his next word. "Brilliant."

I pushed to my feet to lift the pot off the stove. "Dinner is ready."

The meal distracted Piet from his novel at last.

"Do you know what book I should like to read?" Anna asked as I served the soup. "Marie Bashkirtseff and Gustave Flaubert's letters to each other have been published. What a tragic love story."

Marie Bashkiertseff was a Ukrainian artist who'd moved to Paris. She'd died before I went to live there, but I'd heard of her from Theo's friends.

"Died too young." Piet nodded. "What was she, twenty-five?"

Somber silence settled on us once again.

Then, between two spoonfuls, Seb jumped up. "Armand Guillaumin!"

I pressed a hand to my heart. "What about him?"

He'd been Vincent's friend. Theo had sold some of his paintings.

"He won a hundred thousand francs in the French state lottery. I had a letter from him." Envy mixed into Seb's excitement. "He's quitting his job to pursue his art full-time."

The talk turned back to painting.

I enjoyed the gathering with all my heart and hoped it would be the first of many, a more than fair substitute for Theo's circle of artists in Paris. Perhaps even better, for these were all *my* friends—or in the process of becoming friends—even the sometimes pretentious Piet. He had a heart of gold, supporting his widowed sister from what small amounts he earned with his poems.

"Has Gauguin come back from Polynesia?" Jan Veth asked over apple cake, looking at me.

"I have not kept up our correspondence."

The dinner went well, yet I was distracted by the sounds of sawing outside. Janus had accepted my decision, but he was still at the villa at least once a week. Janus was the one who fixed what broke around the house, the one who helped me crate the paintings for shipping, the one who carved little animals for Wil. Every time he strode through the door, Wil ran to him as he should have been running to his own father—a stab of pain in my heart.

"I heard he's courting the milliner's eldest daughter," Anna said under her breath next to me.

Was he? I was happy for him.

Seb strode over to a crate in the corner. "And what is this?"

"Another one of Vincent's paintings. *The Wheat Fields of Auvers*. I am sending it to Amsterdam. I am certain it will find him a champion."

Jan, who'd become like another brother to me, patted my arm. "You are his champion, Jo. No one will ever care half as much for him as you do. No one knows him better. No one carries more passion for his art."

"I need an agent with clout in the business to represent Vincent. I will not be granted as much as an appointment with museum curators. What are my qualifications? None. I am a widow from Bussum who takes in boarders. I am a woman of no consequence with no relevant skills. I can't be Vincent's agent."

"Think of your Mrs. Oliphant writing her many books, doing what she must."

"She is an exceptional woman. I am not."

"All are made exceptional by necessity," Piet, the poet, put in.

Maybe he was right. I would do anything for Wil. If I had to take on a third occupation to feed him, in addition to running the boardinghouse and translating, I would. If I had to crawl on my knees to secure Wil's heritage, I would not hesitate. And if I said I would do *anything*, did that not mean that I would be willing to make myself into the kind of woman who could succeed with this quest?

"All right," I blurted. "I shall represent Vincent myself."

Eight pairs of eyes snapped to me.

Anna was the first to speak. "I'll be happy to watch Wil for you if you have to travel." She put her hand on mine and squeezed. "I tried to make you give up. I wanted to spare you the thankless work and disappointment, but I was wrong. You shall have nothing but support from me from now on."

Seb, who represented authors, asked, "And what is your strategy?"

The question immediately brought all my doubts rushing back. I stared at him, already lost.

He finished his wine and set down his glass. "In my work, I either start an author with the smaller publishers, bank some early successes, and translate that into bigger contracts at bigger places, or go straight to the top. Because once the top publisher shows interest in an author, his name is immediately made. And often, the second-largest publisher will offer an even more lucrative contract to snatch victory from his main competitor, to have that potential next bestseller for himself."

"Vincent tried for the Salon," Max said.

Seb pointed at *The Harvest*. "His work is certainly good enough for the best venues."

"Of course," Jan shot me a reassuring look, "there is nothing wrong with starting small and finding your legs. You could practice on some of the local galleries."

Gratitude filled me. I had losses, but I had not lost hope. I had been tried, but I had also been blessed. "I think..." I drew a bracing breath, my heart beating too fast. "I shall write an introductory letter to the Rijksmuseum in Amsterdam. And then follow it up with a visit. Vincent deserves the best."

"If you need help with the letter," Piet offered, pushing away his empty plate, "I can contribute a poetic turn of words here and there."

My eyes burned. "I think I shall probably need a lot of help."

Dusk began to fall outside, so I stood to light the lamps. I lit all I had, until the house was so bright, it looked as if a new age was dawning in my kitchen.

I had to say the words again. "I will be Vincent's agent." An unheard of audacity from a woman. "I can't wait to see how the gatekeepers of the art world will respond to *that*."

Anna raised her glass. "Let us drink to the battles ahead."

CHAPTER TWENTY-NINE

Emsley

"I'm sorry," Bram told me over the phone, canceling our dinner plans.

I couldn't exactly complain after having just read about Johanna and the hardships she'd faced. She postponed her trip to New York. But she did cross the ocean eventually. I googled it to be sure. I couldn't wait to read about it.

Bram said, "I'm at the emergency room with my grandfather. When he dropped to his knees at Violet's funeral, he hurt his kneecaps. Of course, he didn't tell anyone until he was in too much pain to keep faking being well."

"How bad is it?"

"The doctor is going to drain fluid from both knees. At least nothing is broken."

I was a terrible person for letting Bram's deep

voice get to me when we were talking about an emergency medical situation. And I was wrong to think about him after we hung up, but the electric buzz zipping through my body wouldn't stop. I spent half the night twisting and turning.

And the next night, and the next week.

Bram had to fly to Boston with the heirs of an international client who owned properties in multiple states. He called every day. We talked for hours. I distracted myself from missing him by working on setting up Ludington's New York branch. I reached out to clients and advised them on the location change, talked up new opportunities the city brought, assured them that we'd still be working with their Hollywood supporters. Most celebrities were bicoastal anyway.

On Saturday, I crawled out of bed at dawn. I wanted to finish a good chunk of housecleaning before Strena's show at the MoMA that afternoon.

I drank coffee, ate leftovers, took care of Lai Fa, and then I dragged myself back upstairs to pack up Violet's office. By noon, I was almost finished, everything in boxes except for the paintings on the walls. I had to buy some Bubble Wrap for those. I didn't want to damage any of the pieces.

The terrible little painting I'd found in the blue box with the old letters and the green diary, however, was another matter.

I showed it to Lai Fa. "You think cleaning the grime off might help?"

Peep.

The top three search results suggested "gentle soapy water." I carried the painting to the kitchen, Lai Fa close on my heel.

I grabbed the bottle of Dawn dish detergent.

Peep?

"If it's safe for wildlife being saved from oil spills, it's safe enough. They use it on seabirds."

That seemed to reassure her.

I cleaned one corner. The bedspread under the sleeping baby improved considerably. Encouraged by the progress, I washed away the rest of the grime.

The poor kid still looked as pale and stiff as an auction paddle. The artist didn't have much technique. I set the painting next to the sink to dry, just as the doorbell rang.

"Probably Bram."

We flew to the door, Lai Fa literally, and came face-to-face with Trey.

Determination flattened his lips as he looked past me. "Are you alone?"

"If this is about business, you need to talk to my lawyer."

His gaze snapped to mine. "Do you want me to leave Diya?"

The question surprised me so much that I drew back, which he took as an invitation.

He strode past me, and when he saw that nobody else was there, he whipped around. "I need you."

A few weeks ago, I would have fallen for that line and the desperate tone with which it was delivered. But I had changed since Violet's death. I wasn't quite a warrior woman riding her horse naked into battle, but I was more than I had been when I'd left LA.

"You need me for what?"

"Look, Diya and I… I'm sorry."

I shook off the hand he put on my arm. "No."

He bent his head in that looming-over-people stance of his. "When did you become such a bitch? You used to be a nice girl."

"I used to trust you." I flashed him a sweet, sweet smile. "Then I wised up."

"You're being vindictive. You owe me another chance."

"I don't owe you anything. Get out of my house."

"You're still grieving. You're not thinking straight. Let me explain."

"I swear, if you're not out of here in the next thirty seconds…"

He opened the door, but stopped on the threshold. "You could marry me. Then we'd own both Ludington's offices together. We could open a third one in Seattle. Expand. I feel like with you, I could build something. I'm talking about serious money."

My phone rang. For the moment, I ignored it. I might not have known yet how my future would unfold, but I knew one thing: Trey was *not* going to buy me. I put a hand to his chest and shoved him out. "Go away."

I closed the door and locked it. *Bam.* Spanked and

walking away red assed, as Sergei would say. I luxu-
riated in the moment another second before I picked
up the phone.

Strena said, "Vivian has the flu. I need you to
stand in as her replacement."

The gears grinded in my brain as it switched
tracks. "I can't be naked in front of people."

"It's not *naked*. It's art."

I thought of Violet's *Excalibur*. The woman in the
painting didn't live in her comfort zone. She was
fierce. She didn't wait for things to happen to her. She
rode headlong into battle.

Had I not always wanted to be like Violet? Before
the brain cells responsible for common sense could
protest, I blurted, "All right."

Jo Bonger and I were going for it. All the way.

"Thank you. You need to shower and shave,"
Strena rushed on. "Everything. And no body lotion,
or the sugar mixture won't stick. Come as soon as
you can. Don't drink anything. The show can't be
stopped for a bathroom break. I'll put your name on
the list at the staff entrance in the back."

Click.

Wait. What? Wait!

I shot a desperate look at Lai Fa. "Is this too soon
to regret that I said yes?"

Because I did regret it. Truly. Sincerely. Immediately. What had I been thinking? I couldn't do this.

I called Strena back, but the line was busy. I called
her again two minutes later, from the kitchen, after

serving Lai Fa some chicken feed on an old porcelain plate. My call went to voicemail.

"She's probably busy setting up for the show." Or maybe her battery had gone dead. I didn't leave a message.

"I have to go over. I don't want Strena to be waiting for me, then if I don't show up, it'll be too late to call in someone else."

I was sweaty and dirty from the day's cleaning, so I ran upstairs to shower. A glance at the mirror over the sink set me at ease. No way would Strena put me in her show. The bags under my eyes were so big, they exceeded airline carry-on limits.

I shaved and used no lotion, in case somehow my participation became a matter of life and death, or tranquilization was possible. I skipped my second cup of coffee for the day.

On the way to the museum in the Uber—leaving Lai Fa the run of the house—I felt fairly safe. Strena would take one look at me and seat me in the audience. She was an artist. She had to have some care for aesthetics.

"Strena has a show today," the driver said as he drove past the endless line of people waiting up front.

"You know Strena?"

"She's a celebrity." He pulled over. "Why do you think half of New York is here?"

I walked to the service door in a daze.

"Name?" A college girl in a NYU T-shirt asked, wielding a clipboard.

"Emsley Wilson."

She checked me off. "Oh, you're a model. Do you think Strena will give autographs to the staff afterwards?"

"I honestly don't know. I'm just a last-second replacement."

Another girl, same T-shirt, led me inside, bouncing down the hallway. "You are sooo lucky that you work with her."

We hurried down narrow hallways, arriving at a door that had a sheet of printer paper taped to it with STRENA and the date.

"Good luck!" The girl bounced away with a manic wave.

I almost told her to wait for me. I was only going to be there a minute, just to tell Strena I couldn't do the show. *This is so not me. I'm sorry. I'm not Violet.*

I opened the door.

Explain. Apologize. Run.

That was the plan. Except, I didn't see Strena anywhere.

Monique, in a red silk robe, flew over. "Come on. Makeup. You're late." She dragged me to a clothes rack. "Strip." And then she pointed at a box of white robes next to the rack. "Hurry."

"I don't think—"

"No time to think. You have to do it. There's no one else."

Someone called her name from the other side of the room. She squeezed my hand in encouragement and took flight again.

I drew a deep diaphragm breath. Then another. By the third, I accepted that I couldn't leave without messing up Strena's big night. I fixed Violet's painting, *Excalibur*, firmly in my mind.

"Could you please point me to the dressing room?" I asked the next person who zipped by.

"This *is* the dressing room. You okay?"

No. Not okay. Not even remotely right.

I turned my back to the others. *Better.* I quickly changed into a robe before I could freak out completely. I'd barely tied my belt before Strena sailed through a set of double doors in the back. She scanned the models one by one, nodding.

Then her gaze snapped to me. "Makeup!"

A woman in her forties materialized from thin air, black yoga pants, fitted black T-shirt, shaved head. "Tiana." She shoved a rolling chair in my direction. "Sit."

"I didn't have a good night," I told Strena. "I'm sure you wouldn't—"

"Last-second jitters. Everyone has them. Did you remember not to use body lotion?"

"What about my face?"

"I never obstruct the models' faces. The world has done that long enough, emphasizing women's bodies, as if our faces are interchangeable."

The makeup artist dabbed a cooling cream under my eyes that tingled. "Hemorrhoid ointment," she said. "Brings down swelling."

Strena patted my shoulder. "You're perfect."

I was bewildered. "We've never practiced."

"All I need you to do is stand still. The other models will go through their routine. Don't try to copy them. I'll adjust."

"But—"

She strode away. "Time to move, people!"

Tiana held up three caramel triangles. She immediately started squeezing adhesive on the first from a bottle she pulled from her pocket.

I scampered back. "What happened to the bikinis?"

"Those are for practice." Her smile was nothing but patience. "This is the real deal. Let's hop to it. Breasts first."

She was so no-nonsense, I didn't know how to protest.

Violet would do this in a blink. I opened the robe on the right side first, then the left. Tiana pressed the coverings in place.

"Stay still for a few seconds, please. It's fast acting." She covered me up so I wouldn't have to move my arms.

"Thanks."

"Do you need to go to the bathroom?"

"I'm good."

"Okay. Legs apart."

If I weren't so dazed from lack of sleep and lack of coffee, I would probably have run away. As it was, I seemed to be always a step behind. By the time I could have worked up any serious objections, my last piece of covering was in place.

Who was this person letting someone do this to her?

Long before I could answer that question, Tiana said, "Okay. Go, go, go."

I gingerly followed the others past the same double doors Strena had come through earlier. I couldn't catch my breath. I was being swept away by a hurricane. Strena lived up to her name.

The large space was set up like a circular theater, about a thousand empty seats in concentric circles, a small round stage in the middle, on wheels. In the middle of the platform stood a metal volcano, melted sugar trickling down its side into a basin, then somehow pumped back up so it could circulate. Strena's wand rested on the edge of the crater.

She clapped her hands. "Models, take your places."

Twelve women, including me, stepped onto the stage. Strena arranged us around the volcano at haphazard intervals, making sure to leave enough room between us for her to pass when she did her work. She faced some of us outward, some inward. I was facing the volcano, which I liked. I felt marginally more comfortable presenting my naked back to someone sitting a few feet from me than flashing them my front.

"Robes off, when you're ready. We need to calibrate the lighting and the cameras."

All the other models dropped their robes, white petals falling from almond trees.

Strena shouted instructions, and the spotlights

came on. I squinted at the world-famous art photographer who was adjusting a handful of cameras on tripods around the stage. *Was she...*

"Jordan Kane is here," I whispered at Strena when she walked over to me.

"She's making a series of photographs about the show. Take off your robe, please."

Nobody else had raised a fuss. I let the silk slide off my shoulders and pool at my feet. There. Now Strena would see now how big a mistake she had made.

She tapped the back of my knee. "One foot forward. I want a sense of movement. Arms loose but purposeful. Head up."

"What if I *can't* do it?"

"What if *I* can't do it?" She moved on to the next model, calling back, "Queens don't think those thoughts."

An hour passed before Strena was satisfied with our poses, and Jordan Kane with her camera placements.

"Stay on the platform," Strena told me as I put on my robe. "I want you to get used to the movement. The others have practice."

She signaled, and the stage slid toward the double doors that had been left open. The whole thing ran on a rail. It smoothly rolled out of the auditorium, back into the prep room.

The doors closed behind us.

"All right, people." Strena sent off a quick text. "Our audience will be seated shortly. Models, you have thirty minutes to move around and stretch your muscles. I suggest you take it."

I wanted to talk to her, but Jordan Kane walked over to discuss something with her, and I felt too intimidated to disturb them.

The half an hour was half a second. Then we were ordered to disrobe, step back onto the platform, and take our places.

Strena stopped by to give me a reassuring nod from the ground.

The prep room was plunged in darkness.

The buzz of the audience on the other side of the doors built and built, and a terrible, horrible thought hit me in the gut.

"Tell me Bram isn't here," I whispered.

"With his grandfather and his cousin, Sergei. I sent them tickets."

"If I could see, I would run away."

"Why do you think I'm standing next to you?"

The doors opened, and the stage glided forward in the dark, slowly, smoothly, thank God, or I might have fallen on my face.

In seconds, we stopped.

Perfect silence, but I could sense the people in the room, holding their breaths. I was an inch from hyperventilating.

Music started, a primal melody, ancient flute and drums. A light dawned above, like a sunrise. People in the audience gasped.

When Strena walked in like a queen, a thunderous applause erupted, men and women calling her name. She stepped onto the stage, gave a gracious bow, and then she began.

Because I was facing the volcano and her, I could see most of what she was doing, and I finally understood it. With the music and the lights, the way she moved with an audience to watch, her act was more than performance art. She was a shaman, a creator goddess. She transformed us.

She worked on one model for a few minutes, then the next, then the next, a dance, guiding our female bodies through metamorphosis. She created something extraordinary, not a spectacle, but an all-immersive experience. She wasn't merely transforming her models. She was transforming the entire room, her audience.

The lights changed, and her patterns emerged, grew, moved. She told a story, from the first mother all the way to the first woman in space, which was me, constellations glowing on my body. Yet she was the sun, around which we all revolved, reflecting her brilliance.

After Violet's death, part of my despair came from thinking she was lost to the world, that I wouldn't see an artist like her again in my lifetime.

Now I understood that Violet had been a shining link in a chain of exceptional, admirable women. And there would be more, with Strena in the lead. Violet wasn't gone. Her spirit was in the room with me.

I blinked hard, trying not to cry, and realized some people in the room were sobbing.

The ninety-minute performance passed too fast and too slow, outside time, like a dream.

The music reached a crescendo, high notes flying to the ceiling, a flock of rising birds. The clapping of wings came from the thunderous applause from the audience.

For a moment, it all held, the planets stopping their rotations. Then the music died, and darkness fell again.

I kept my balance as the stage rolled out and the doors closed behind us. The lights came on in the prep room. I felt emotionally drained, but at the same time, my body buzzed with a wild energy, recreated.

I searched for Strena, but she was still out there. More applause. People called her name.

When her assistants materialized with trays to peel off the sugarworks, I was still flying near the ceiling.

"Want to see what you look like before I help you clean up?" Tiana asked.

"Yes, please."

She pulled a tablet from her bag and clicked on the camera.

I stared at the screen. "Wow."

What I'd thought was a shooting comet running down the middle of my body, from the hollow of my throat to below my belly button, looked very much like a sword. "Excalibur."

And if that wasn't enough… I touched a finger to the elaborate V over my heart. *Violet.*

While I fought tears, Tiana put the tablet away

and began peeling planets off my stomach, careful not to break them. "Was it as scary as you thought it would be?"

"It was transformative. Are these saved?"

"They're eaten." Tiana laughed. "For as much as these patrons paid, they're served a gourmet meal. They're moving over to the dining room as we speak. Dessert is organic coconut ice cream with crumbled sugarworks from the performance."

"Whose idea was that?" The extravagant touch wouldn't have occurred to me in a million years.

Tiana flashed me a *Who do you think?* look. "It symbolizes humankind's unchecked consumption of our resources until nothing remains." She looked toward the double doors. "Here she is."

Strena walked in, glowing, carrying an armload of flowers, which she began distributing to her staff. "Thank you, everyone. The success of the show is yours as much as mine. I couldn't have done it without you. You were all brilliant."

Of course, we clapped, half-blind as if we'd stared into the sun too long.

"Are you all right?" She checked on me.

"Thank you for allowing me to be part of this. It's…" My throat burned. "I feel reborn."

"Thank you for trusting me."

A long moment passed between us before I glanced down my body. The ornamentation had been removed, and suddenly, I noticed my nakedness again. "Is there a shower?"

"My only request that the museum couldn't accommodate. There are plenty of wet wipes."

I could see the other models who were already using them.

"I don't think I'm comfortable with spending another ten minutes naked. Mind if I take a robe?"

She picked the silk up from the floor where I had dropped it prior to the performance. "All yours."

I wrapped the robe around myself. If I put my shirt on over that, I'd look as if I were wearing a shirt over a wrap dress. "Thank you. Again. I'm going to miss you when the house sells and we have to move out."

She tilted her head. "You could assume Violet's mortgage."

"Me and what millionaire friend?" I considered her. "How would you feel about renting the fourth-floor studio long-term?"

"I'm going to be doing larger works next. I already rented a warehouse."

So there went that.

"I wouldn't mind renting the two gallery floors," she said then. "I hate a gallery closing. Especially Violet's. I'm part owner of a place in Harlem, but it'd be nice establishing a toehold in the Village. Let's talk about this later. Right now, I'm supposed to be giving interviews." She stepped away. "The rest of the team are going out to eat. I'm sure you'd be more than welcome. Why don't you go with them?"

"I need to go home and take a shower." Everybody was great, but I wasn't part of the team. I was a last-second addition. I didn't want to intrude. And I didn't want noise and crowds. I wanted a minute to process what had just happened, that I'd done this thing I wouldn't have thought I could do in a million years.

"I'll walk out with you." Strena helped me with my shirt. "The press is in the lobby. It'll be faster for me to walk around the building than to walk through."

A minute later, we were marching down the hallway.

"I've been reading the Dutch letters you gave me," she said. "They seem to be corrections. Like Clara is talking about Jo's life, and Jo is telling her, no, that happened later, or earlier, or no, I never said that. Does that make any sense?"

"Like Clara was writing Jo's biography?"

"Exactly."

One piece of the mystery solved. I'd told Strena about the little green book when I'd given her the letters. "Do the letters say what the connection is between Jo and Clara?"

"Jo refers to Vincent and Theo in the letters as *your uncle Vincent* and *your uncle Theo.*"

"This is so helpful. Thank you. Wait till I tell Bram."

"What's going on with you two?"

"I don't know. I like him. Too much, too fast."

"Don't believe in that. It's like looking at art. When you know, you know. Someone either speaks to your heart or they don't."

"If they do?"

"Like art, you take them home and keep them. Everything else is a waste of time."

Maybe she was right. "He listens. He cares. He has ideas. He helps, but he doesn't push. It's up to me, everything. He—"

We reached the door and burst outside.

Bram was there. "Congratulations on the show, Strena." Then he shot me a hopeful smile. "Can I drive you home, Emsley?"

He wore an even nicer suit than usual, fitted, no tie, the top button of his shirt open.

Strena raised an eyebrow at me. But instead of commenting on Bram, she said, "Thank you, Emsley." And then she hurried away.

While I stood awkwardly in front of Bram, painfully aware that I didn't have on underwear.

CHAPTER THIRTY

Johanna

December 1891, Amsterdam, Netherlands

What was I thinking, hiring Amsterdam street urchins and leaving Vincent's legacy in their hands?

"Don't drop that!" I leaped back and nearly tripped on the hem of my dress. I had no time to rejoice over my narrow escape. I had to steady the crate the boys were carrying behind me. I had to deliver Vincent's art to our destination in one piece.

The younger one, around twelve, teetered, at risk of falling backwards and plunging into traffic. The barely attached soles of his boots slipped off the curb. I grabbed his shoulder and caught him.

Soot stained his threadbare coat. He must have been hauling coal earlier in the day.

"Careful."

He flashed me a gap-toothed grin, and then he

and his brother marched on, through the throng of ladies and gentlemen out for a walk, while I followed, struggling to catch my breath.

If I could have lifted the weight, I would have carried the crate myself. "Watch it! The contents are irreplaceable."

The scent of burning wood and roasting chestnuts wafted from a vendor up the street. Christmas decorations crowded the shop windows, reminding me of the time when I had visited Dries in Paris and had my first long talks with Theo, the Christmas he'd proposed.

Was he watching me from above? If he was, I hoped he saw that I was doing my best to fulfill my promise. I hoped he could see our little son, napping at my parents' house, under the care of my mother and sisters. I had brought him to the city with me for the week.

Clouds covered the sky, the sun unable to break through to warm the air. I did not take that as an omen. It was just Dutch winter. But I *was* shivering by the time we reached Arti et Amicitiae's white neoclassical building on Gracht Ronkin.

"Please watch your feet," I begged the boys as we headed up the steps.

Arts and Friendships, the Dutch artists' society, had been founded a decade before my birth and offered the most sincere and wide-reaching support to artists in the country. It was also the last place I had not yet begged for help.

I knew from Anna's husband, Jan, that Arti exhibited both members and nonmembers. I even had a letter of recommendation from Jan in my handbag, and another from Richard Roland Holst, whom Jan had convinced to provide at least that much assistance.

I silently rehearsed my well-prepared argument as I climbed step after step, nervous but undaunted. *His homeland must support him... His work will bring glory to our country...*

"*Goedemorgen.*" A gentleman passed me and opened the door for us.

He was a head taller and at least a dozen years older than me, his smile quick, his eyes inquisitive. He reminded me of my Theo. Or maybe I was just seeing Theo everywhere because I desperately needed his spirit to be present with me.

I thanked the man for his kindness. "Dank u wel."

"Madam." He executed a perfect bow, then left me at reception and continued down the hallway, disappearing behind the first door on the left.

I'm here. The paintings are here. We will be seen. Breathe. Speak. "Goedemorgen."

"And you are looking for?" the porter, a much older man with a neatly trimmed white mustache, enquired after an exchange of polite greetings.

"I would like to speak to the man in charge. I am here to set up an exhibit. I am Vincent van Gogh's agent."

The porter stared at me with alarm, as if I had said I'd come to rob the place. "Ladies do not agent, madam."

"And yet I am here. And I am a woman."

He gaped at me, having clearly not expected such blatant resistance.

"I am Johanna van Gogh," I said with impeccable politeness. "Could you please let the person in charge know that I am here to see him?"

"Impossible." He looked at me as if I were Hannibal before the gates. "Not possible, madam."

He seemed quite certain.

I was quite determined, however.

I had *not* come this far to be shooed away within reach of my goal. I opened my mouth to give the lengthy argument I had prepared. But then I thought better of it. I would no longer waste time on convincing obstacles to move out of my way. From now on, I was going to charge through them.

"Very well. I shall find the man myself." I marched down the hallway, glancing back only to urge the boys in our invading army of three. "Hurry!"

The gentleman who had escorted me into the building seemed to have manners. Maybe he would help. I strode straight to the door behind which he had disappeared.

The porter scrambled from behind his desk. "Madam! Madam!"

If he was going to hold against me that I was a woman, I was going to use that he was a man. I ripped my hat off and tossed it behind me.

Courtesy demanded that he stop to collect it. "You lost your hat, madam!"

He picked it up and charged forward again. Too late. My hand was already on the doorknob.

I executed a cursory knock, but didn't wait for an answer. I opened the door and gestured the boys forward. "Quickly. In here."

As soon as we were inside, I closed the door, turning the key.

The porter banged behind me. "Meneer De Jong!"

The room I had invaded had a window on the opposite wall, a fireplace with chairs to my left, and the now-familiar man at his desk on my right.

"No worries, Hendrik," he called out. "All is well."

And while I grasped for an explanation for my audacious actions, he rose to his feet.

The boys drew behind me, likely regretting hiring themselves out to a madwoman. I had second thoughts myself. I shook them off. One did not change one's mind in the middle of battle.

"Forgive me for the intrusion." *Did I truly break into a stranger's office?* I would have to think about that later. Right then, I had to save the moment. "I am Johanna van Gogh, and I require your assistance."

"A pleasure to meet you, Mevrouw Van Gogh. Daan de Jong, at your service. I would be happy to assist you in any manner I can, madam."

"Could you please escort me to the person in charge of scheduling exhibits?"

A playful smile came into his eyes. "I hope you haven't been expecting an imposing figure, because I regret to inform you that you are talking to the man."

Oh, just breathe, for love's sake. I had to look in control instead of scared. That De Jong had not threatened me with the law yet helped.

"I represent the artist Vincent van Gogh, recently deceased."

"I have heard of him." De Jong crossed to the crate the boys had set down. "But I have not had the pleasure of seeing his work."

"Neither has the world. I am here to remedy that," I surprised myself with how confident I sounded. "Please, lay the crate on its side," I instructed the boys.

They did as I'd asked, and I opened the clever latches Janus had constructed so I wouldn't need to bring tools with me. Once the lid was off, I unwrapped, then lifted out the first canvas.

The windows showed a gray and dreary sky outside, but suddenly, the room filled with sunlight. Instead of bringing the small prints and paintings I had sent around in the past, I brought larger works this time. As quickly as I could, I unpacked the crate, leaning the three canvases against the back of the man's desk.

"Ah. I see. I see indeed." Meneer de Jong's gaze paused on the stark blues and yellows of *The Starry Night*. "And what village is this?"

"A village born of the artist's imagination. To a degree." Vincent had painted the sky from his window at the asylum at Saint-Rémy. There had been no village, however, outside. He added in Saint-Rémy, on the other side of the building, from memory. "Isn't the contrast beautiful? The sky in motion, swirling with the mysteries of the universe, while the village is peaceful and asleep."

I had no technical knowledge of art, nor could I analyze Vincent's skill as an expert. The best I could do was share how the painting made me feel.

"I have often wondered whether the duality represents Vincent's tumultuous thoughts and dark imaginings, sharing space with the inner peace he was so desperate to achieve. The two are balanced on the canvas, living in harmony."

I half expected De Jong to tell me I was talking nonsense, but he nodded. "Millet also has a *Starry Night*. Have you seen it?"

"I have not had the privilege."

"I had a glimpse when it was sold through Goupil. I believe the piece ended up with the Scottish writer George Craik, and it's still in his family. Millet's version is more subdued, almost monochromatic. This one is altogether brilliant."

He moved on to *Blossoming Almond Tree*.

I was there to convert the man, so I had to speak. "Every time I see the awakening branches, no matter how bad things are, the mood of the painting makes me look forward to the future. The unfurling buds symbolize new life, new hope, a rebirth of the tree." I cleared my throat. "Vincent hoped for a rebirth himself. He found a new way to paint in Arles." He'd written about how different the light was in the South of France, how magnificent and perfect for his art. "If only he had more time left, he could have…"

"We could have had more of this."

"Yes." Oh thank heavens, the man understood me. Air rushed into my lungs. I was unsteady with relief.

De Jong progressed to scrutinizing the *Sunflowers*.

"Vincent painted the flowers more than once," I kept going. "Two of the paintings are with the artist Paul Gauguin. He loved them so much, Vincent gave them to him as a gift."

"Why a plant that came from America, and not one of our native flowers?"

"He wanted a fresh subject?" I improvised. "The flowers migrated across the ocean to thrive on the continent. As Vincent hoped to thrive in France. Those strong roots and thick stalks have a sturdiness about them."

De Jong stepped closer to the canvas. "He used nothing but shades of yellow."

"And yet the painting lacks for nothing. It's complete. It is almost as if the artist is saying, *Hope is all you need*." This I said from the deepest recesses of my heart.

"Do you think the painting is about hope?"

"Yellow is the color of the sun. We survive the cold and the darkness of the night in the hope that the sun will rise in the morning."

"My goodness, you didn't mention you were a poet." The man cast me a curious glance that quickly changed into a look of approval.

I relaxed. "Vincent said the sunflowers turned toward the sun in gratitude." Confidence bloomed slowly in my chest, unfurling like the golden petals on the canvas. "I have more of his work."

De Jong carried his gaze from one painting to the next, then the next. "Meneer Van Gogh had a distinct style, I'll give him that."

I advanced, while I was brave enough to do it. "I am here to ask you to sponsor him with an exhibit."

De Jong offered a smile. "I cannot say I see everything you do in the paintings, Mevrouw Van Gogh, but I do see the effect they have on you, the passion and loyalty they inspire. Even love. And who am I to say they will not have the same effect on our viewing audience? Certainly, it is worth giving Meneer Van Gogh a chance."

I bit the inside of my cheek so I wouldn't cry. After all this time... *Did you hear that, Theo, my dearest?*

"I cannot guarantee interest, of course," De Jong warned.

"I understand. A chance is all I ask. I am convinced that if we bring the works in front of an audience, the pieces will speak for themselves."

"You are a determined woman."

And what could I say to that? "If you hear a voice within say you cannot do something, then by all means, do that thing, and that voice will be silenced."

"Wise words."

"Vincent van Gogh said them."

De Jong gestured at the two armchairs by the fireplace on our left. "Why don't you sit, madam, and tell me about the man?"

CHAPTER THIRTY-ONE

Emsley

I stood on the sidewalk outside MoMA with Bram, pressing my thighs together. I would have given my little red auction hammer for a pair of granny panties.

Especially, when Bram Sr. and Sergei walked up to us.

"Don't worry, dear," Bram Sr. said, reading the discomfort on my face. "I didn't see anything. Every time Strena worked on you, I removed my glasses."

"I didn't," Sergei volunteered with an enthusiastic grin.

"Quit provoking your cousin." Bram Sr. tapped Sergei's shin with his cane. "My knees hurt. I'm ready to go home."

"Are you all right?" I asked the older Bram. "Should you even be walking?"

"I'll bring the car around." Sergei maneuvered around us, winking back at me, "Great show. I hope you'll do it again."

"I'll bring my car too." Bram went after him and punched him in the shoulder, leaving me alone with his grandfather on the sidewalk.

I wanted to take advantage of the few minutes we'd be alone. "About Senator Wertheim..."

"Terrible accident at the funeral."

I lowered my voice. "We both know it wasn't."

"Yes. Well, I suppose. What I started, you finished." He flashed a satisfied smile. "How did you figure out it was him?"

"New Year's Eve party, Vanderbilt Mansion. I counted back to the year, then searched for old photos on the internet."

"I'm impressed. I've been working on it for decades. Knew who was at the party, had a short list of suspects. I kept bringing them up to Violet to see who made her flinch. I watched whom she avoided. Unfortunately, I suspected the wrong man first." He fell silent for a moment while an ambulance screamed by. "You wouldn't know him, an up-and-coming singer in those days. He fizzled out eventually. He showed up at a soiree at Violet's, and Violet cringed away from him."

"Did you confront him?"

"Stabbed him with a butter knife."

A shocked laugh escaped me. "So the rumors of a stabbing at the brownstone were true."

"You think it's funny." Bram Sr. turned baleful.

"But he needed stitches. Violet ended up having to paint his portrait so he wouldn't press charges. She'd only flinched away from him because he was coming from a drunken party and he stank."

"I went to see Wertheim," I blurted.

"Did you kill him?"

"No!" I laughed again, because he didn't look the least appalled. "I told him I knew what he did and that I thought he was scum."

"I wish you'd taken me." Now he looked upset.

"It was a spur-of-the-moment adventure. How did you figure him out?"

"He was on my list. And then, at the funeral, I asked him how he knew Violet. He said when they were young, he courted her."

"Who didn't?"

"He said he still had her wrap from a party they went to at the Vanderbilts. Hung on to it all these years for the good memories attached to it. He made overtures after his wife died, but Violet never returned his calls."

"I wonder why." Anger edged the snark in my tone.

"I think he convinced himself over the years that she'd been too shy, needed a small push. Girls said *no* so they wouldn't look like bad girls. That's how a lot of guys back then justified…"

Sergei pulled up to the curb.

I tamped down my murderous impulses and opened the passenger-side door for Bram Sr., and then I hung on to the doorframe as he eased in.

"There's something else I wanted to ask you. Do you know anything about a box of old letters and a little green book Violet had?"

"The ones she kept in that blue box? She found them under a loose windowsill when she had to replace some of the original windows that capitulated to dry rot."

Sergei watched us curiously, but didn't ask any questions. Instead, he said, "By the way, I just received an offer on the carousel. Nine hundred and fifty."

My lungs exploded. "Thousand?"

"I'm holding out. Another interested party popped up. Just wanted you to know."

"Thank you, Sergei." I could have kissed him.

"One piece of bad news. You're now officially my client, so I can't seduce you away from Bram."

Then they were away, Bram pulling up behind them.

"What were you and my grandfather conspiring about?" he asked as I slipped into the car, my mind spinning.

"Old stories about my grandmother." Maybe someday I would tell him, but not right then.

"Because you looked like you might be planning your next attempted murder."

"That was a strictly one-time deal."

"As a representative of the law, I'm glad to hear it." He deftly pulled into traffic. "But if you think anyone deserves to meet a grim end, I trust you, and I'm willing to help."

"I wouldn't involve you in anything illegal. Good-looking men don't last long in prison."

"Point there. All right. I'll stay out of trouble so I can post your bail."

His words reminded me of my grandmother so much, my heart squeezed.

Traffic was impossible, a glut of tourists. I clutched my robe closed over my thighs, while Bram concentrated on not hitting people who insisted on darting in front of us and demonstrating a complete lack of survival instinct.

"Should we swing by the Thai place for dinner?" he asked when we stopped for a red light.

I couldn't imagine getting out of the car. "I need a shower. I have leftovers in the fridge. If day-old pizza is okay."

"Perfect." He seemed to want to be back at the house just as badly as I did.

The mention of Thai food, of course, brought up memories of our canceled plans the week before. An awkward silence settled in as we took off again. I wondered if he still wanted to eat in bed.

I turned on the radio.

The two hosts of a show were talking about Strena's performance. I quickly changed the station.

"Don't you want to hear the critics?"

"What if they say it was sublime except for that one short dumpling-looking chick?"

"Dumpling?"

"My father's nickname for me. In high school, it made me want to take a bubble bath with a toaster, but I've embraced the truth since. I'm loosely in the dumpling category. Not a giant Chinese soup dumpling, but definitely a few sizes above gnocchi. People who spend half their life in their office chair and the other half at champagne receptions don't generally have an athlete's body." The words just poured right out of me.

"When the lights came on and I saw you, I almost choked to death," Bram said. "Nearly as bad as when you opened the door in a T-shirt without a bra the morning after we met."

I covered my face. "You noticed that?"

"Do I have a Y chromosome?"

I twisted to the side window and considered jumping from the moving car. "I was hoping that you missed that."

"I was pretending hard." He gave a strangled laugh. "At least I had that as training for today. It takes skill to look an art connoisseur when you feel like…"

I waited for him to finish. When he just shook his head, for some weird, suicidal reason, I asked, "How close were you sitting to the stage?"

"Thirty feet? I couldn't have handled any closer." Bram navigated traffic, silent for a few seconds before he asked, "Are you going to do it again?"

"No," I said on reflex, then thought about it. "All my life, I wanted to be like Violet, free and wild, but somehow, I ended up like my mother. Practical, methodological, crossing my t's and dotting my i's."

"All good traits for a business owner."

"I want to take more chances."

"You're running away to join the Carnival in Rio?"

"That's the other extreme. I think balance is the key."

"So that's a definite no on another naked show?"

His overexaggerated disappointment made me smile. A long string of *noooos* was on my tongue, but my phone pinged with a text. "My mom. Wants to know if I'm finished with the house yet."

I texted back. *Almost.* Then I added, *Do you know who owned Violet's house before her father?*

His father. Albert. Why?

Just checking out stg. And before him?

Nobody. He had the house built for his wife.

"Everything okay?" Bram asked.

I gave an absentminded nod, my mind on the mysteries of the past. And it stayed there for the rest of the drive.

Then we were at the house, Bram going inside with me, and I was very much in the present. The then and there was just fine.

He picked up Lai Fa and scratched her head. "You do what you need to do. I'll warm up the pizza." But instead of walking away, he touched my neck. "You have a…"

"What?"

"A piece of something stuck here." He picked a nearly translucent whirl of crystallized sugar off my skin. Instead of heading to the garbage with it, he put it on his tongue. "Sweet."

And just like that, I couldn't breathe.

Lai Fa flew off to chase an ant.

"Any more where that came from?" Bram's tone dipped. "May I check?"

"Make your bid."

"Everything."

"Going once. Going twice. You win."

"I'm going to have to take your clothes off." He said it like a disclaimer. How very lawyerly.

"In the foyer?"

"I can lick that sugar off you here as easily as anywhere else. Why make the bedroom sticky?"

"Solid argument. I can see you convincing a jury." I let him unbutton my shirt.

Surprise.

The sex was incredible.

And showering together in Violet's giant clawfoot tub wasn't a hardship either. I'd never done that with anyone before. I could see the appeal.

We ate the reheated pizza in the small downstairs kitchenette, me in one of Violet's Old Hollywood-style robes, Bram in his slacks and shirt. Unbuttoned. No undershirt.

Because we live in a generous universe that keeps on giving.

Lai Fa joined us, pecking at the crumbs at our feet, a luminescent moment. Bram kept looking at me, a smile playing on his lips. "Sergei said there's interest in the carousel. You could renegotiate with

Trey. Pay him off and keep Ludington's. Both coasts."

"I don't want to have to spend half my life going back and forth between New York and LA. I think I'm going to buy this house. If I can assume the mortgage."

As the words left my mouth, happiness flooded through me.

This is what it feels like when you make the right decision.

Bram leaned across the small table and kissed me. "You look especially beautiful when you're in the middle of conquering the world."

His words went straight to my heart. They brought to mind Johanna Bonger, who'd fought her own share of battles. I pushed my empty plate aside and pulled over my laptop.

Bram reached under the table and ran a hand up my thigh. "If you're going to work, I haven't done enough to scramble your brain. And that would mean I have to take you straight upstairs to bed."

My fingers tripped, then tripped again as they danced across the keyboard. "I want to look up Johanna Bonger for a sec. Strena translated the letters. Clara was writing Jo's biography. Your grandfather told me Violet found the papers hidden in a windowsill. Clara must have a connection to this house. Right?"

Bram moved his barstool next to mine so he could see the screen, then dropped his hand back between my legs. If we ever ended up living together, we were definitely going to need separate home offices.

I scrolled, distracted enough to nearly miss the link I was looking for. "Jo came to New York in 1914. After she made Vincent famous in the Netherlands, she made him famous in Belgium, France, and England. All of the continent. And then she came here and did the same."

Bram's fingers stilled. "Do you think she lived in this house?"

"Maybe?" I read on. "The website says one of her nieces accompanied her on her trip. Clara Bakker." I scrolled. "Johanna returned home in 1919, but there's no further mention of the niece."

I picked up my phone and texted my mother.

Do you know your great-grandmother's maiden name? The one who lived here?

You need this in the middle of the night?

Yes.

It was 7:00 p.m. I waited as the seconds ticked by, then her response popped onto the screen and stole my breath.

Clara Bakker. She was a Dutch immigrant.

I showed Bram the screen.

"You think," he said, "Violet knew all along that her grandmother was Johanna van Gogh-Bonger's niece?"

"Why would she keep that a secret?" But then I knew. "I've been reading through old newspaper clippings about Violet that Strena gave me, articles titled 'Heiress of Department Store Empire Dabbles in Art,' 'Warhol's New Sidepiece Also an Artist,' and others. For most of her life, Violet was defined by the men in her life. If this came out," I gestured at the screen, "for the rest of her life, it would have been 'Van Gogh's Great-Grandniece Tries Her Hand at Painting.'"

"I didn't know Violet was an heiress to a department store empire."

"My great-great-grandfather lost almost everything in the Great Depression. I think the house was the only thing Violet inherited at the end."

"I'm glad, or the letters and diary might have been lost to the family. If Clara Bakker was Violet's grandmother, then that makes you..." Bram's hand slipped higher on my thigh.

"Johanna Bonger's great-great-great-grandniece? Sorry. I don't know how many greats." I couldn't deal with the thought, so I gave him a hokey smile. "For a while, I was hoping I was Vincent's descendant through a secret love child. But I think this is even better. I'm related to some seriously amazing women."

Bram pulled me over onto his lap and wrapped my legs around his waist. I wrapped my arms around his neck.

"Emsley Wilson." He kissed me. "You *are* an amazing woman."

CHAPTER THIRTY-TWO

Johanna

January 1892, Amsterdam, Netherlands

"Was my papa a bad man?" Wil asked, the two of us alone in the otherwise empty train compartment.

I was so mired in nerves, I didn't immediately answer. I was distracted by worries over Vincent's first official show, our destination. *Dear God, let him be well received.*

"Mama!"

My breath hitched at the pinched look on Wil's little face. "No, my sweet. Your papa was a great man."

"Did somebody take him?"

"No, my sweet. He fell ill and died. He is in heaven."

"Like Mevrouw Ballot?"

My boarder Mevrouw Ballot had become sick at

the beginning of winter. She had gone into the hospital after New Year's and passed away. Wil and I missed her. We adopted all her cats.

"Yes."

"Can we send them letters?"

My son had seen me write to so many people, I wondered if someday he would be saying, *All I remember about my mother is that she was always writing letters.* "Not to heaven, no. I am sorry."

He looked out at the platform, where moments ago, the police had taken away a drunkard. He pondered my words so hard, his little forehead wrinkled.

"Why don't you draw me something?" I handed him a piece of paper and a stubby pencil from my bag.

He cast one last hopeful glance at the platform for further entertainment, then began drawing squiggly shapes and other doodles, half the lines running off the paper.

"Your uncle Vincent loved to draw. And paint too."

"Did Papa paint?"

"No, my love. Your papa sold paintings."

"I sell my painting!" Wil beamed with pride, his brilliant blue eyes shining as he pushed the scribbles toward me.

"All right." I reached into my bag for a biscuit. "I will pay you one of these."

"I want two!"

He rarely did anything without bargaining, from

going to bed at night to washing his face in the morning. Since the skill was much needed in life, I didn't discourage him.

He tasted his biscuit, then immediately offered it back to me. "Mama too."

"Thank you, darling." I took a pretend bite, chewed, then kissed his head.

"Was Grandfather a painter?"

"Your father's father was a preacher," I told him as the train whistled. We were leaving at last. "He taught people about God."

"I forgot. Sorry, Mama."

"That's all right." Not the first time we'd had this conversation, and probably not the last.

Many of his little friends had family nearby, grandparents, aunts and uncles on the same street, or sometimes even in the same house. They had cousins over to play every day. Since Wil didn't have that, I did the next best thing and made sure that at least he learned about his father's people. My mother, during our visits, made certain Wil learned about mine.

"Do you remember what I told you about your great-uncle?"

"He sailed on a ship."

"He was an admiral in the navy."

"What else?" He loved this game.

The enthusiasm on his sweet face made me smile. "One of your great-grandfathers was bookbinder to the king."

"Did he go to the palace?" He grinned wide, his

mouth stuffed with biscuit, dropping crumbs all over his lap.

"What did I say about talking with your mouth full?"

He pressed his lips shut and chewed with great effort.

"Well done." I reached across to tousle his hair. "Yes. He went to the palace all the time."

Not that I knew that for a fact. Willem Carbentus was my mother-in-law's father, and I had never met him. All I knew about him was that he had framed our country's first constitution, which Theo's mother had recounted to me proudly, and I had told Wil many times. I was determined not to let my son feel the shadows of his ancestry ever, but to paint in his mind a line of great men to inspire him.

"You have his name," I told him. "Willem."

"But I was named after my uncle. Vincent Willem van Gogh."

"You certainly were."

He puffed out his chest. "Will I meet the king?"

"We have a queen now, love. Young Queen Wilhelmina, with her mother Queen Emma as regent, remember? Only great men receive the honor of meeting the queen. If you want to meet her, you must become a great man."

"When I go to the palace, I will take you too, Mama," he told me with confidence.

"Thank you, Wil." He had inherited his father's generous heart. *Nothing else, please,* I silently begged God. *With that good heart, please let the similarities end.*

Anna entered the compartment just as the train lurched into motion, steadying herself on top of her seat. She and her husband, Jan, had run into a friend as we had boarded the train. They'd stopped to talk in the corridor outside while we had waited for our departure. My friends were coming along to support me at Vincent's exhibit at Arti.

"What a good boy," Anna told Wil as she sat in the seat next to him. She'd left her daughters home with her mother.

Wil was too lost in his doodling to respond.

Anna smiled at me. "Nervous?"

"I might faint."

"There will be many fine gentlemen there to catch you, I am certain."

"I'm not going husband hunting." I gave a desperate laugh. "I have spent all these months in Bussum and but grieved and tried to replace Theo with other men."

I stopped when I realized how that sounded. "In the sense that I spent all that time trying to find someone else to champion Vincent. And now I've decided to carry on Vincent's legacy myself."

Anna nodded.

"And I replaced Theo in the family, being both mother and father to Wil. Instead of Theo, I am the one teaching my son about his heritage. And I replaced Theo's income with income from the villa. You see, I have already replaced Theo in so many ways. I cannot bear the thought of replacing him in *every* way."

"I'm sorry. I worry that if you don't fully settle in at the villa, if you have nothing to tie you to Bussum, you might leave. I wish, selfishly, for you to stay."

"I *am* settled. And reasonably content. I like to think that Theo is watching me from heaven. He will be part of my life forever. And I cannot let Vincent go either. You cannot keep one without the other. They go together. They always have. They are part of me. I will not rest until everyone knows Vincent's name. I want to bring him to the world."

Anna smiled.

"I am obsessed. Oh, you can say it."

"You are dedicated."

"Someday, when our country is mentioned, people will think of Vincent first. Men and women will come here to see his paintings. He will have his own museum. My children's children will live to see it."

"His own museum, then? With nothing but his own art? But museums collect hundreds of artists."

Ordinary museums. But not the one I dreamed of.

I thought of Vincent's exhibit at our Paris apartment. None of us had been there. Vincent had died shortly before. Theo was locked up and raving, months from his own death, and I had been with him, visiting when they would let me. The show at our apartment had been attended only by Vincent's closest friends.

"A museum for him only, in Amsterdam, with visitors from as far as America standing in line in front of the doors," I told Anna. "They will do that for Vincent."

"If you say so, Jo, I believe it. And if there is such a museum," she said, reaching across to squeeze my hand, "I predict it will be your doing. They will write books about you, Johanna van Gogh-Bonger."

Such silliness. But before I could protest, Jan came in and sat next to her, and Anna's attention switched to her husband.

"What have you two talked about all this time?"

"Pigments."

Anna flashed him an indulgent look, which only encouraged him, so he recounted his conversation with his artist friend in its entirety for our benefit. And then he described, in detail, his friend's greatest works and the nuances of his technique, putting little Wil to sleep. By the time Jan finished, the train was pulling into Amsterdam.

My nerves attacked anew as we deboarded. "What if nobody comes?"

"Dries!" Jan waved next to me and sprung forward.

The sight of my dear brother, who was making his way toward us on the busy platform, settled my nerves a small measure.

As soon as he reached us, he took my still-sleeping son from me. "I have a carriage waiting for us outside the station."

We bustled through the crowd together. All around us, family members were embracing each other, mothers shouted for their children, porters jostled forward, laden with luggage. Steam engines whistled. I didn't attempt to talk to Dries over the cacophony of noise.

"You've done it, Jo," he said once we settled into our conveyance. "You must be excited."

"Petrified. But even if today is an utter failure, I shall go on. This is what I have learned," I told him. "Refusals will not kill me. Ridicule will not kill me. My feelings might be hurt, I might be embarrassed, I might want the ground to open beneath my feet, and others might wish the same for me, but I will not die. I will keep trying. I will live in gratitude, my face pointed toward the light."

He squeezed my hand. "Then there is nothing to be scared of, is there?"

Maybe so, yet I held my breath as we turned the last corner.

I stared at the men and women waiting in front of the door, a veritable crowd. "For Vincent?"

"He has the only exhibit today." Dries grinned.

Then the horses stopped, which woke Wil. I took his hand and led him to the end of the line, dazed.

Before I could recover, Daan de Jong was running out to greet us. "Mevrouw Van Gogh! Oh, madam, you are here. Splendid! Have you seen the line? I let a journalist friend in as we set up the works two days ago, and he wrote us up in yesterday's paper. Look!"

He ushered us past the waiting crowd and into the exhibit itself, and it was as if my words to Anna on the train had sprung to life.

My friend and I looked at each other with tears in our eyes.

"A great success, madam." De Jong threw his arms wide. "The critics all call Vincent van Gogh brilliant."

You must do lighter, Theo had admonished Vincent in his letters in the beginning. *More color.* And Vincent, with all that darkness inside him, journeyed from the muddy browns of *The Potato Eaters* to the still-brown houses in the back, but colorful tulips in the front of *Bulb Fields*, then to the vibrant light and joy of the *Sunflowers*—pure color, pure light.

That light shone from all the paintings that graced the walls.

We walked around as if in a dream, Wil's hand held tightly in mine. When people heard I was of the family, they came over to congratulate me.

Some were artists I knew, Holst among them. How good it felt to hear them praise Vincent, those who had in the past called him a talentless hack.

"Triumphant," Dries crowed. He pointed at a small group at the head of the room. "More newspapermen. The exhibit will be written up in every paper."

A tall, severe gentleman interrupted us. "Mevrouw Van Gogh. Might I trouble you to discuss an exhibit later this year in Pulchri?"

And it went on and on. Gallery owners sought me out. Before the day finished, I placed ten paintings with Buffa in Amsterdam, and twenty with Oldenzeel in Rotterdam.

I'd never wished more for Enrique Gaspar's time machine. I wanted to travel back for Vincent and Theo and whisk them forward. But as much as I wished to do so, I couldn't gift this moment to them.

Yet when I lifted my son into my arms and turned slowly around in the middle of the room, showing Wil the paintings and the crowd that admired them, I felt both Theo and his brother with me.

I hugged my little son closer. "See, Wil? This is your Uncle Vincent."

And then, when nobody was looking, I whispered to the ceiling, "I love you, my dearest. Be at peace."

EPILOGUE

Emsley

On the first anniversary of Violet's death, Strena, Bram, his grandfather, and I drove out to the cemetery. My father and mother were coming down from Hartford on the weekend and were visiting Violet then. After Mom told me over the phone that they were coming, I asked her if she would still want to know who her father was—if it was possible to find out.

She told me she had to think about it.

As I was trying to figure out what I'd say if her final answer was yes, a cab pulled up and Diya jumped out with a large bouquet. She was working for a startup in Silicon Valley that was disrupting the fast-food industry. I'd kept in touch with her. Life was too short to hold grudges. She was in New York for a meeting, and when she called and invited me to coffee an hour earlier, I told her where I was going. She asked if she could come along.

Trey had transformed Ludington's LA into a political polling company, then renamed it after himself. Ludington's New York was the only Ludington's, and I liked it that way.

I'd let Trey go. I had everything I wanted.

Bram Sr. stepped forward and laid a bouquet of red roses on the grave. "Senator Wertheim had a fatal heart attack. I thought you'd like to know. He didn't suffer enough. I'd say kick his sorry ass, my dear Violet, if you run into him, but I know you went to different places."

Strena popped the cork from the Veuve Clicquot she'd brought, handed the bottle around, then poured the rest of the champagne on the grave. "I reopened The Gallery Velar. We had a record showing this week. Every piece of artwork sold. We were written up in the *Times*." She shook the last drops out of the bottle. "Also, I know I promised to look after your granddaughter, but she's pretty dope. Girl can take care of herself. She had the brains to hook up with a decent guy who only occasionally gets on my nerves."

Bram gave her a slight bow, and when Strena moved back, he stepped up in her place. He laid his own bouquet of roses, then rested a hand on the headstone. "Remember when you said you were going to hook me up with your granddaughter? And I said I was fine alone? I was wrong and you were right. I know women like to hear that."

He moved aside, and I pulled a snow globe from my bag, a perfect miniature carousel inside the glass. I shook it, then set it on top of Violet's gravestone.

"Ludington's is a success," I told her. "We're giving the big auction houses a run for their money. And I had my inaugural benefit auction." I pulled a check for one hundred thousand dollars from my back pocket. "For stroke research. I'm dropping this off today, but wanted to show it to you first. More to follow." I stashed the check away then drew a deep breath. "About your friends... Mrs. Yang and Louis both recovered enough to leave the center. They bonded over the grief of losing you. They're getting married next month in Miami. Mrs. Yang took Lai Fa with her. She's a happy chicken, on her way to being an Instagram star. Oh, they went to Vegas right after they left the center, and Louis won a major poker game. I hate to tell you this, but all that time you won at cards, I'm pretty sure he let you beat him."

I swallowed a heavy lump of grief. "I like living in the Village. The house is great. I redecorated it. I hope you don't mind." *Okay.* "Don't freak out. I made the fourth floor into a Violet Velar Museum. Open every Saturday and Sunday. I had a security system and professional temperature and humidity control installed. Some of your old students volunteer on rotation. I have about two dozen of your paintings on loan from your most ardent collectors, and in the middle of the room, Strena made a 3D installation from your old clippings and photographs."

I picked up the snow globe, shook it again, and this time, I wound it up too. Wurlitzer music filled the air. "You're a tourist attraction. If it bothers you, you can haunt me."

Strena gave me a hug. "I think she'd like being a tourist attraction. I have to go. I'm meeting a new artist at the gallery. I think she'll be a good fit for the next group show."

"If you like her, I'm sure she's great."

Strena said goodbye and walked away, all style and grace and stiletto heels.

Diya laid her flowers next to the others, then stepped back to me. "I'm sorry about Trey, Em. I apologized over the phone, but I want to do it again, in person. I was so stupid. I was in love with him for so long, my feelings blinded me."

I walked us away a few feet. "What do you mean *so long*?"

"Remember how I was dating Christopher in grad school, then he took us to meet his roommate, Trey? I knew ten minutes in that I'd picked the wrong guy."

"Why didn't you say something?"

"Trey only had eyes for you. And if I tossed Christopher like that, Trey would have thought I was some sorority slut anyway. He asked you out, and you kept saying no. I thought maybe I could break up with Christopher after a few weeks. But then, the night I was going to talk to Christopher about splitting up, you said yes to Trey."

"You could have told me."

"I didn't want you to be alone. I thought you deserved someone great."

"You did break up with Christopher."

"It wasn't fair to string him along."

"You were secretly in love with Trey for the past six years? I had no idea. I'm sorry. I just had my nose in work all the time."

"You know, a little TAFB can be healthy."

"Bram and I are learning life-work balance."

He needed it as much as I did, considering how many hours he clocked at the firm. But we tried to see each other as much as possible, helped by the fact that we were living together. We did have separate home offices.

"Anyway." The corners of Diya's mouth tightened. "I don't think Trey ever really loved me."

"He didn't deserve you."

"He didn't deserve you either. I'm glad you're with Bram. He looks at you like you founded the American Bar Association.

I laughed.

Her expression softened. "I'd like to see you again when I come up to New York next. And I'd like you to come and see me if you're in California."

"Let's do that." I hugged her. I'd missed her. I was grateful to have her back as a friend.

After she left, Bram came over. "What was that about?"

"Clearing some air."

Bram Sr. was whispering something to Violet's headstone.

"Should we leave too?" I asked him. "How is the knee?"

He'd long recovered from his fall at Violet's funeral, but had reinjured his left knee the week before, under mysterious circumstances.

"Good as new." He flexed his leg. "We can stay as long as you'd like. Well, within limits. I do have a lunch date."

Bram and I exchanged a look.

"Someone new?" I asked.

"Same gal as last time." His smile was pure male satisfaction. "Things are progressing."

I wondered if that had something to do with his knee injury. If so, I didn't want to know it.

Sergei's BMW rolled up the crushed gravel behind us and stopped to park in the spot Diya's cab had just vacated.

He carried a wrapped package under his arm, in addition to a fat oversized envelope that he handed to me. "Sorry I'm late."

"What's this?"

"Johanna Bonger's letters to her niece. Authenticated. Bam!"

"I'm holding historical treasure?"

"Don't have a heart attack yet. There's more." Sergei's fingers trembled as he loosened the string around the other package.

I'd never seen Sergei nervous before. It made me nervous in turn. "What is it?"

I knew the small painting that emerged, the poorly painted baby on the blue bedspread. The painting was too ugly to hang, so I'd passed it to Sergei to see if it might be worth something just based on age.

"An original Vincent van Gogh," he whispered. "An old buddy at Christie's certified it. They would love to have it as the highlight of their fall auction."

My heart stopped.

Bram took my hand, flashing his cousin a look of pure suspicion, as if he suspected a ploy on Sergei's part to seduce me away. "Are you sure? It doesn't look like a masterpiece. I always thought the poor kid looked dead."

A dead child. My heart stopped. "I know who that is." And it made me want to cry. "Vincent's older brother who was stillborn. Vincent was named after him. Jo talks about him in one of her letters."

"He's meant to look dead?" Bram scrutinized the figure. "He does look a little better than when he was covered in grime."

My brain was in a parallel universe as I said, "I washed him with Dawn."

Sergei stilled. "You mean metaphorically? You took the painting to Central Park and held it up to the rising sun to consecrate the day, like a spiritual experience?"

I covered my face with a hand and spoke through my fingers. "Dishwashing liquid. In the kitchen sink."

"Christ." He huffed out a shocked breath.

I had nothing to add, not even when Bram gave

me a comforting hug, doing his best to keep the horror off his face.

"So," Bram Sr. said with caution, "Violet had an original Vincent van Gogh and just kept it quiet?"

Her last gift to me, her last secret, I thought, as a soft wind swirled around me, almost like a hug.

While Sergei grumbled, "Anybody surprised, raise their hand."

THE END

AUTHOR'S NOTE

This is the book that broke me.

Two years ago, I saw an art documentary briefly mention Johanna Bonger, and I knew I wanted to write about her. There was only one problem. I write genre fiction (under the pen name Dana Marton): fantasy, romance, suspense. I don't write historical fiction. I don't write women's fiction. I don't write stories based on true events.

I threw myself into the work anyway, settling on a past-present dual timeline. I thought that Jo's story was so sad, it needed a lighter counterbalance in the form of a modern-day heroine. Since Emsley is an auctioneer, I had to do some research for her, but the effort paled in comparison to the research I had to do on Johanna. Especially because her descendants kept her diaries locked away, granting access to no one, not even academic researchers. So I went about painstakingly collecting tidbits of her life through a multitude of sources, a reference here, an anecdote there. I combed through hundreds of letters between Vincent and Theo for mention of her. Older books were my best sources, but they were out of print, unavailable in ebook format, and were selling in the hundred-plus dollar range each. (I'm pretty sure I currently have the best Van Gogh library on the East Coast.)

The story I came up with helped me get a wonderful agent. Submissions went out to twenty publishers. All wanted the manuscript. I'm not saying I was envisioning a bidding war (I was), but I was hopeful.

Then the first rejection came in. Then the second. Then the third. Then the nineteenth. The last publisher kept considering it for well over a year. I became convinced that my writing was bad. That I couldn't write. That I shouldn't write again.

I ran out of money. (I depend on a regular publishing schedule.) I started looking for jobs online. After close to two decades of being a full-time author, for the first time, I seriously considered quitting. But Jo kept whispering to me from the past. *You can do it. Just do it yourself.*

She never quit.

How could I? Wasn't my whole point to learn about this indomitable woman and introduce her to others?

I emailed my agent. I withdrew the manuscript from submission. The story was mine again, its fate in my hands. But I couldn't do this alone. I asked my readers on Facebook to give me an opinion on the project. Several angels volunteered to do a quick read, and they encouraged me to move forward. Without them, you would not be holding this book in your hands.

Now here we are. You've read the book. I hope you liked it. I hope Johanna inspires you as much as she inspired me. If you end up embarking on a new adventure, or sticking with an old one, because of her, please let me know. I would love to celebrate your success with you.

And if you'd like to be part of getting her story out there, would you please leave a review online? Would you recommend this book to your friends? I would love for people to learn about her and remember her name. I think she has a lot to teach us, even in this day and age. Words can't express how much I'd appreciate your help.

Thank you so much for giving THE SECRET LIFE OF SUNFLOWERS a chance!

With endless gratitude,

Marta Molnar

Author

Please sign up for my newsletter at www.MartaMolnar.com

P.S.: About a month after I finished writing the book, while I was still cross-eyed from all the research and broke from having to build my own Van Gogh library, Jo's descendants decided to release her diaries to the public and put them all online. They are available for free, in English. In an easy-to-search format.